HUNTED

HOSTAGE RESCUE TEAM SERIES

KAYLEA CROSS

HUNTED

Copyright © 2014
by Kaylea Cross

* * * * *

Cover Art & Formatting by
<u>Sweet 'N Spicy Designs</u>

* * * * *

ISBN: 978-1502894014

Dedication

A big shout out to the men and women in the military and law enforcement, working hard to keep us safe. Thank you for your service!

Kaylea

Author's Note

Can't believe this is the third book of the **Hostage Rescue Team** series already! And, *Hunted* is my 25th book! Time flies when you're having fun, right?

Well I certainly did have fun pairing Bauer and Zoe together. The thing I love most about this couple is that they both have so much to teach each other, and even though Bauer is jaded and cynical, he's still willing to learn from Zoe and allow himself to grow.

Happy reading!

Kaylea Cross

Prologue

Sixteen months ago

Somewhere down the long, dimly-lit hallway, a door opened and closed. Measured footsteps echoed against the jail's concrete floors and walls, coming toward him, slowing as they reached his cell.

"Bauer."

Clay Bauer turned his head at the brusque male voice, not bothering to sit up from where he was laying on the hard cot installed into the cement wall. Fifty-three hours he'd been locked up, after a single, frantic phone call to his best friend, the only person who might be able to help him now. The judge had finally set the bond yesterday afternoon and given him a court date three months out.

The jailer stopped on the other side of the iron bars and cut him a hard look. "Get up. You made bail." *You sorry piece of shit.*

The guy didn't say it, but he didn't have to because the disgust in his eyes said it all. And even though Clay was a full head taller and probably outweighed him by a good forty pounds, that look made him feel two inches tall.

Gathering himself, he pushed to a sitting position, ignoring the protest of his bruised, aching muscles and the throb of the scratches in his skin. It felt like he'd gone three rounds in the ring with another fighter. In a way, he guessed he had, but it hadn't been a fair fight. He'd been forced to take all the blows without being able to strike back.

That wasn't going to gain him any sympathy, however, with the judge or anyone else. Not that he wanted any. Having someone feel sorry for him on top of all this just might break him. And he was already closer to being broken than he'd ever been before in his life, even back during BUD/S when he'd been pushed past every limit he'd thought he had. He'd made it through and earned his Trident. He'd get through this as well.

Clay gripped the edge of the bunk so hard his knuckles turned white as an increasingly familiar flush of humiliation burned in his cheeks. The irony wasn't lost on him. He'd been taken prisoner before during the grueling mental and physical stress of the most intense SERE training the military could throw at him and never once felt this beaten down.

Parts of the Navy SEAL Code ran through his head, mocking him.

I serve with honor on and off the battlefield. The ability to control my emotions and my actions, regardless of circumstance, sets me apart from other men.

Uncompromising integrity is my standard. My character and honor are steadfast. My word is my bond.

Funny how being arrested and locked behind bars could make a man wither in his own skin.

"Who paid it?" he managed to rasp out.

The jailer shrugged in a dismissive gesture. "Doesn't matter. Let's go." He waved a hand impatiently for Clay to get up, his whole attitude making it clear that if it were up to him, he wouldn't be letting Clay out anytime soon.

Clay pushed to his feet and crossed to the door as the guard unlocked the cell. The bars slid aside with a heavy clang and Clay stepped out into the gray hallway, followed the guy down it and through another locked steel door. In the office portion of the jail, a female officer doing paperwork glanced up at him, her face tightening with disdain before she looked away. His jaw clenched. How many of them knew why he was in here?

Clay kept his head high despite his embarrassment and refused to look at any of them. He read and signed the documents put in front of him, took his wallet, watch and phone, listened to the instructions about the conditions of his bond. Finally the guard led him through the office into a waiting area. When his gaze landed on the two men standing there, his throat tightened and he had to look away, unable to meet their eyes because he was fucking terrified of what he might find there.

"You look better than I thought you would," Matt DeLuca, his boss and the CO of the FBI's Hostage Rescue Team said in a chipper voice.

Clay stuck his hands in his pockets and looked anywhere but at them, painfully aware that the bruises and scratches on his face and arms were visible. The cops had documented them all when they'd arrested him, but he hated that the two men in front of him could see them.

Normally he didn't give a shit what other people thought of him but with these guys, he did. And he was afraid this would cost him their respect. "Yeah. Thanks for getting me out."

"No worries, man," Tuck, his new team leader said in his Alabama drawl. Rather than try to say something funny to lighten the mood, he stepped up and clapped a solid hand on Clay's shoulder. "Let's get you the hell outta here, huh?"

Clay nodded, grateful they were making this easy on him but knowing he was eventually going to have to divulge every last detail to the both of them, and the entire command. He'd sooner face an enemy ambush. Alone. The scratches on his neck and arms stung like hell but what burned more was knowing that his entire career was now in jeopardy.

DeLuca led the way out to a black agency SUV and got behind the wheel. As Clay opened the back passenger side door he saw Tuck studying the marks on him. The deeper ones had made him bleed. He had more on his upper chest and shoulders. As far as injuries went, they were nothing compared to what he'd endured before. And yet they'd already scarred him more deeply than any of the others.

"You need anything for those?" Tuck asked.

They'd put some antibiotic cream on them when they'd brought him in. "No." Fuck, he hated this. He slid into the back and shut the door, wanting to get back to his apartment so he could hole up alone, shut off his phone and destroy a bottle of Jack.

"You hungry?" DeLuca asked as he steered out of the parking lot.

"No."

"I'm stopping for coffee," he warned. "You should eat something."

He wound up sipping a coffee and eating the bagel DeLuca shoved at him, though it tasted like cardboard in his mouth. They drove in silence across town and back toward Quantico, where Clay lived in a studio apartment near base.

Two miles from his place he couldn't take the uncertainty anymore. "Am I off the team?" More than the possibility of a conviction once this went to court, and a fuckload more than the certainty that his sham of a marriage was finally over, the thought of being booted off the team over this latest incident set off a hellish grinding sensation in the pit of his stomach.

DeLuca didn't try to sugar coat the situation. "Officially, you're on leave for the time being. I'm gonna do everything I can to smooth this over, but the rest will depend on what the courts decide."

That was months away, Clay thought in despair as he glanced out the window. His emotions were so jumbled he damn near felt numb at the moment. "So I'm fucked."

Tuck shifted and leaned around to peer back at him from the shotgun seat, his dark blond brows drawn together in a pissed off scowl. "No, you're not. Those are defensive wounds and we're gonna document every single mark on you so we've got our own evidence," he said, indicating the livid scratches Eve's perfectly French manicured nails had gouged into his skin two days ago.

Clay tore his gaze away from Tuck. The guy was more than Clay's team leader, he was one of his best friends, and since he'd served with Delta before coming to the FBI, Clay considered him a god. He fucking worshipped both men in the vehicle. That they were seeing him like this, at his absolute worst, was more than he could take.

He closed his stinging eyes and rubbed his fingers over them. It was all going to come out anyway. Every ugly, sordid detail. Better to tell them the worst now, so they knew what he was facing. "I grabbed her. Threatened her." And that made him a fucking statistic. Yet another former Spec Ops member arrested for domestic violence. He didn't even know how to process that, let alone go about forgiving himself for it.

"Threatened her how?" DeLuca asked in a sharp

tone.

Clay sighed and leaned his head back, keeping his eyes closed so he wouldn't have to see the men's reactions. "I hadn't changed the locks yet. She came in the bathroom as I was getting out of the shower." She'd caught him off guard, then cornered him. He would have left but there was no way she was letting him out of that bathroom without a fight and he'd wanted to avoid a physical confrontation.

Little good that did you, huh?

"She threw a punch at me and everything went from shit to shittier."

"Jesus, she's whacked," Tuck muttered.

"Yeah," Clay agreed. It had been bad. When she'd kept on attacking him he'd finally grabbed her and used his strength and skill to stop her, something he'd never believed himself capable of until now. "I couldn't get past her without hurting her so I had to restrain her. Pinned her to the wall with my hands around her wrists. I definitely left marks." She probably had others on her upper arms and back, too, from him grabbing her and the force with which he'd slammed her up against that wall.

And God help him, in that moment as he'd stared down into her furious face he'd been more tempted to put his hands around her throat and squeeze than he had been to kill some of the insurgents he'd hunted during his tours back in Afghanistan.

A deafening silence filled the vehicle at his announcement.

Clay felt the burn of tears, swallowed the lump in his throat before he forced himself to say the rest. "I kept her pinned there and said I could kill her for what she'd done."

More silence, and this time the shame he'd been holding at bay swamped him, flooding through his body like hot lava. He knew exactly how bad this was, what would go against him in court. He was big. Six-four, a whole ten inches taller and ninety pounds heavier than his petite, estranged wife. His whole life he'd been aware of his size, had grown to be aware of his own strength and what it could do to someone. He'd been brought up to respect women, to never raise a hand to them. As a SEAL, he'd been relentlessly trained to have control over that strength, to earn his Trident every day.

Guess every man had his limit. Much as it shamed him that he'd given in to his anger, Eve had finally managed to shove him head first over his. Even so he was fully aware that there was no excuse for what he'd done. His skin prickled with humiliation.

He blew out a shaky breath and continued, glad he couldn't see DeLuca and Tuck's faces. "The second I did it I knew I was fucked." He'd snatched his hands away from her like she'd burned him and staggered back, a sick sensation in his gut at the gleam of satisfaction in her eyes. As though he'd just given her her fondest wish.

And in her twisted little mind, he'd done exactly that. He'd allowed her to push him until he self-destructed, effing up his life. She knew as well as he did that a conviction would mean his career was over.

How the fuck he hadn't seen the sickness inside her until it was too late, he'd never know. The signs of her mental illness were there all along if he'd been paying attention. Tuck had seen it, had warned him early on, but he'd refused to listen, too blinded by lust and what he'd thought was love to see the reality right there in front of him. He owed Tuck a thank you and an apology for that. "I went and sat on the front step and waited for the cops to come get me," he finished, a wave of exhaustion hitting him.

It had taken Eve all of three seconds to dial 911. He'd cooperated fully with the officers. The cops had taken one look at the marks on him and taken her into custody too, but by then she'd been hysterical, screaming that he'd beaten her, showing them marks he knew damn well he hadn't put on her. It had hit him then just how much she hated him. She was willing to mark up her own body and get arrested in order to ensure his destruction.

Standing with a cop in front of his apartment building, she'd watched them take him away, a smug smile on her face as they cuffed him and stuffed him into the back of a squad car. Basking in the knowledge that she'd just manipulated him into destroying his life.

Clay had never hated anyone as much as he did her in that moment. The knowledge shook him as much as the charges now laid against him.

Domestic abuse.

Assault.

He mentally cringed. Didn't matter what had led up to it or what Eve had lied about or done to him, at the end of the day, that's what he was facing. Christ, had he really sunk to this level? The thought shook him to the core. He felt like he didn't even know himself anymore.

And now he had to face whatever consequences his actions brought.

Up front, Tuck made a frustrated sound and shook his head. "We both know what you've gone through, man. Evers too," he said, referring to another of their teammates. "I know it looks bad now, but the truth will come out in court and whatever bullshit story she's giving won't hold up. Hell, we'll all testify about what's been going on and the kind of man you are, every last one of us. You're not a fucking wife beater, Bauer. We've got your back."

One side of Clay's mouth twitched in a sad smile. "Thanks." He turned his head to stare back out the window, that sick, hollow sensation continuing to burn a hole in his gut. Didn't matter how many people were willing to stand up and testify on his behalf. He was terrified that the judge would take one look at him, read the word SEAL in his records, and believe every fucking lie Eve gave in her statement.

If that happened, barring some kind of miracle, life as he knew it was over.

Chapter One

Present Day

"Hit it."

At the stern of the Zodiac, Clay cranked the throttle and opened up the outboard engine. The boat's rigid rubber bow lifted as the craft picked up speed, skimming over the crests of the low swells.

He grunted as they slammed down into a slight trough, the impact jarring enough to make him grit his teeth as that all too familiar ache shot down his spine and into the back of his right leg. Not as bad as it had been at the start of his recovery from spinal surgery three months ago, but enough to remind him he wasn't a hundred percent yet and would probably never be again.

Sweat beaded his face and body. In this humidity he was goddamn sweltering inside his BDUs and body armor, but after all the training and punishment his time in the Navy had put him through plus this latest injury, the physical discomfort barely registered on his torment scale. Focused on getting his team in position as fast as possible, he pushed the lingering pain in his lower back aside and locked in for this joint training op.

Damn, if felt good to be back in action again. He'd been sidelined since the surgery, and at the start of his rehab he'd been afraid he'd never make it back to operational condition. It was September, the day had been still and hot and the cool breeze as they skimmed across the waters of the Gulf felt good against his face. A few scattered clouds above them slid across the quarter moon, obscuring it, but there was enough light for them to be able to work without NVGs.

Seated directly ahead of him in the boat, Tuck and Evers scanned port and starboard respectively for any threats. Schroder, the team medic, was at the bow, ducked low against the wind, gripping the rope tight to steady himself each time the bow thudded on the crest of a swell. The other three members of their seven-man assault team followed in another Zodiac, M4s slung across their backs.

One-point-seven klicks ahead in the dark water, their unsuspecting target awaited them. A DEA FAST team was approaching from the opposite side. Clay and his team would take the vessel; the DEA boys would take the crew.

A few hundred meters away from the vessel, Tuck gave the signal for him to cut the engine. Clay throttled back to minimize the noise and the bow came to rest on the water's surface, the sound of the motor quiet as they neared the target. The small cruiser sat still in the water, only a single light visible in the cabin, behind the bridge.

"One sentry on duty," Tuck confirmed in a murmur via his earpiece as he gazed through the binos. Looked like the rest of the crew—five more drug runners with ties to a terror group in Central America, according to the intel—had all hit their racks and nobody was expecting company.

17

Just the way Clay and the others liked it.

"Blade two, this is Blade-one actual," the DEA FAST Team leader said through their earpieces. Other DEA members were stationed even farther back and the HRT's tactical helicopter unit was on standby back at Keesler Air Force Base. "We're in position and have you in our sights. Verify range to target."

"Coming up on the starboard side of her stern, hundred and fifty meters and closing," Tuck answered in a low voice.

"Copy that. Intel says there might be two other vessels inbound."

"Roger." Tuck turned and nodded at Clay, who cut the engine. In a synchronized motion, the guys up front picked up their paddles and began rowing toward the target boat, their blades cutting into the water in near silence.

Once they were close enough to drift the remaining distance, Clay and the others ducked down low in the Zodiac, going to radio silence and using hand signals only. Inside the target vessel Clay could see the sentry moving around the cabin. An outer hatch opened and the man stepped through, binos raised to his eyes as he scanned the water off to the starboard.

Clay brought them soundlessly alongside the vessel out of sight, the rubber siding of the Zodiac nudging the stern of the boat with a soft bump. His heart rate remained steady, his breathing calm. Out here on the water in a maritime operation, he was in his fucking element.

The other Zodiac arrived behind them. Two guys got the boarding ladders ready. Tuck confirmed with the DEA team that they were in place and ready to board, then motioned for them to wait while he did one last visual sweep.

They were all on guard, all locked and loaded, but

as team leader the timing was his call, as was the responsibility of whatever happened here. Tuck was the most experienced operator Clay had ever worked with and knew he would never send any of his men into harm's way without making absolutely sure he'd done everything possible to ensure their safety. Even in training.

The sentry remained up near the bow, peering out into the darkness, his back to them. They were still undetected. Clay brought his weapon up and took aim at him, centering his sight between the man's shoulder blades.

Tuck raised his right arm, brought his hand down in a sharp chopping motion, fingers extended forward.

Execute.

Blackwell locked the hooks of the boarding ladder over the side of the vessel's railing, the quiet clanks barely carrying in the still air. Vance took point, scaling the ladder in seconds while Blackwell held the ladder steady. The rest of them kept their weapons trained on the deck to provide cover. Cruz went next, then Schroder, Evers and Tuck.

Clay went up last, climbing the aluminum rungs of the ladder as quickly as he could. On deck his teammates had fanned out around the stern, every one of them crouched slightly, weapons up.

The squawk of a radio sounded from where the sentry had been. Male voices speaking rapid Spanish punched through the quiet, followed by rapid footsteps and the sound of the steel hatch slamming shut.

Element of surprise gone. Now the success of the op depended on swift, violent action.

"Go," Tuck ordered.

They moved as a unit toward that hatch door. The breaching team set a charge on the hatch, blew it with a loud bang that echoed in the quiet. The instant Blackwell kicked it open, raised voices and the roar of gunfire shattered the night.

Stacked up along the starboard wall, Clay maintained his place at the rear of the line, keeping part of his attention on what was happening ahead of him, and part behind him to make sure their six was secure even though he knew the DEA team was providing cover.

Vance took point again. The team surged through the open hatch, returning fire with the same simunition rounds the bad guys were using, while Cruz yelled over top of the noise in Spanish.

"FBI, FBI! Everybody down on the floor!"

By the time Clay got through the hatch, it was practically over. Four crewmen lay face-down on the steel deck inside the wheelhouse, three of them hit with yellow dye from the simunition rounds. The captain, a man they'd codenamed Juan Valdez, lay crumpled on his side against the port-side wall with two shots to the chest. Dead. All the HRT members were unscathed.

Fucking A.

Just as the noise died down, Clay's ears caught the faint scuffing sound coming from outside. Instantly he whirled and crouched in the open doorway, the muzzle of his weapon trained sternward. The man holding an AK froze in shock when he saw him.

"Drop it and put your hands up!" Clay growled, aware that one of his teammates was in position behind him, moving alongside to provide backup. Language barrier or not, there was no mistaking what he'd said.

The man hesitated an instant, must have realized he was the only crewman left, and made a fatal mistake by raising his weapon in an effort to get a lucky shot off. Clay fired twice in a controlled burst, the double tap hitting the guy dead center mass before he could fire a single shot. He stumbled back with the impact and dropped to his side, unmoving.

Clay shot to his feet and rushed over to kick the man's weapon out of reach. It clattered over the steel deck, hitting the wall with a thud. The crew member didn't even twitch.

He looked up to find Tuck behind him, providing cover, and nodded. "Clear."

"Clear," Tuck echoed. "Cruz, Blackwell. Get out here." The two members exited the wheelhouse a second later. The FAST team leader arrived to take charge of the prisoners and help search the ship.

"Let's go," Tuck said. Together they moved through the rest of the vessel, checking each and every room and storage closet.

"Clear," Clay called out from the engine room, the last room to check. Tuck strode in, glanced around briefly and gave a satisfied nod. Now it was a search and seizure operation. He and Tuck searched the room for drugs and weapons.

"Think I found the mother lode," Cruz called out from down the hall two minutes later.

"That was fast," Clay muttered. He and Tuck followed the sound of Cruz's voice to the head at the end of the hall. In the brilliant beam of the flashlight he held, Cruz nodded toward a panel set behind the toilet. "Take a look."

They both stepped closer. Tuck let out a low whistle and Clay finally saw the duct taped bundles stacked inside the stash site. Clay reached up one hand to yank at the panel. The faux wood material came away in a big chunk, exposing yet another large stack. And another. He yanked again. Another.

"Jesus," he muttered. He was no expert on the street value of drugs, but there had to be at least ten million dollars' worth of cocaine in here.

Tuck was silent a moment as he surveyed the stash,

then contacted the remaining teammates still in the wheelhouse. "All clear." He tapped his earpiece to change frequencies. "This is blade two actual. Target is secure. All crew members accounted for. And we've found the cargo."

"Roger that," the FAST Team leader responded, a smile in his voice. He appeared in the doorway a minute later and slapped Tuck on the back, his grin showing up neon white against the camouflage paint on his face. "That was fucking awesome to watch, man."

Ever the humble operator, Tuck merely nodded by way of acceptance. Clay and his teammates stood at the stern as the wounded and dead crew members—who were actually DEA officers posing as tangos for the training op—lifted their heads from where they lay and started talking shit amongst themselves.

Clay smirked at the good-natured ribbing, still juiced from the rush of the op. Other officials began arriving to document everything. That was their signal to take off.

Clay and the others climbed back aboard their Zodiacs. He opened up the throttle and zoomed back to shore. DeLuca was waiting for them at the dock, along with other FBI, DEA and Homeland Security officials.

DeLuca's hard features eased into a grin when they pulled up alongside the dock. "Good night's work, I'd say."

"Yeah, not bad," Tuck said as he climbed out of the boat, his grin as wide as DeLuca's. The CO shook each man's hand then ushered them toward the waiting van. Fifteen minutes later they were inside a private room at Keesler for their debriefing and after action report.

An hour after that, DeLuca straightened from where he'd been bent over a folder of documents, closed the front cover and gave them all a smile. "Go on and get outta here. Report back at oh-eight-hundred hours.

Meetings with the DEA people will go until around eighteen-hundred, I figure. Guess I don't have to ask where you boys are heading after that, do I?"

Clay opened his mouth to say a smart-ass reply but DeLuca held up a hand before he could get a word out. "I don't even wanna know. I'll be in New Orleans for the security conference this weekend. Feel free to come by and buy me a beer."

When he walked away, Tuck turned to Clay and Schroder. "You guys still coming into town with me?"

"I'm in," Schroder said, hazel eyes bright with excitement. "You're still meeting up with your cousin, right?"

Clay's head snapped around to stare at him and he shot the former PJ a hard look. What the hell did he know about Zoe, and why did he seem so happy about the prospect of seeing her tonight?

Her face formed in his mind. Pale skin, red and black-dyed hair, sultry golden eyes that saw right into him. Saw right *through* him, and she didn't seem to mind his brusque, rough edges. And her body. Fuck, those long, strong legs and full hips he'd wanted to feel beneath his hands. Under *him*.

No, he didn't like the gleam in the young medic's eyes at all when he mentioned Zoe. The raw, territorial reaction came out of nowhere, catching him off guard.

"Bauer, you're in too, right?" Tuck asked.

Clay met his gaze, kept his expression impassive even as he experienced a simultaneous shot of anticipation and dread. "Yeah, I'll go." Wasn't like he had anything else to do, and despite all her weird quirks, he liked Zoe. More than he wanted to, and sure as hell he should be beaten with a tire iron for thinking the way he had about the woman Tuck considered a sister, let alone for all the filthy, X-rated things he'd imagined doing to her.

"Good. Zo's been looking forward to seeing you."

Clay didn't reply as he followed Tuck and the others back to the van. Zoe was... Well, there was no one like her. To be honest, she confused the hell out of him. Without even trying she made him want her so much it was all he could do to keep his hands off her. She also had a knack for making him feel like an uneducated idiot compared to her, and it had nothing to do with her being three years older than him. The woman's brainpower was a little intimidating, to be honest.

He wasn't the best judge of character, but from what he'd seen of her and what he'd heard from Tuck and Celida, Zoe was one of those rare people who said what she meant and meant what she said. And by all accounts, she was loyal. Something as rare as diamonds in this world, at least in Clay's experience. But he'd witnessed that loyalty firsthand.

Resting in the back of the van with his eyes closed as they drove back to their hotel, memories flashed through his mind. Zoe's face lighting up and the way she'd rushed over to hug him when he'd gone to pick her up from the airport as a favor to Tuck back in June. That smile on her face had seemed genuine, as if she'd truly been glad to see him.

Her finding him alone and naked in the hot tub at his and Tuck's place a few nights later. The unmistakable female appreciation and interest in her eyes when he'd climbed down the steps with nothing but a towel wrapped around his waist.

They'd watched a movie together, her just three feet away from him on the other end of the couch. She'd looked so...soft, that night. So feminine and sexy, that hard-edged attitude dimmed until it was all he could do to keep from reaching for her, twining his hands in that thick, shockingly bright, red-streaked hair and kissing that smart mouth.

But most of all, he remembered her being at his hospital bedside after he'd been injured on his last op.

The hostage rescue mission at a federal bank eight weeks ago had gone to shit when the hostage-taker had detonated his explosives wired into the building's windows and doors, collapsing the tunnel Clay and the others had been waiting in to do the breach.

He barely remembered anything after that except for the hellish pain in his back, in his legs, that wouldn't stop. When he'd woken in the hospital that first night in a haze of mind-numbing pain, Zoe had been right there to help him. She'd come back the same day of his operation, too, and visited him twice more before he was discharged.

The last time he'd seen her was at her uncle's— Tuck's father's—funeral. He'd been two days post-op and even grumpier than usual because of his pain level. When she'd showed up at his house to drive him to the church, the sight of her in that filmy, black Victorian Goth dress had taken his breath away.

She hadn't seemed to hold his gruffness against him, even standing quietly in a corner at the reception after the graveside service, enduring his silence because she'd known he was in pain and didn't want to socialize, and that he couldn't sit down without being in agony. They'd e-mailed and talked over the phone a few times since, but he'd been careful not to encourage the interest she clearly broadcasted.

And the books she'd left him before she'd gone back home to New Orleans. That had been one hell of an eye-opener, because mother of Christ, the woman had a brilliant, dirty imagination.

He wasn't much of a reader but when he did it was usually biographies, historical stuff or Spec Ops thrillers. Romantic horror wasn't even remotely on his interest spectrum but he'd read all three books Zoe had given him because *she'd* written them and for some reason he'd wanted to know that part of her. The sex scenes had played on the screen of his mind like a high definition porno flick long after he'd read them.

He'd replayed them at least a hundred times since when he was alone in bed and needed to take the edge off, except he always imagined it was him and Zoe in place of the main characters. Each time the need she'd awakened inside him only seemed to get stronger.

And therein lay the dilemma.

There was no question that he wanted her, more than he'd wanted any other woman in recent memory, but that was where he drew the line. He couldn't just fuck her and walk away, and that was all he had to offer a woman these days. His disastrous marriage and divorce had damaged him and he knew damn well he wasn't ready for another relationship. Might never be. Zoe deserved better than what he could give her. If he acted like a prick and gave into temptation and took her to bed, Tuck would cut his heart out for hurting her.

That wasn't why Clay wouldn't make a move on her though. The truth was he didn't ever want to see those pretty golden eyes fill with hurt because of him. He knew all too well what it felt like to be hurt by someone you cared about, and Zoe cared too much about people, including him for reasons he'd never understand. So he had to keep his distance.

And since he'd just agreed to see her tomorrow night, that had to mean he was a fucking closet masochist or something.

Back in the hotel in Biloxi, Clay stripped and stepped under the hot spray of the shower in the room he was sharing with Tuck. He groaned at the heat and pressure of the water pounding against his sore back and shoulders. The instant he closed his eyes, however,

Zoe's face came to mind again. Smiling, laughing at something he said, the knowing gleam in her eyes challenging him. Clay's muscles tensed. Molten heat and need erupted inside him, making him hard all over.

He leaned forward and braced one palm against the slick fiberglass wall as the water pounded over his back. The door was locked and even though he should probably feel guilty as fuck for fantasizing about Zoe like this when Tuck was just in the next room, he couldn't help himself.

Blocking out the twinge of guilt needling his conscience, he grasped the length of his hard, swollen flesh and let his favorite fantasy unfold. Zoe on her knees in front of him, hands secured behind her back. Her wildly-colored hair wound into a knot at the top of her head, those heavily made up eyes gazing up at him with lust and desire as her luscious lips closed around the head of his cock.

Clay stifled a groan and stroked harder, faster. The fantasy raged on in vivid detail. He could hear the wet slide of her mouth on him, feel her lips and tongue working the ultrasensitive spot beneath the head just before she bobbed down and took him deep.

His back arched, a raw gasp tearing free of his chest. A warning twinge of pain shot down his lower back, into his thighs as scar tissue and newly healed muscle and tendons pulled, but the pleasure obliterated it all. His free hand curled into a fist against the wall. In his fantasy his fingers wound around her hair. He squeezed tight, holding her head and mouth just where he wanted them, watched as that flare of heated awareness and languid acceptance appeared in her gaze when he seized control. He shuddered, squeezed his eyes shut as the pleasure bordered on pain.

And when he came deep in her mouth, despite his iron control and vow to remain silent, two desperate syllables rasped out of his tight throat.

Zoe.

Chapter Two

Zoe pulled at the high collar of her black, ruffled Victorian-style sleeveless top and blew out a sigh as she shifted her weight to counteract the streetcar's change in momentum when it slowed at the next stop. Even though she had her hair secured into a messy bun at the back of her head, the tendrils around her face and nape were limp and stuck to her skin.

Summer in New Orleans was notoriously hot and steamy. Even though it was September, the temperature was still damn near unbearable. Not for the first time she wondered what the hell had possessed her to decide to stay down here instead of moving to a cooler climate where her hair didn't frizz every time she went outside. The humidity was going to kill her yet, just see if it didn't.

With the streetcar halted, the slight breeze that had been coming through the windows stopped and without it the atmosphere inside went from uncomfortable to intolerable. It got even worse when she had to press up against a heavy-set man in front of her in order to allow a mother and her two young children by so they could get to the door.

The man looked down at her with a wry smile, face

shiny with perspiration and sweat stains marking the armpits of his shirt. "Summer in N'Awlins," he murmured, his gaze taking in her newly purple-streaked hair and Goth outfit and makeup. Not that she cared. She was used to people staring at her and didn't give a damn what they thought. Some were more ignorant than others, of course. *Is that a costume? Aren't you a little early? Halloween isn't for a few months yet.*

Or her favorite: *Are you a vampire?*

The locals usually didn't say dumb shit like that because New Orleans was called the Big Easy for a reason and the city was okay with all lifestyles. Tourists and strangers when she ventured outside the city, however, were a different story.

"Gotta love it," she agreed as she stepped back, "else you're gonna hate it." And lord, did she hate this part of it. She couldn't wait to get back to her new air-conditioned apartment she was renting in the Quarter and climb into a cool shower. She had big plans tonight and she wanted to look and smell her best when they happened.

Because whether the man in question knew it or not, they *were* happening.

The streetcar began moving again, starting up that blessed wisp of a breeze through the windows. The air streaming in was hot, but at least it was moving across her skin and brought a slight measure of relief.

She actually loved her weekly commute, though.

Out the window across the aisle from her she watched her favorite part of the Garden District pass by. Beautiful, stately homes with well-manicured gardens and lawns that looked like they'd been sheared with scissors, some pre-dating the War Between the States. She'd used a few of the houses in the district in her novels, though usually she set the homes in the swamps and bayous just outside of the city. Way spookier that way, and the setting helped give her the dark and creepy vibe she aimed for in her books. Her fans loved her settings as much as they did the tortured heroes and kickass heroines, and Zoe loved delivering.

Just as the streetcar began to slow for its next stop, her cell phone buzzed with an incoming text. She pulled it out, aware of the surge of excitement in her veins, but it quickly dimmed when she saw the text wasn't from her cousin, Tuck. It was from a woman she'd talked to a couple of times at the women's shelter where she volunteered. Normally she didn't give out her number to anyone but Leticia was a special case and Zoe had been trying for months without success to talk her into leaving her boyfriend and stay at the shelter until they could come up with a permanent solution.

I'm at the house, the text read. *They told me you just left.*

Zoe typed a response. If she could convince Leticia to stay at the shelter, then she had to go back. *I'm about fifteen mins away. Want me to come back?*

No. Can we talk when you get a chance though?

There was no way she was going to say no, not when she'd begged the woman four times already to leave her current situation and get her and her son to the shelter for help. If she was there now, this had to be important. *Sure*, she responded.

The streetcar's brakes let out a high-pitched squeal as the vehicle slowed to a stop to pick up a passenger. Zoe hitched her black leather satchel higher up on her shoulder and stepped past the heavy-set man to get off. The air outside was still just as heavy but without all that body heat surrounding her to make it worse, it felt like heaven.

Stepping off the sidewalk onto a patch of brown, brittle grass beneath the shade of a huge, spreading live oak, she called the number on screen and Leticia picked up on the second ring.

"Hey."

"Are you okay?" Zoe asked her.

"Yeah. Xander and me are fine, we just arrived a few minutes after you left."

"Sorry I missed you. Do you need anything?"

"No, everyone here's been real nice. They're making Xander some mac and cheese right now, his favorite."

Zoe smiled. "That's good. Will you be staying the night?"

A huff of ironic laughter answered her. "Longer than that." She paused. "I left him, Zoe. For good. I'm not going back there, ever."

Zoe closed her eyes in relief. It had been necessary, but still incredibly brave of Leticia to take her ten-year-old son and leave her abusive, waste-of-skin, controlling boyfriend. "I'm proud of you."

"Thanks," Leticia said with a little laugh. "I'm proud of me too."

Unease tightened her stomach. "Did Carl... Did anything happen to make you decide this?"

Another pause, and Zoe could feel Leticia's hesitation before she answered. "He tried to go after Xander."

Zoe sucked in a breath, her spine going rigid as her eyes narrowed and her fingers tightened around the phone. *That piece of shit.*

"We were arguing again and he got physical, then Xander tried to get between us to protect me. Carl sent him flying, would have beaten on him if I hadn't screamed at Xander to run. Luckily the neighbors heard us this time and when they showed up Carl took off. Right then I realized I couldn't afford to wait any longer. My baby's the most important thing in the world to me—he deserves to live without fear."

"And so do you," Zoe added, unable to hide the edge to her voice. She'd been volunteering once a week at the shelter for more than a year now, and too many times the women she'd come into contact with there actually believed that they deserved the treatment their abusers dished out. It made her furious. No woman or child should ever have to live in fear of a beating or worse from a man in their life when he lost it.

"Yeah, I know."

But Zoe got the feeling Leticia *didn't* know it. Not yet. She would though, eventually, when she'd had enough time and distance from Carl to see everything clearly. "Did you go to the police?"

"Yes, and I got a restraining order like you told me to."

"Good." She glanced at her watch. Ten minutes to six. "Listen, I can still come in, it's no problem—"

"No, we're fine. But thanks. Just…you're sure this place is secret, right? I mean, even the cops, they don't know where it is, right?"

One of the reasons she'd refused to leave before was because she was so afraid of Carl and his connections across the city. It was no secret that some politicians and cops down here were known to be corrupt, and even though Leticia hadn't said who Carl was or what he did, clearly she believed the strings he was capable of pulling were powerful ones.

"Right. Only the workers and the women who stay there know the location, and we're all bound to secrecy. You and Xander will be safe there," Zoe promised.

A loud sigh filled the line. "Be nice to feel safe enough to sleep through the night for once. Maybe not tonight or even the next one, but hopefully in a few days it'll sink in that we're not in danger anymore."

Zoe hated that she and Xander had lived that kind of life for so long. "Do you have a plan in mind yet?

Where you want to go?"

"I'm not going back to Tennessee. He'll look for me there, track down my family. He *knows* people, has connections all over the South, and a lot of them owe him favors. Trust me when I tell you, I have good reason to be scared of him."

Jesus, who was this guy? "Then we need to start thinking about somewhere else you could go. A different city for sure, but out of state would be even better. We've got contacts through social workers, even the FBI—"

"*No*. No Feds or cops or anyone else like that." Her voice was so panicked that Zoe felt a chill run down her spine. "Just you and whoever can help me here. That's the only reason I came in. I trust *you*."

"Okay, it's all right, I won't say anything to anyone," Zoe said, rushing to soothe her. Her cousin Tuck was on the FBI Hostage Rescue Team and his girlfriend, Celida—who was also Zoe's best friend—was an agent too. They'd have solid contacts to help her, but she wasn't going to break Leticia's trust. "I'll be in first thing in the morning to talk everything over with you. Okay?"

Maybe by then Leticia would realize she needed more help than Zoe or the others could give her, and she'd allow Zoe to contact Celida about this. Maintaining Leticia's trust was key, however, and she wouldn't rush her into a decision. One false move and the woman could bolt, disappear without a trace with her son. Maybe Carl would find them again. Zoe couldn't let that happen.

"Thanks, I appreciate it," Leticia said softly.

"It's the least I can do," Zoe insisted. "I'll have my cell with me if you need anything, okay?"

"Nah, I don't wanna bug you, you've already done so much to help us. I'll see you tomorrow though?"

Zoe didn't miss the uncertainty in the question. Leticia may not have had many people she could count on in her life, but Zoe and the others at the shelter were solid. They wouldn't let anything happen to her on their watch. "Bright and early."

As she tucked her phone back into her bag she felt lighter, as if an invisible weight had been lifted from her shoulders. The streetcar had just come into view at the far end of the road when her cell buzzed again. This time when she pulled it out she smiled at the sight of Tuck's name on the display.

We just finished up. Heading into NOLA now. We still on for tonight?

She snorted. Was he kidding? *Uh, duh. YES!* she typed back.

Got Bauer, Evers and Schroder with me. Be at your place around nine.

She didn't know who Schroder was but guessed he must be one of their teammates. Bauer and Evers, though, she knew. And she'd like to get to know one of them a whole lot better.

A buzz of excitement hummed in the pit of her stomach as she texted again. *Sounds good. I'll be ready.*

Ready as in looking fabulous and set to make a move on a certain sexy former SEAL with questionable social skills, she thought with a satisfied smile. His rough edges didn't bother her. He'd been through a lot. They were different, but they also had a lot in common. They'd both been divorced, for one, though hers looked freaking amicable compared to his. And she knew damn well he wanted her, no matter how aloof he seemed.

In a way he was like Leticia, jaded and street smart and didn't trust easily. Zoe was determined to win him over, show him not all women were manipulative and calculating psychos like his mentally unstable ex.

Putting the phone away as the streetcar ground to a

halt in front of her and opened its door, Zoe climbed the steps, imagining the look on Bauer's face when she showed him just how *interested* she was and took them firmly out of the friend zone this weekend.

****

Carlos parked in the back alley and climbed out of the car with a foreign ball of unease grinding in the pit of his stomach. All the blinds on the front of the house were drawn. His sixth sense kicked in. It had kept him alive in many dangerous situations before so he never ignored it. And right now it was telling him that she was already gone.

He entered the gate at the side of the wooden privacy fence encircling the property. The neighborhood was good and even though he'd offered to buy Leticia a house multiple times, she'd always turned him down, preferring to live in this modest place and pay her own rent. Her independence was one of the things he loved most about her. Now it threatened to take her from him for good.

Opening the side door with his key, the stillness hit him. He closed the door behind him, the sound seeming to echo in the absolute silence that surrounded him. His hand shook as he shoved the key back into his front pocket. Jaw clenched, he flipped on the kitchen light. The dirty dishes in the sink were a dead giveaway. As was the milk carton still on the granite-topped counter.

She'd gone. He'd bet right after he'd taken off yesterday.

A deep, burning rage lit up in his chest. The heat of it seared him as he stalked through the kitchen to the family room. He paused, his gaze stuck on the fireplace. All the framed photos of them were gone. His hand balled into a fist at the thought of her wiping the images of them away.

His boots thudded over the hardwood as he strode down the hall to the master bedroom. The bed was perfectly made, not a single wrinkle in the coverlet. He stepped to the bathroom, noticed immediately that her makeup case and toothbrush were missing. A sick feeling of dread took hold, smothering the flames of his anger. Pushing open the door to the walk-in closet, he held his breath and flipped on the light.

A gap on one of the shelves caught his attention. There were several gaps in between the hangers on the rod next to it as well. He glanced up at the top shelf, noticed the largest of her suitcases was missing. Oh yeah, she was gone all right. And from the looks of it, not just for the weekend.

Disappointment and betrayal warred inside him, along with a heaping of guilt. He'd made her run. He'd scared her away by being too forceful too soon. She was different than any of the other women he'd been with, more headstrong and confident. He'd known early on that she wouldn't come to heel quickly or easily, which was half the reason he'd wanted her so bad. She was the only woman who'd ever stood up to him and held her ground, even knowing him and his reputation. What he was capable of. He loved that about her.

But now she'd left him. Run from him with her mouthy brat who had caused all this in the first place.

He'd teach her there was nowhere she could go that he couldn't find her. And when he found her...

He shut off the light and closed the closet door. If she came back he didn't want her to know he'd been here. He couldn't risk spooking her to bolt again before he caught her and taught her a lesson. No woman ever walked out on him.

Locking the front door behind him, he let himself out back through the side gate, his attention snagging on the garbage can lid sitting askew next to the garage. Walking over, he lifted the lid, every muscle in his body going rigid when he saw the broken picture frames inside. Pictures of them together, the images obscured by the shatter marks in the glass. All from the fireplace, the few from her bedroom.

The symbolism of it hit him in the chest with the force of a bullet. She'd not only run from him, she'd thrown them away.

He dragged in a slow, deep breath to ease the pressure in his lungs, the fury choking him, and dug his phone out of his hip pocket. "She's gone," he said when Rick answered.

"Sorry, man," Rick said, sounding apologetic.

Carlos swallowed past the thickness in his throat. "Trace her phone and find out where she is."

"Hang on." The sound of fingers clacking on a keyboard came in the background.

Carlos stood there waiting in the smothering heat, and even though his body was sweating, inside he was ice cold. His jaw tightened again as he stared down at the ruined photos.

Tossing the lid aside, he tucked the phone between his ear and shoulder and tied the black plastic bag shut with an angry tug, then yanked it from the can. He wasn't leaving them here for anyone else to find. Later he'd come back and sweep the place for other personal stuff that might hint at his connection to Leticia, wiping any fingerprints and erasing himself from the house. DNA was a problem, but he had the resources and he'd call in a cleaning crew to scrub any evidence of his presence from the premises.

There could be no proof left behind once he located and went after her.

"You sure you put the tracker on her phone?" Rick asked.

Carlos straightened, held the phone in his hand once more. "Yeah, why?"

"It's not working. Think she might have found it and disabled it?"

"No." He'd put it inside the SIM card slot himself when she wasn't looking. "She might have ditched it and gotten a new one though. Trace her call records. Find out who she's been talking to and where she called from. Call me back once you find something." Jealousy, suspicion swirled in his mind. If she'd been calling one guy more than any other, he'd find out. If the guy had touched her, he was a dead man walking for touching what was his.

Carrying the trash bag, Carlos stalked to his truck. A nondescript ten-year-old Ford pickup that was perfect for his latest undercover role. He'd gotten so good at playing parts over the years that he actually believed his own cover story. Leticia had fallen for it too, falling in love with the bad boy image the job required. But she didn't realize just how bad he could be, or all the criminal connections he had access to because of his role.

She was going to find out the truth firsthand soon enough.

Chapter Three

At a little past nine that night Clay stood sweating on the cracked sidewalk out front of Zoe's place with Tuck, Evers and Schroder. He knew she'd moved here from Mid-City to rent a place a couple months ago, soon after his surgery. The noise of the French Quarter surrounded him with the smoky sounds of jazz coming from a band playing around the corner and the laughter and chatter from the tourists filling the cramped streets. Underlying the tantalizing scent of food coming from the restaurant down the street, the faint scent of overripe garbage hung in the still air.

"Move over and gimme some room, man," Schroder said to him, bumping his shoulder into Clay's to get him to step closer to the wall.

"Find your own spot, it's too damn hot for you to stand so close," Clay muttered, but stepped aside anyhow. They were all crowded together in the little patch of space created by the wrought iron pillars supporting the balcony above them, to allow the flow of pedestrians to walk past. It was wide enough that it blocked the stream of the streetlamp coming from behind them.

"Quit your bitching. We're in New Orleans, baby.

They call it the Big Easy for a reason—this town's full of food, jazz and women. Who cares about a little humidity?"

Ignoring the jab, Clay peered through the black wrought-iron gate at the entrance of Zoe's place that served to block the pedestrian traffic from entering the historic brick building. He sincerely hoped she had better security upstairs, because anyone with a bolt cutter could cut through that flimsy-ass lock she had on there, and anyone with some training could blow through it with a couple well-placed kicks.

He lifted his gaze from the combination lock holding the thing shut and looked through the arched entryway to the far end. Warm lamplight filtered down through what appeared to be a courtyard nestled in the center of the building. The sound of trickling water came from whatever lay on the other side of the far brick wall.

Two dings sounded and Tuck lifted his phone to read a message. "She's on her way down," he told them, and put the phone back into his cargo pants' pocket.

Clay edged back from the others. And it was absolutely *not* because he was nervous about seeing Zoe again, he assured himself.

Tuck's dark blond head lifted, his gaze shifting to the inner courtyard. "Here she comes."

Clay's muscles tightened slightly in anticipation just before her voice called out. "Hey, y'all. Glad you could make it." The low, husky edge to it made his heart beat faster.

"Good to see you, cuz," Tuck drawled, a big grin on his face.

"You too, handsome." A slender hand appeared through the wrought iron gate. She fiddled with the lock that was seriously going to give him sleepless nights and a moment later the gate swung open with a metallic creak. Zoe stepped out onto the sidewalk and hugged her cousin, and Clay felt his heart stutter.

Her hair was black with chunks of deep purple this time, pulled up into a loose knot at the back of her head that left the graceful sweep of her throat exposed...right down to all the cleavage she was showing off in the purple corset she wore.

His tongue got stuck to the roof of his mouth for a moment as he stared at the mounds of her breasts, pushed up so lovingly by the bodice, the indent of her waist highlighted by the way it cinched inward before flaring out over her hips. She was smaller on top and bigger on the bottom and he loved her curves. The black ruffled skirt she wore hit her at mid-thigh, exposing miles of pale, smooth legs set off by killer black, spike heels. Her toenails were painted a shocking purple too, and she had what looked like little crystal bats on the strap overlying her toes.

She looked over Tuck's broad shoulder, spotted him, and the smile that lit up her face was like a sucker punch to the solar plexus. "Hey, you," she said softly, stepping back from Tuck to approach him.

When she got within five feet of him he could smell the faint scent of her perfume. Something sultry and exotic and mysterious, light enough that it made him want to lean in to press his nose against the side of her throat and breathe more of it in. "Hi," he managed, suddenly feeling too fucking awkward. She was tall for a woman, around five-ten or so, with a solid frame. Even though he knew she wasn't delicate, he was afraid to touch her. Zoe had no such reservations, however.

She walked right up to him, that warm smile in place, golden eyes sparkling against the heavy black makeup surrounding them, and reached up to wrap her arms around his neck. "It's good to see you," she said in a low voice, pressing those luscious curves against him as she squeezed him tight. Still a hugger.

Clay knew he should pull away, but she felt so damn good and she seemed genuinely glad to see him so he didn't want to hurt her feelings. And if he was honest, he'd been looking forward to this moment much more than he'd ever admit. "You too." Oh, hell, she smelled delicious and her genuine warmth thawed the cold place inside him.

Zoe pulled back and grinned up at him, the little diamond stud in the right side of her nose winking in the lamplight. "Hard to believe, but I think you're even bigger than the last time I saw you." Her eyes trailed appreciatively over the line of his chest and shoulders, skimmed down to his waist. A surge of blood shot southward, making his jeans uncomfortably tight. He shifted again and cleared his throat, bringing her gaze up to his once more.

"Been working out a lot since I started rehab."

"Mmm, yeah, I can tell." The sultry edge to her voice made him think of hot, sweaty sex. Of her tangled naked with him in her bed upstairs. The flirtatious light in her eyes told him it was intentional.

Shit. He glanced at the others, who were watching them with interest. Schroder was checking her ass out. When he looked up and noticed Clay watching him, Clay shot him a warning glare before indicating him and Evers with a nod. "You know Evers already, I think, but not Schroder. Nate's our medic."

"Nice to meet you," the former PJ said, taking a step forward to offer Zoe his hand.

"Likewise," she said, shaking it. When she withdrew, she looked back at Tuck. "You boys hungry or do you want to just hit a bar?"

"Bar," Tuck and Schroder both answered at the same time.

Zoe grinned and gestured northward. "Right this way."

Tuck slid an arm around her shoulders as they started up the sidewalk.

"Are we going to Bourbon Street?" Schroder asked from behind them.

Zoe looked over her shoulder at him and made a face. "If you want to, but honestly, Bourbon's pretty gross."

Clay agreed, but snorted. "You live less than a block away from it."

That keen gaze zeroed in on him. "Doesn't mean I go there. That's for the tourists." Her eyes shifted to Schroder, softened with a smile. "Let's try the place I have in mind and if you still want to, we can do Bourbon after."

"I gotta do Bourbon at least once," Schroder said, keeping in step with them. "Bauer, you been there?"

"Yeah, once." He was aware of Zoe shooting him a glance, but didn't look at her as he kept walking.

Some of his SEAL buddies had dragged him from one end of Bourbon to the other back at his bachelor party two days before he'd gotten married. He'd been drunk before they'd started, and so wasted by the time they'd left their second bar that he didn't remember anything about the rest of the night except for puking his guts out in the gutter at some point before they'd literally carried his ass to a cab and gotten him back to the hotel. Eve had been there waiting after her bachelorette party, pissed that he'd left her alone for the whole night.

He'd crawled to the toilet, utterly miserable; she'd tossed a towel at him and slammed the bathroom door shut in his face. He'd spent the night with his cheek pressed to the cool, tile floor, alternately cursing himself and throwing up until he thought his insides would burst.

"Just down this street," Zoe called back as they turned the corner. Up ahead he saw the sign for Pat O'Brien's. They made their way to the back of the bar and found a table for them all to sit at. Zoe stayed next to Tuck, but her eyes followed Clay as he rounded the table to sit at the far end.

"So what's the specialty here?" Schroder asked, looking like a kid in a candy store as he glanced around the busy bar.

"You gotta have a hurricane," Zoe told him. "They're strong, but you guys are big boys so I'm sure you can hold your liquor better than I can."

"Hurricane it is." Schroder jumped off his chair. "I'll get the first round. You guys all want one?"

"Sure," Tuck said. Zoe and Evers nodded too, then Schroder looked at Clay.

"Beer," he said.

"Seriously? So boring."

"Beer's good." He was pretty sure he'd had more than a few hurricanes at his bachelor party, and a couple of those damn absinthe things too.

As Schroder went off to the bar, Clay tried not to focus on Zoe. She was talking with both Tuck and Evers, who flanked her, her husky laugh at whatever they were saying tightening his insides. Schroder was still at the bar when she looked over at Clay. "You okay?"

"Fine."

She studied his face for a moment. "You just seem really quiet. Even for you."

"That's Bauer, life of the party," Tuck said dryly.

Rather than laugh it off, Zoe got up, came around the table and pulled out the seat beside him. When she had something to say, she didn't pull punches. Clay braced himself for a full interrogation but she merely lowered herself into the chair and leaned toward him while Tuck and Evers talked. Before she could say anything, Schroder came back with the drinks.

"Hurricane for the lady," he said, giving her a wink, his damn dimples creasing his cheeks.

"Thanks, hon," she said softly. Bauer thanked him for the beer and when everyone had their drink Zoe raised her glass. "To rough men who stand ready in the night to visit violence on those who would do us harm," she said, quoting part of the famous saying by some author whose name Clay couldn't remember. Zoe would know it though. She knew all kinds of random facts, that busy mind never stopping.

Tuck and Schroder grinned at her and they all raised their glasses with a chorused, "Cheers."

They clinked glasses and Zoe took a sip of hers while the three men across the table started chatting amongst themselves. "So," she said to Clay without looking at him. "How's your back these days?"

"It's good."

She turned those gorgeous eyes on him. Most of the guys in the vicinity had checked her out at least once already, but a few were staring at her with open curiosity. He didn't like it. "Yeah? Good enough to let you get back to work?"

"I'm back already. Our team's in a training cycle right now, so it's perfect. Gives me a few more weeks until we go to either operations or support."

"That's great. But how are *you* doing?"

He blinked at that. "Good. Why?"

She shrugged. "Not sorry you came here tonight?"

She read him easily. He didn't want her thinking it had anything to do with her though. Clay looked away, out across the bar to where a band was setting up to play. "You know how I am." He didn't like crowds, didn't do social niceties. Mostly because he just didn't see the point in putting out the effort.

"I'm beginning to think I actually don't, no."

At the teasing note in her voice he shifted his gaze back to her and felt that all too familiar zing of attraction in his gut when their eyes connected. "You know me a lot better than most people."

She gave a nod of acknowledgement. "I'll take that as a compliment."

She should. Since the divorce he'd made a point of walling himself off from others, especially women.

Silence began to spread between them. Reminding himself of his manners, he took a sip of his beer and lowered the bottle, his thumb sliding over the condensation on the glass. "What about you?"

"I'm great. Working on my next book."

His mind went right back to those insanely hot sex scenes. "I read them all, by the way. The ones you left for me." She'd e-mailed him some research questions over the past few months too, and he'd always wondered if it was a convenient excuse for her to keep in touch.

Her eyebrows shot upward. "You did?"

He nodded, one side of his mouth turning up at the surprise on her face. "Yep, all three."

"The entire book, or did you skim?"

"Cover to cover."

She set down her drink, turned to face him fully, her eyes wide. "Wow. And? Do you need therapy now?"

A reluctant chuckle eased from him. She smiled in answer, her eyes sparkling. "No. Wasn't what I was expecting, though." That was an understatement.

Her smile widened. "Hot, huh?"

Grinning at her smug expression, he looked back down at his beer. "Yep. Helluva lot darker than I expected, too. And gorier." He gave her a sidelong glance. "Never knew you were so bloodthirsty."

She seemed to take that as a positive, because she laughed softly. A beat of silence passed, and when she spoke her voice was quiet, barely carrying over the noise of the bar. "What did you think of the hero in the third one?"

The one with his very favorite sex scene. "He was

okay. Why?"

"Just okay?" She didn't sound offended, just curious.

He struggled for something more complimentary to say. "I liked the action parts in that one the best." Mostly the action in between the sheets, but he wasn't going to say it.

She sat back, looking supremely satisfied. "Thanks." Actually, she looked like she was sitting on a big secret.

It made him curious. "What?"

"Was just thinking about that hero. He's very special to me."

He didn't respond, wondering what was going on in that razor sharp mind of hers. She scared him sometimes she was so freaking smart.

Her lips curved in a soft smile. A private smile, just for him and he felt an electric zing travel through him. "He reminds me a lot of you."

Clay cranked his head around to stare at her, unsure he'd heard her right. "Me?"

She nodded once. "You."

He frowned, trying to remember who the hero had been. He couldn't remember the guy's name, just that he'd seemed fairly competent, tactically speaking, and that he'd had insanely hot, rough sex with the heroine. "Why?"

Her bare shoulders lifted, drawing attention back to the creamy skin of her neck and shoulders and tantalizing curves of her breasts pushed up by the corset. "Because you've got a lot of the same qualities he does."

At that cryptic comment Clay felt his face grow hot as he sat there, clueless as to how to reply, and though he wanted to know what she meant, he wasn't going to press for details. She saw him as heroic? Even though he was usually gruff, cynical and rough around the edges?

Though if she knew about what had happened with Eve, he doubted she'd still see him that way. "Thanks," he said, not knowing what else to say.

"Don't thank me, it's just the truth," she said, turning back to her drink. "Celida reads all my stuff and she saw the similarities too. Guess you must have rubbed off on my subconscious while I was writing that one. Anyway, I only told you because I thought it might be kind of cool for you to read how someone else sees you through their eyes." Before he could respond she refocused her attention on his teammates across the table and leaned in to engage in their conversation.

Clay took another pull of his beer as the rest of them talked, mulling over her words. Now that she'd told him, it was kind of cool to know she'd based one of her characters on him. But how far did it go, and what did it mean? She wasn't spinning romantic fantasies about him, was she? Because shit, he was so not a romance hero and he didn't want her to be disappointed when she realized that.

Romance heroes didn't get arrested and thrown in jail for alleged domestic abuse. And since Zoe had practiced family law, she'd no doubt have seen all kinds of that shit. He would hate his past to change her opinion of him.

Even as he thought it, Clay mentally shook himself. She wasn't going to ever see that side of him, so it didn't matter, did it?

The band started up, a drummer, fiddler and guitarist playing some lively Irish-sounding jig. Zoe made a sound of pleasure that hit him square in the chest and straightened. "I love this song!" She shot him a smile, raised one dark eyebrow. "Wanna dance?"

His muscles grabbed. Hell, he hated to disappoint her even this much, but he'd sooner undergo an interrogation than set foot on a dance floor. "I don't dance."

The other eyebrow shot up to join the first. "Ever?"

He shook his head, aware that the others were staring at him.

"He doesn't, but I do," Schroder said, already rising from his chair. "Come on, sweetheart, let's show these boys how it's done." He came around the table and offered her his hand, those goddamn dimples doing their magic, and Clay's hand tightened around his beer.

"Love to," Zoe said, taking his hand.

As she left the table and let Schroder escort her across to the small dance floor where other people were already dancing, Clay braced himself for the moment when she turned and gave him a look to either guilt him or rub in the fact that she was dancing with his teammate. Try to make him jealous, show him what he was missing in an attempt to get him to cave and go out there, to take Schroder's place. Or start some other manipulative mind game some women liked to play.

It didn't happen.

Not only that, but as the third song faded into the fourth and Zoe showed no signs of slowing down, she didn't glance his way even once. It was obvious she was enjoying the hell out of herself, and so was Schroder. And his teammate wasn't the only one who couldn't take his eyes off her. Other men around the bar were watching her too, eyeing her as she swayed and shimmied in that sexy outfit and heels.

Despite himself, Clay found his attention kept getting dragged back to her too. Out on the floor dancing like that she was damn near mesmerizing. Her pale skin practically glowed under the lights. Watching her move, all sinuous, confident grace, he couldn't help but think back to her books, especially the third one. Was that the kind of sex she liked? Edgy. A little rough.

He liked sex that way, raw and primal, but he'd

been careful to tone that part of him down during his marriage because during the increasingly rare times that Eve had shown any interest in sex, she'd wanted slow and sweet. There was definitely a time and a place for slow and sweet, but so many times he'd been forced to rein that more dominant side of him in so he wouldn't scare or offend her. Looking back, they hadn't been compatible at all in most ways, and the lack of sex had been another nail in their marriage's coffin.

Clay finished off his beer, watching Zoe. He couldn't be sure, but he got the feeling she wouldn't balk or be scared if he let his rougher side out in the bedroom. Hell, he was pretty sure she'd welcome it.

His groin tightened at the thought and he shifted in his seat to ease the suddenly snug fit of his jeans. Dammit, he had to stop letting himself go there in his mind. She wasn't for him, plain and simple.

"Yo. Bauer. Hello?"

He looked across the table to find Evers snapping his fingers in Clay's face to get his attention. "What?"

"I'm getting another round. Want another one?"

He glanced back at the dance floor. Zoe and Schroder were still going strong. "Sure."

As Evers left to go to the bar, Tuck leaned back in his chair and followed Clay's gaze, a fond smile on his face. "It's good to see her loosen up like this."

Clay shot him a surprised look. Since when was Zoe in need of loosening up? "What's that mean?"

Tuck turned his head toward Clay and shrugged. "She doesn't go out to bars much. Likes to keep to herself. Introvert. You know how she is."

No, Clay realized with a start, he didn't. Tuck's description of her didn't mesh at all with the confident, outspoken woman Clay had come to know. Or thought he'd known, anyway. Now he was even more fascinated by her.

The fifth song came to an end and finally Schroder escorted Zoe back to the table, a hand on the small of her back. Clay studied his teammate's face. The former PJ was leaning close to Zoe, grinning at something she said, his body language protective, almost possessive.

Something raw and territorial lit up inside Clay, its ferocity taking him off guard. His teammate wasn't doing anything wrong. Clay couldn't fault him for his clear interest in her, and Schroder was a good guy, but he still wanted to walk over there, yank that guiding hand off her, and replace it with his own.

God, you're so fucked up.

Thankfully Evers returned to the table with the next round just as Zoe and Schroder sat down, preventing Clay from having to analyze his unconscious reaction. They spent the next hour shooting the shit—well, Clay mostly listened and tried not to keep looking at Zoe—then Schroder slapped his palms to the wooden table.

"Bourbon Street," he declared, his too bright eyes telling Clay the medic was feeling his three hurricanes. "Who's in?"

"I'll go, for a while," Evers said.

"Not me," Zoe said with a smile. "This was my biannual dance fest, and now I'm going to go home and work."

"Work," Schroder said in a confused voice, his expression making it clear how disappointed he was that she was leaving. "It's almost midnight."

"I know, but as you can plainly see I'm a creature of the night and it's when I'm most creative." She shrugged. "If it ain't broke…"

"Zoe's a writer," Tuck said over the noise of the band when Schroder continued to look confused. He started to push back from the table. "I'll take her home then meet you guys. Bauer, you want to go with them, or—"

"Bauer can take me home," Zoe interjected, and they all looked at her. She stood, slipped the strap of her purse across her bare shoulder. "If you don't mind," she added, looking down at him with a question in her eyes.

He should say no. It was on the tip of his tongue to refuse, make some excuse about having to go with the others, but the words wouldn't come. Instead he found himself nodding as he pushed back from the table and stood. He looked at Tuck. "I'll text you once I'm done, meet up with you guys."

Tuck was no idiot. His gaze shifted from him to Zoe and back, then he nodded. "Sure." He came around the table to give his cousin a hug, kissed her cheek. "See you later."

"Yeah. Come by when y'all are done barhopping if you want. I'll still be up. I can make you guys some coffee before you hit the road."

"You're a gem, Zo."

"I know," she said, giving him a bright smile, the easy affection between them making something in Clay's chest tighten. Hell, she'd even won over his mother in the short time they'd spent together when Clay had first been released after his surgery.

Zoe turned to him, her smile dimming a little. "Shall we?"

Clay nodded and followed her toward the door without a word. He stayed right behind her, his big frame opening up a path for them, casting warning looks at two guys he saw gawking at her breasts. Others stared at her with open curiosity, sweeping the length of her body to take in her outfit.

Clay hated both reactions, even though she didn't seem to notice them or care. The air of unshakable self-assurance in who and what she was only strengthened the protective urge inside him. Instinctively he stepped closer, until he could feel the warmth of her body against his side. With every step he battled the need to put a hand on her cinched waist in a clear gesture for every man in the room to stay the hell away from her.

He was still at her back when she turned down a darkened alley, he assumed for a shortcut, and reflexively grabbed her shoulder to halt her when he saw two people arguing up ahead. Zoe stiffened when she noticed them—a woman up against the wall, the man with a hand around her throat. The guy froze and turned his head to look at them.

Clay pushed Zoe behind him and stood his ground. "Let her go." The words came out more of a threat than a warning and when the man shifted Clay could see the pistol held in his grip.

He reached back and gave Zoe another push in a silent command for her to run. She didn't, instead staying riveted in place behind him. His body was tense, ready to lunge for the mugger. Though he was armed, his weapon hidden in his waistband, if he pulled it things would only escalate and he didn't want Zoe anywhere near this asshole if a shot was fired at them.

Pinned against the wall, the young woman stared back at them with wide eyes, hands clutching her purse. A high-pitched, frightened sound squeaked from her throat. As if the noise startled the man into motion, he gave the woman a shove, sending her sprawling to her knees, turned and ran for the opposite end of the alley.

Clay took off after him, sprinting past the woman, his gaze locked on the mugger, who wheeled to the right at the end of the alley and disappeared from view. It wasn't until he'd turned the corner in pursuit that his brain finally caught up with his instincts. The woman was okay and he couldn't leave her and Zoe back in that alley undefended. He skidded to a stop, jogged back to them.

Zoe was on her knees next to the woman, talking

quietly. She stopped when Clay got close, looking up at him in the dimness. "She's not hurt from what I can tell. Just shaken up."

Nodding, he crouched down in front of the woman. "Can you stand up?"

She bobbed her head once, shoulder-length blond hair swishing around her face and pushed to her feet. "He c-came out of nowhere," she quavered, her whole body shaking as she held her purse to her chest.

"Did he take anything?" Clay asked, pulling out his phone.

"N-no. Thank God you showed up when you d-did."

Zoe set a comforting arm around the woman's shoulders and rubbed her hand over her upper arm as Clay dialed 911.

"No," the woman said, taking him by surprise. "He didn't take anything and it was too dark to get a good look at him. This night has been eventful enough without me having to go to the police station to file a report. If it's all the same to you, I'd much rather just go back to my hotel."

Clay exchanged a look with Zoe, who nodded and he relented with a sigh. "We'll get you a cab."

"Thank you." The woman allowed Zoe to lead her back to the main street, arm wrapped around her.

As soon as they'd put her into a cab, Clay turned to face Zoe and put his hands on his hips. "Why the hell didn't you run?" he demanded. "The guy could've taken a shot."

She raised her chin and met his gaze without flinching. "So I should've just left you there alone? He could've shot you as easily as he could've shot me."

He aimed a glower at her. "I'm trained. You're not."

"You're also *unarmed*. At least I had this," she said,

holding up a canister of pepper spray he hadn't seen her pull out of her purse.

Staring at the small cylinder, he had to fight back a snort of incredulous laughter. He was glad she had sense enough to carry it with her, but seriously? That against a gun? He shook his head at her. "I'm always armed, Zoe." And he knew how to disarm someone with his bare hands if necessary. "Let's get you back to your place."

Before she found any more trouble.

Chapter Four

Zoe stopped at the entrance to her place and reached for the combination bicycle lock holding it shut, her hands slightly unsteady from the adrenaline rolling through her veins. Every cell in her body aware of Clay standing just a few feet behind her, a silent, looming presence. He was still angry, but he could just get over himself anytime now. Even though the incident in the alley had scared her, running away and leaving Clay to face the threat alone was completely insulting to everything she stood for.

"Want me to do that?" he asked, obviously seeing her hands were unsteady.

"No, I'm good."

"It's normal to feel like that," he said, causing her to glance up at him. "Adrenaline crash."

"I'm fine. Just angry that piece of shit and others like him are still walking free in this city." She went back to working on the combination.

He made an impatient sound as she fumbled with the last number on the lock. "Please tell me you've got an alarm system or something inside? Because that pathetic excuse for a lock is enough to give me nightmares."

Smothering a grin, she angled a look at him over her shoulder, unprepared for the way her belly did a somersault at the sight of him standing there. Six-four and probably two-thirty, his dark hair cut into a skull trim that made his angular features even sharper. Those electric blue eyes bored into her, intense and assessing, the soft, black cotton of his T-shirt stretched taut across the sculpted muscles in his chest and shoulders. The grim set to his expression should have made him look even more foreboding but somehow only made him sexier.

Oh, lawd. "I do."

Helpless to stop herself, she snuck a quick glance down his arms, hungrily taking in every dip and swell of his biceps and triceps, then down to the flat, hard stomach before stopping at his hips. She wanted to keep going but ogling him this way wasn't going to help her cause for getting him to go to the next level with her.

She forced her gaze back to his face, met those vivid eyes and felt an answering echo deep inside. Much as he tried to hide or ignore it, she knew she wasn't the only one affected, either. She'd seen the way he looked at her a few times tonight, as if he was imagining what they'd be like together in bed.

She already knew the answer to that. Freaking *amazing*.

"Despite what just happened, this part of town's pretty safe and there's always lots of foot traffic around so if anyone tried to break in someone would notice," she said as she finished unlocking the gate. Unwinding the chain from one side, she swung the intricate wrought iron aside with a metallic squeal and held it open for him. "Right this way."

He hesitated for a moment, his eyes meeting hers, and she could tell what he was thinking. He'd walked her home, had assumed she'd let herself in the gate and then he'd leave once he knew she was safe.

Zoe had other plans in mind. She waved him in. "Come on, I don't bite." *Unless you want me to.*

His lips twitched, the barest hint of a smile, and he stepped through the gate, securing it behind him with a clang. She liked the sound of him locking the two of them in here alone, away from the rest of the world. As he stepped forward the curved entryway immediately felt smaller with him standing in it, his wide shoulders blocking her view of the street behind him. "Just for a bit," he said.

Ignoring the comment, Zoe headed through to the courtyard. The trickle and splash of the fountain grew louder until she rounded the corner and the courtyard opened up. Old, weathered brick walls lined all four sides, right up to the top of the two-story building. Pots and hanging baskets dotting the space overflowed with fuchsias, impatiens and Boston ferns she hand-watered every couple of days. The private haven smelled cool and damp, a refreshing change from the scents found just outside her front gate.

"Wow," Clay said as he got his first look at it. "Very cool."

"Isn't it? I love it here." She gestured to the table, chair and ottoman she'd tucked into one shady corner. "I get sunlight here from about eleven to five or so, but most of it stays near the top of the walls. I usually have my morning coffee down here or up on the balcony, then sit here with my laptop where it's nice and cool." He nodded, still taking in the space. "The rest of the place is even better." She unlocked the bright cobalt-blue door set into the rear brick wall and pushed it open. A swish of blessed coolness greeted her, courtesy of the air-conditioning.

She flipped on the light switch inside the door, disarmed the security system and stepped aside to let

Clay in. He came through into the foyer, surveyed everything with a single visual sweep. His movements, body language and expression were as economical as his language, she'd noticed. He gave what he needed to get his message across, nothing more, nothing less.

"This is mostly just storage and stuff down here," she said, moving past the heavy antique wooden furniture. "The owner's a collector, left most of his stuff here for me to use. He's got some amazing pieces, but I had the movers put out my favorites and shift everything else out of the way because most of the furniture's too heavy for me to move by myself."

The ancient wooden stairs creaked beneath her feet as she ascended them, the faint mustiness of an old home underlying the scent of the Murphy's Oil Soap she used to clean all the wooden surfaces. At the top landing she moved toward the galley-style kitchen set into the back of the apartment and turned to face him. "So, this is me."

Clay turned in a slow half-circle, taking in the place. "Yeah, it is." His gaze landed on the far wall of the living room, fastened on the framed vampire print she'd hung over the couch. "Very you."

It was. The interior was painted a deep, rich red, almost a burgundy. The perfect backdrop for her assortment of spooky décor. Bats and skulls and ghosts, a few Victorian-era items that tickled her fancy or sparked her imagination. Clay walked over to the bookshelf on one wall, perused the leather-bound volumes she'd lined up there. "Pretty dark stuff, Zoe."

She shrugged. "I like dark." And she *really* liked the darkness standing in front of her right now. Not dark merely because of his hair color and tan skin, but because of the darkness he carried inside him. A fellow loner, like her.

He stopped in front of her collection of ravens, all perched atop the bookcase to keep watch. She stepped closer, wondering what he found so fascinating about them, and caught the faint twitch of his mouth that she now understood was his smile. "What?" she asked.

He turned his head toward her. "You're a raven."

She blinked. "Pardon?"

He nodded up at the little murder of crows she'd created. "Dark hair, observant. Scary intelligent."

"You think I'm scary intelligent?"

He made a little noise of affirmation and kept studying the birds. "I watched a documentary a few weeks ago on crows. The things they do are incredible."

Zoe crossed her arms. "That's true. But they're also incredibly opportunistic and like shiny things."

He turned back to her, amusement lighting his eyes. "What, you don't like shiny things?"

"Well, some—" She broke off as she realized what he'd said. And, more importantly, *not* said. "Wait, so you're saying you think I'm opportunistic too?"

"No, I *know* you are," he confirmed, taking her aback as he mimicked her stance and folded his arms across his chest, drawing her attention once again to those beautiful muscles. He lifted a dark eyebrow in a gesture she could only describe as sardonic, yet there was still a gleam of male interest in his eyes. "You really going to stand there and pretend you didn't bring me up here hoping to get me into bed?"

Well, wow.

His directness momentarily put her at a loss for words, something that rarely happened. For two seconds she thought about protesting, laughing it off, but decided that would not only be immature, but stupid. Clay was jaded, had some serious trust issues with women in general. Thanks to Eve, he thought she and most of her gender were manipulative and conniving. Zoe wasn't going to prove him right by lying now. Her whole plan was to show him she was nothing like his ex, so meeting his directness head-on was the only way.

"Nope. Not denying it. So how do you feel about that, then?"

His other eyebrow rose and she knew she'd surprised him with her bluntness. Good. She had plenty more surprises in store for him if she had anything to say about it. If he'd just give her a chance.

He looked away. Disappointment hit her like a fist, surprising in its strength. "You know why that can't happen."

"You're worried about what Tuck will think," she guessed. It sure as hell wasn't because he didn't want her. She knew he did, and the way his eyes kept dipping to her cleavage was in direct contrast to his words.

His gaze slid back to hers. "It's not gonna happen, Zoe." The words were sure. Final.

She tilted her head. "You're not even going to tell me why?"

"Doesn't matter why. We're not going there."

The disappointment swelled, growing into something sharper, something resembling loss. Until that moment she hadn't realized just how much she'd pinned her hopes on the chance of a fling that led to more with him. Part of her was convinced that once he let her in that far, she'd have a shot at the rest. Though she wanted to press, find out what the problem really was, she sensed if she pushed now he'd pull back into himself and she'd lose him for good.

Taking a deep breath, she gave a small shrug as if it didn't matter and turned toward the kitchen. "Okay." The hardwood floor was cool beneath her bare feet as she headed for the fridge. "I'm kinda hungry. Want something to eat?"

"No, I'm just gonna meet up with the guys," he said, already texting one of them on his phone.

Realizing that all her plans for the night had just

gone up in smoke, Zoe pulled out a platter of chilled watermelon and set it on the counter. As she was pulling back the plastic film covering it, her cell rang inside her purse, hanging from the post at the top of the stairs. She crossed to get it. It was rare for her to get a call this late at night so she expected to see Celida's number on the screen, but instead saw it was a fellow volunteer from the shelter. She took the call and answered.

"Hey, glad I caught you," Liz said, sounding a little out of breath.

"Everything all right?"

"Not really. It's Leticia."

Zoe stilled. "What's wrong?" She was conscious of Clay looking at her but didn't glance at him.

"She's gone."

"What? Gone where? Did he find her?"

"We don't think so. Something spooked her a little while ago. She said she didn't feel safe here, took her son and left."

"On foot?" It was the middle of the night and if her dangerous ex was out looking for her, that seemed like a stupid thing to do. Very unlike Leticia.

"She might have caught a cab, I don't know. I've tried calling and texting but she won't answer. Can you try? She seems to listen to you. See if you can talk her in to coming back in for at least the night and we'll talk about her options more in the morning."

"I was coming in to see her first thing," Zoe said, alarmed at this turn of events. If they lost contact with Leticia now, they'd likely never hear from her again. "I'll call her."

"Thanks."

"No worries. I'll let you know if I get hold of her." After she disconnected, she immediately pulled up Leticia's number from her call display.

"Everything okay?" Clay asked from over by the

bookshelf.

"Bit of a work emergency."

"A writing emergency?" He sounded confused.

"No, at the women's shelter I volunteer at." She waved at the stairs. "You go ahead, I have to make a call. I'll lock up after you leave."

"I'll stay."

She didn't ask why, not wanting to waste time even though she was curious, and stepped out through the sliding glass door onto the balcony, sitting on the quilt she'd spread onto the antique daybed before dialing. She almost sighed in relief when Leticia answered. "Are you and Xander all right?"

Leticia let out a long exhale. "Yeah, we're fine."

"Are you guys somewhere safe?"

A short laugh answered her. "There's nowhere safe anymore."

Zoe frowned, not liking the edge of panic she heard in the woman's voice. "Why did you leave the shelter?"

"Because staying in one place for too long makes me feel like a sitting duck. I won't risk my son's life that way."

"Okay, I understand," Zoe said, keeping her tone level even though she wanted to reach through the phone and shake the other woman. "Can I still meet with you? To talk?"

A pause. "I can't wait until morning like I originally promised. If you want to see me it'll have to be tonight. Xander's tired, he needs to sleep."

Zoe blinked. This could be her only shot at talking some sense into her. "All right. Where do you want me to meet you?" Leticia named the place and Zoe promised to be there within forty-five minutes. When she walked back inside, Clay was still standing at the bookcase, his brows drawn together in an ominous frown.

"Where are you going?"

"Up to Mid-City. Have to meet someone." She walked past him into her bedroom, took a light sweater from her closet. He was at the doorway when she came out.

"Who are you meeting?"

"A woman."

The frown grew even more foreboding. "Not by yourself."

"Yes, by myself. If I show up with anyone else, especially a man with your size and bearing, she'll bolt, and I can't take that chance." She slipped the sweater on, walked past him to the stairs and put her phone back in her purse. "Tell the guys I'm sorry I couldn't stay until they were done bar-hopping."

He shook his head once. "You're not going out there alone."

While she appreciated the protective side of him, she didn't have time to stand here and argue. "I'm fine. Gotta go." Under normal circumstances she would have hugged him goodbye. She loved to hug, got a kick out of seeing Clay have to give into politeness and allow the contact, but after the way he'd rejected her she wasn't in a hugging mood.

He took a step toward her, caught her arm. "It's the middle of the night and we already saw one mugging up close. There's no way in hell I'm letting you meet whoever it is you're meeting alone."

She shot him a glare. "I used to live in that neighborhood, and I can take care of myself."

"With your pepper spray," he said, disdain dripping from every word.

"I'm not going to need it," she insisted, pulling her arm free.

He blocked her from going down the stairs, his expression fierce. "I'm serious, Zoe. You don't go there alone. If you don't want me with you, then ask Tuck.

Pick one of us. Or I'll call him myself."

Struggling to suppress the snap in her temper, Zoe let out a deep breath. "You wanna come with me then?" Unfortunately that held none of the sexual innuendo she would have liked.

"Yeah, I'll go."

At least he cared enough to be concerned about her safety. She just wished it wasn't because of his loyalty to Tuck. "Then you have to stay out of sight when I meet her. If you screw this up and she runs, I swear to God I'll—"

He snorted. "I'm pretty good at the whole staying out of sight thing," he said, his bland tone pointing out that he was a former SEAL.

"Fine." Shouldering her purse, she started past him and down the stairs, actually relieved that she'd have him nearby. "Let's get moving. I don't wanna be late."

Chapter Five

C arlos pulled into the rest stop off the highway, parked in the shadows near a group of trees far away from any other vehicles, and cut the engine. Two minutes later, headlights appeared in his rearview mirror. The car turned into the rest stop, drove slowly toward him and parked to the right of his truck. He verified that the driver was who he'd been expecting, then got out. The smell of hot pavement and fresh cut grass swirled around him as he rounded the back of the truck.

Standing beside the car, his contact acknowledged him with a nod.

Carlos didn't bother with any social niceties. With a man like this they weren't expected anyway. "Did you find anything?"

Gill, an Indian immigrant in his early twenties, glanced around to verify that no one was watching or listening in before responding. "Her cell phone was deactivated this evening around six p.m.," he said in a strong accent. "I can't tell if she merely turned it off, or if she's permanently disabled it. She might have bought a new one, or a throw away phone."

"You could've told me all that over the phone," Carlos growled, growing impatient. The longer Leticia had in terms of lead time, the harder it would be for him to find her. "What else have you got?"

Gill stuffed his hands into his pockets. "I traced her

bank account activity. She withdrew two thousand dollars cash from her account at a downtown bank two hours ago. No credit card activity since yesterday and if she's paying cash now it's going to make her harder to track."

Carlos's hands tightened into fists at his sides. He'd put that money in her account last week to help her pay for her kid's fucking braces. Now she was trying to use it to escape him. By trying to support her financially and be a nice guy, he'd given her the means to run. "What else?"

Gill reached through the open driver's side window and withdrew something. A file. "I printed off a copy of her phone records for the last month. I took a look through it, highlighted numbers that seemed to keep coming up. See if you recognize any of them, and if the patterns make sense to you."

Carlos took the file and started scanning the contents, but there was really only one thing he was interested in. He flipped to the last page and read the final bit of the log. One series of texts and an incoming call jumped out at him immediately. He didn't recognize the number but the communication had taken place around four, two hours before her phone was deactivated. And it was also the last number she'd contacted. "Start with this one," he told him. "Find out who it is, get an address or place of work if you can."

Carlos immediately began searching through the rest of the pages for the number. Her mother's number came up a few times, as did her work and two of her friends' numbers. The unfamiliar one was there too. It showed up from time to time over the past month. Nothing too overt, but clearly Leticia knew the person well enough. If he found out it was another man who'd been trying to lure her away, Carlos would kill him.

He exhaled to ease the pressure in his chest cavity.

"She's still in the city." He was sure of it. There was no way she'd go back to Tennessee to stay with her mother. It was too obvious a move and she knew he'd check there. Besides, Leticia's mother was a drunk and she wanted nothing to do with her. It was the reason she'd left home with her son and moved down here in the first place. "Call me when you find out."

Gill nodded and opened his car door. "I'll be in touch shortly."

"I want this by the time the sun comes up."

Gill's eyes flashed up to Carlos, his trepidation clear. "I'll do what I can."

Carlos wasn't worried about the man slacking on the job. He was in too deep, owed Carlos too much, and knew if he disappointed or crossed him, he'd either wind up dead in an "accident" or turned over to the Feds for fraud and cyber crimes. He knew none of that needed to be reiterated now.

Carlos started around the back of his truck, paused when Gill didn't move. Facing him, he arched a brow. "Problem?"

He rubbed the back of his neck. "You said there was a boy."

"Yeah, so?"

"Well I just… You're not going to do anything to him, are you?"

"Not your problem." A wealth of warning filled the words.

Gill shifted, swallowed. "No. It's just…" He searched Carlos's face for a moment, as if looking for reassurance that nothing would happen to the kid.

Carlos couldn't give him anything of the sort. Leticia loved that kid more than anything and if using Xander for leverage was his only way of getting her back, he'd do it. Whatever it took to make her stay.

If he let her live after the way she'd betrayed and

humiliated him.

Giving Gill a cold look, Carlos stalked around to the driver's side of his truck. He waited with the engine running, the burst of cool from the air-conditioning drying the perspiration on his face. He watched the car pull out of the rest stop and drive west on the highway until its red taillights disappeared in the distance. Only then did he start his engine and drive east, back toward downtown. With that amount of cash in hand, Leticia could have caught a bus or bought a plane ticket.

His gut said otherwise. That would make her too easy to track. No, he was sure she hadn't left town yet. But his window of opportunity was getting smaller and smaller with each passing hour.

He kept the radio off as he drove, the rhythmic sound of the tires on the asphalt soothing him. Was she lying in a bed somewhere, too afraid to go to sleep for fear of him finding her? Just the thought of her being in another man's bed was enough to have his hands clenching around the steering wheel.

Ahead of him down the dark ribbon of highway, the city of New Orleans glimmered. Somewhere in the glow of those lights, Leticia was hiding.

But she wouldn't stay hidden for long.

****

Even though Clay was next to her in the backseat of the cab, Zoe was nervous enough that she kept darting glances in the rearview and side mirrors. Not that Leticia's psycho boyfriend knew about her or this meeting, but the woman had made the man sound so scary that the mere thought of getting more deeply involved in all of this put Zoe on edge.

Clay noticed her looking but didn't say anything, instead shooting her a subtle frown. Even with the added risk of Leticia bolting if she caught sight of him, Zoe was glad he'd come.

At the meeting location the driver pulled up at the curb in front of a narrow, two-story Victorian-style house in a quiet, residential neighborhood. "You'll wait here?" Zoe asked him.

"You've got my cell number programmed into your phone, right?" he said instead, dodging her question.

She nodded. "I'll be as quick as I can. Clay, she can't see you. It's important."

"She won't see me. But there's no way I'm waiting in this cab." He reached across her and popped her door open. "Text or call me once you make contact. If I don't hear from you in five minutes, I'm coming after you." A warning and a promise, and even if it was domineering of him, she knew he was only insisting on this for her own safety.

"Okay." She got out and hurried up the sidewalk, around the back of the house. Away from the soft illumination of the streetlights out front, the shadows seemed to close in on her. A dog barked from a yard a couple houses over. Rounding the corner of the sidewalk that led to the wooden privacy fence encircling the property, she looked around.

"Over here."

She glanced toward the rear fence where the female voice had come from. Leticia stepped out of the shadows, hair and the upper part of her face hidden by a gray hoodie. "Thanks for coming." She turned and spoke behind her. "It's okay, Xander, you can come out." The boy appeared behind her, a living shadow.

"You guys still okay?"

They both nodded. "Thanks for coming," Leticia said, dropping her gaze to the ground as though she was too ashamed to meet Zoe's eyes.

"No problem." Zoe crossed her arms and looked around. "Do you have friends or relatives here?"

"No, but I used to work here when I cleaned houses and I knew it was a safe place to come." Leticia blew out a breath and stuck her hands into the kangaroo pocket on the front of her hoodie.

Zoe stepped closer, lowered her voice so it wouldn't carry. "What scared you so much tonight?"

She lifted a shoulder. "I was watching from the windows in the guesthouse out back. Thought I saw a car circle by a few times and I got nervous."

More than nervous, if she'd decided to take off with Xander at that hour with no plan and no place to go. "I want to help," Zoe said softly. "But I feel like we're both in way over our heads with this already."

A humorless laugh. "Yeah, I know." She wrapped an arm around her son's shoulders, brought him close and pressed a kiss to the top of his head. "I'm so sorry, buddy. This is all my fault."

"It's okay, mom," Xander said. "Don't worry."

Zoe wanted nothing more than to swoop in and rescue them both, but she couldn't do that. "You didn't get the restraining order, did you?"

Not meeting her eyes, Leticia shook her head.

Zoe pushed out a breath, disappointed but not all that surprised. "Why not?"

The woman lifted her head, stared back at Zoe with haunted eyes. "I already told you. He's too dangerous. If I go to the cops, he'll know. They'll even help him find me. So I lied and told you I got it."

It made Zoe's skin crawl to think of cops so corrupt that they'd help a criminal hunt down a woman he'd battered. But this had to go way beyond the local police, and that in itself was a huge red flag. The way Leticia acted, this guy had connections to all the powerful and important people along the entire Gulf Coast, maybe farther. What the hell had Leticia gotten involved in?

"We need help," she said simply, appealing to

Leticia's common sense. "There are people who can help you. Not the cops." She had to be careful about her wording here. "I know a few people personally who can give you and Xander the help and protection you need." Leticia started to shake her head, but Zoe kept on. "These are people I know well, Leticia. People I trust my life with."

The woman hesitated, still staring at her. "Who? Are they law enforcement?"

"Federal agents."

She gave a bitter laugh, looked away again and tightened her hold on her son. "He'll know them."

"Even if he does, these people aren't corruptible." Normally she wouldn't reveal any of this to an outsider, let alone someone she didn't know all that well, but this was important and Zoe was getting desperate. There was no way Leticia's ex had ties to Tuck, Celida or Clay, yet she seemed so terrified that he might. Zoe wished she had a name, so she could find out exactly who they were dealing with here. "One of them's my cousin, one is my best friend, and the other—" She took a deep breath, prayed she wasn't about to lose Leticia over this. "—is waiting in a cab around the corner."

Leticia's head snapped up. Her eyes widened in horror, in betrayal, and she instantly took a step backward, dragging Xander with her as if she expected men to come racing at her at any moment.

Zoe held up a hand to stop her, her heart aching for the woman. "I told him to stay where he was. He doesn't know who you are or why I'm here. He's not even from the area, he lives on the East Coast and is only in town for a few days. But he's a good man and I promise you he's no threat to you or Xander. He'll know how to help."

Leticia shifted and the faint moonlight illuminated the right half of her face, showing the tears glimmering on her lashes. "I don't know where to go."

"I know." Zoe reached out a hand for her. "Come with us. We'll drop you off at the shelter for the night. I won't let my friend see which house we go into. We'll make sure we're not followed by anyone, my friend will keep watch on the way there and once I get you settled, you and Xander can get a good night's sleep for once. In the morning you can let me know whether you want me to ask my cousin and friends for help."

If this Carl guy was as bad as Leticia seemed to think he was, he likely had a lengthy criminal record. The FBI might be willing to help out with protective custody or even WITSEC in exchange for her testimony to put Carl away. That would depend on how bad the agency wanted him, though. "You can think about where you want to go tomorrow, but please don't try to run now. It's the middle of the night and you just said yourself that you don't have a plan. For Xander's sake, come back to the shelter and think things over. It's not safe for him out here either, especially at this time of night."

Leticia drew in a shaky breath, released it slowly, and Zoe knew the mention of her son's safety had just clinched the deal. "I can't go back to the shelter even if I wanted to. They explained the curfew thing when we got there and told me how strict it is to protect the other women and children already staying there. They won't let me back in now."

"I've already talked to the woman who runs it, and cleared it with her. She's waiting for my call to let her know whether you're coming back."

Leticia swallowed. "The guy waiting in the cab. You really trust him that much?"

"I do." Gruff and antisocial as he was, she knew Clay was a good man. And crap, she hadn't texted him yet. She pulled out her phone. "I promised I'd text him to let him know I'm okay. I'm not telling him anything about you still." She typed in a quick message, held it out to Leticia in case she wanted to check it herself but she shook her head.

His response came back a second later. *OK*

The curt, no-frills response made her smile a little. So Clay.

Putting her phone back into her purse, she looked at Leticia. "Well? What do you want to do?"

The woman glanced down at her son, seemed to exchange some kind of unspoken message with him, then met Zoe's gaze and nodded. "Okay. We'll come with you to the shelter. But only for tonight."

Relieved, Zoe relaxed and gave them both a smile. "Sure." She held out an arm, beckoned them both closer. "Come on. Right this way."

Chapter Six

C lay didn't like it, but he reluctantly stayed put in the cab while Zoe took the woman and kid to wherever she was taking them. The urge to get out and follow to make sure she was safe was strong, but the neighborhood here in the Garden District was quiet. And since most properties here probably cost more than ten times what he'd make in this lifetime, he was pretty sure Zoe could walk to and from the shelter alone without getting assaulted.

At the twenty minute mark he started to get antsy, but he'd seen how reluctant the mother had been to get into the cab with him in the first place, so he figured Zoe was likely still talking to her and getting them set up for the night. How the hell had he not known that Zoe volunteered at a place like that? Tuck had never mentioned it, and neither had she in any of their e-mail exchanges over the past couple months.

It didn't surprise him that she'd work at a women's shelter though. Her background in family law made her interest in the cause understandable. For all her quirks and sharp tongue she had a huge heart, and seeing her go out of her way to help the woman and child tonight touched something deep inside him. That cynical, cold

part of him that had taken over more and more, partly because of what he did at his job, and partly because of what he'd experienced in his personal life.

"How much longer?" the cabbie groused, shifting restlessly in the front seat.

"Dunno, but she already paid you to wait, so she'll be out when she's ready," Clay told him, not taking his eyes off the sidewalk where Zoe had disappeared around the corner. He'd give her another half an hour before he got concerned enough to send a text. If she didn't answer that, he'd go find her, instructions to stay put or not.

Fifteen minutes later, she appeared at the opposite end of the block and headed for the cab, her silhouette unmistakable. He inwardly smiled at the change in her route, approving of her awareness. Both she and the shelter seemed to take their secret location and confidentiality policy seriously. A good thing if they wanted to guarantee the safety of the women and children inside.

He popped the door open for her and Zoe slid into the backseat with a sigh. "Sorry about that. Back to the Quarter, please," she said to the cabbie, and rattled off her address as she settled back against the seat. Her light, exotic scent rose up to tease him, intensified by her body heat.

The cabbie did a U-turn on the wide, tree-lined street and headed back the way they'd come. Clay stole a look at Zoe as they left the Garden District. She had her head back against the seat, eyes forward and she seemed lost in thought. "They get settled okay?" he finally asked.

"Yeah, but they won't be there long." She didn't sound happy about that. When they passed by a streetlamp he could see the furrow between her brows.

"Something wrong?"

Her head turned, those pretty golden eyes focusing

on him. "I'm worried."

"About them?"

A nod, and her gaze shifted away toward the cabbie, who was now talking to someone using his hands-free device. Even though he was on the phone, when she spoke next it was in a hushed tone. "Without going into too much detail, the guy she's running from sounds like really bad news. She refused to go to the cops because apparently this guy is tight with at least some of them, and even though things she's told me make me think he must be a criminal, she makes it sound like he's got an in with every level of law enforcement in the region."

A warning tingle started up at the base of his neck. Had Zoe just put herself in danger by helping them? "Is there any way this guy knows you're involved with her case?"

She met his eyes briefly before looking back out the windshield. "No. But the way she talks about him makes me wonder who the hell he is and what he does. Or what he's done, for that matter. I wish I had a name to go with the reputation. Then I could figure out how to help her."

Well, he, for one, was glad she didn't have a name and wasn't going to be able to dig any deeper. She'd been a practicing lawyer until recently, so if she'd had a name there was no way she'd let it go until she had all the answers she wanted. But he still wanted to be sure. "So you're done with them now, right? You saw them safely to the shelter and now you're out of the picture."

She hesitated. "Technically."

Oh, hell. "Zoe." He waited until her eyes swung to him once more. "If this guy is dangerous and the woman is a flight risk, you need to stay out of it now. Let the social workers or whoever handle this if she won't go to the cops."

She shook her head, the angle of her chin defiant,

and checked to make sure the cabbie wasn't listening in. He wasn't, because he was still on the phone. "It's not that simple. I'm the only one she trusts. If I'm the only one she'll turn to for help, I can't say no and just cut contact with her. No one but the owner, the volunteers and the women we shelter knows where the house is. It's privately owned and operated, so we have strict rules and have to sign a confidentiality agreement when we apply.

"All of us are fully screened, including in-depth background checks. My degree and past work in family law actually helped me get accepted. The cops don't know where the house is, the neighbors don't know what it is, and even the social workers don't know where it is. Whenever one of them has a new case for us, either the owner or a volunteer always meets the woman needing help and her social worker at an unrelated location first. If we decide to take them in, the women have to sign the same agreement we do and sign off on all the rules and stipulations. That makes our shelter one of the safest in the state, and it's why I wanted to work there. We make a difference in people's lives."

It was clear she was proud of her work there, and rightly so, but he wasn't liking the sound of this particular case at all. He also knew that arguing with her about dropping the case was futile. One of the things he admired most about Zoe was her unyielding loyalty. In this case, however, he was getting concerned that it would become dangerous.

He let it go, for now, the silence settling over them as the cab headed back toward the French Quarter. They'd just turned onto Canal Street when his cell buzzed with an incoming text from Tuck.

Schroder's let the good times roll a little too much. Some guys keep trying to pick a fight with us. You back yet?

He'd sent a picture of Schroder with the message, his mouth wide open in a humorous expression of glee that told Clay their medic was feeling no pain at the moment. The sight of his calm and easy going teammate pissed out of his mind amused him. He smirked as he typed in his reply.

Better roll him on outta there then. Want backup? We're close.

Sure. We'll meet you out front. Tuck gave the name of the bar. Clay asked Zoe where it was.

"At the far end of Bourbon. Think they really stopped at every bar on the way to Lafitte's?"

Clay vaguely recalled the place from his last trip here. "Looks like." He instructed the driver to drop them off close to the bar and a few minutes later he and Zoe stepped out onto the corner of Bourbon and St. Philip.

Loud music pulsed from inside Lafitte's Blacksmith Shop Bar and it was so crowded people were spilling out of it onto the sidewalk. Clay stepped up close to Zoe and wrapped his hand around her bare upper arm, trying and failing to notice how soft her skin was as they walked toward the crowd assembled in front of the bar. People paused to watch two men wearing red afro wigs and matching costumes hamming it up as they performed a choreographed dance for their audience.

"Do you see them?" Zoe called above the music, craning her neck to see over everyone.

"I see Evers." His dark-haired teammate was standing on the sidewalk about ten meters west of the bar entrance, talking to two big guys. Clay waved to get his attention and Evers waved them over. With a guiding hand against the small of her back, Clay led Zoe through the groups of onlookers watching the show and over to where Evers stood.

Evers smiled and indicated the two men with a nod. "This is Hunter Phillips, co-owner of Titanium

Security," he said, gesturing to the sharp-eyed, dark-haired man.

"Clay Bauer. I recognize you from back in the day," Clay said, holding out a hand. Phillips had been a Teams guy before becoming a security contractor.

"Yeah, I've seen you around, I think last time at a training thing up north," Phillips said with a smile. "Good to know we're well represented over there at the agency."

Clay grinned. "You know it." He was proud to represent the SEAL community.

"And this is Gage Wallace, Titanium's 2IC," Evers said, indicating the broad-shouldered redhead with fully tatted arms next to Phillips.

"Former 2IC," Wallace corrected. "I'm a glorified desk jockey now."

Phillips raised an eyebrow at him. "There was no desk out in the field last week while you were running the newbies through their paces."

"Okay, I'm *mostly* a glorified desk jockey," Wallace qualified, shaking Clay's hand.

Clay was very much aware of Zoe standing beside him, noted the way the men gave her appreciative looks and was strangely relieved when he saw they both wore wedding bands.

Not that rings meant anything. Guys could cheat just as easily as women could, and he'd seen it happen a lot in his line of work when guys were away from home, either on the road for training or overseas on deployment. Eve had accused him of cheating plenty of times, even though he'd never touched or flirted with another woman the whole time they'd been together. The ironic thing was, while he'd been loyal to her and their marriage, she'd never believed it.

"This is Zoe Renard, Tuck's cousin," he told them, mentally shoving his ex-wife out of his mind. They were done. Eve was part of his history and he'd moved on.

No, you haven't. If that was true, you wouldn't have turned down the woman next to you.

Zoe offered a smile as she shook the men's hands, and Clay had to remind himself exactly why he'd turned her down earlier. Because he genuinely liked her. Admired her. He even enjoyed being around her, which was something he couldn't say about most people, and he had a feeling they'd be more compatible in the bedroom than either of them realized. Could he really only do one-night stands anymore? He didn't know, because he hadn't tried anything else.

A dangerous thought, because part of him really wanted to try for more with Zoe.

"Nice to meet you both," Zoe said. "Are y'all in town for the security conference Tuck told me about?"

"Yes, ma'am," Wallace said. "Got a few of our guys here with us." His light blue gaze shifted to Clay once more. "You should come by with Tuck and Evers tomorrow, meet us for a drink in the hotel bar."

"Maybe," he answered evasively, then glanced behind him at the bar entrance again. "You seen Tuck and Schroder recently?" he asked Evers.

"Not for the better part of an hour now." He turned to leave. "I'll go get them."

"Nah, I'll do it." Clay turned and automatically put his hand on Zoe's back again, not wanting to leave her here making small talk with these guys while she waited for him to get the others.

Up ahead the male dancers had finished but people were still milling around on the sidewalk and out on the street where groups of tourists in horse-drawn carriages were snapping pictures of the famous bar. With his size it was easy for him to maneuver through the crowd but he put Zoe directly in front of him so he wouldn't lose sight of her and made sure no one hassled her. She drew stares at the best of time, but in that corset she was a fucking man magnet, and he didn't want anyone in here trying to get grabby or gawking at her cleavage.

They'd just pushed through the last few people to the bar's entrance when a group of guys suddenly tumbled out backwards. Zoe froze and leaned back to avoid a collision with one of them but Clay caught her shoulder and spun her out of the way. The last guy in line put a hand out to steady his friend in front of him and pushed him forward. All four of them were red-faced and shouting at whomever they were arguing with back in the bar. They stalked back inside, their body language and expressions making it plain that they were about to start something.

Clay slid his arm around Zoe's shoulders and entered the bar, keeping her close, but a glance toward the rear of the dimly lit bar showed Tuck and Schroder standing with their backs at the far dark brick wall, and the angry men heading straight for them. Tuck saw them coming and tensed, stepping in front of Schroder to intervene. He said something to the group, but they didn't stop.

"Ah, hell," Clay muttered, stopping where he was. He didn't want Zoe anywhere near those guys if they were about to throw down. Tuck's gaze flashed to Clay's for an instant and he rolled his eyes in an I-really-don't-need-this-shit-right-now expression before focusing back on the other men.

"What?" Zoe asked, standing on tiptoe to see better, then gasped when she figured it out. "Is it them?"

He switched her to his left side, away from any danger of fists and elbows if things got ugly. "Yeah." The man in the lead of the group was toe-to-toe with Tuck now, thrusting his finger into the air inches from Tuck's face. Tuck remained calm, hands at chest level, palms out, and shook his head. Clay couldn't hear what the other guy was saying but it sure as hell wasn't friendly and then Schroder stuck his head around Tuck's shoulder and said something that made the others surge forward.

Shit. He released Zoe, body tensed for action. "Stay here while I—" He never got the chance to finish.

One of the guys threw a punch at Schroder, who, even drunk managed to duck out of the way in time. Tuck caught the guy's wrist and said something, his brows lowered in a menacing expression that Bauer recognized as don't-fuck-with-me. He shoved the guy's arm away and reached back to grab Schroder by the back of the neck.

Clay kept going, just in case, aware that Zoe was trailing after him but didn't stop her, not wanting to take his eyes off the other men's hands.

Tuck had taken one step toward the exit when the next guy in line decided to take a shot. His fist came back, cocked and ready. Clay automatically lunged over and grabbed him from behind, locking his arm around the guy's chest, trapping his arms against his sides. The guy's head snapped around and he glared at Clay for an instant before he tried to come up swinging.

Blocking the punch easily, Clay tossed the guy off to the side. The man reeled backward, arms outstretched. Clay saw Zoe there an instant too late, watched her eyes widen and her arms come up to shield herself a moment before the guy crashed into her.

They both tumbled backward and hit the floor, Zoe on the bottom, the impact throwing them into the legs of a wooden table hard enough to topple over the drinks sitting on it. The people sitting there shot out of their chairs and swiveled to see what was going on.

Fuck.

Enraged, Clay rushed over and ripped the guy off her, tossing him aside without caring where he landed, and crouched down in front of Zoe. He cupped a hand around the back of her neck, concerned she'd hit her head. Her eyes were clear though, the pupils even. "Are you okay?"

She sat up and put a hand to her cheek, nodded at him with wide eyes before darting a look over his shoulder where the sudden increase in volume told him Tuck and Schroder had seen the incident and weren't happy about it. "Just stay the fuck back," he heard Tuck warn, and Clay recognized that steely edge to his voice. "We're leaving. Get out of our way."

Ignoring the others, Clay slid his hands under Zoe's arms to pull her from beneath the table. "Come on." Gently hoisting her to her feet, he pulled her hand away from her face where a bright red mark stood out over her cheekbone. God dammit, he should have thrown the guy harder.

He brushed a thumb over it and searched her gaze, and leaned forward so he wouldn't have to shout over the music. "Hurt?" She'd hit the floor pretty hard and then skidded into the table, and that guy had to weigh around two hundred or so. Her bun had come loose, several chunks of black-and-purple hair now streaming over her shoulders.

"It's fine," she mumbled, her voice husky, expression a little dazed. "I think the back of his head got me."

Mouth compressed into a flat line, Clay kept his body between her and the assholes responsible for all this as he turned to face the rest of the room. Bouncers were already escorting the other guys out the back. Tuck was almost to him, pushing Schroder toward the exit, and though the drunken assholes were still glaring holes in the backs of their heads, at least they weren't going after his teammates anymore.

"She okay?" Tuck asked Clay as they reached him

and Zoe.

"Yeah. Let's get her the hell outta here." She'd had a helluva night already.

Tuck didn't answer, simply propelled their medic out of the bar and onto the sidewalk with a hand flattened between his shoulder blades. Outside, Schroder wrenched away from him and gave the hem of his T-shirt an angry tug as he glared at their team leader. "It wasn't my fault."

"Never said it was, but you're drunk and that was gonna get ugly in a hurry."

Apparently appeased by the lack of blame, Schroder turned his attention to Zoe. "Sorry about that." Clay knew the instant he noticed the red mark on her cheek. Schroder's expression tightened. "You all right?" His eyes zeroed in on the mark and he took a step toward her, his hand lifting toward her face as though he was going to touch her.

Something in Clay bristled at the idea of anyone else touching her right now. He wrapped a proprietary arm around her shoulders and brought her in tight to his side, silently warning Schroder not to try it.

"I'm fine," she said, but to Clay's surprise, pressed closer to him. Automatically he tightened his hold on her. He couldn't help but notice the way she fit against him so perfectly, warm and soft in all the right places.

Schroder looked at them both, blinked once, and stepped back in clear acknowledgement of Clay's unspoken claim.

Zoe sighed. "I'd like to get home now, though. Had a long and…eventful day."

"Sure," Tuck said, his gaze shooting from her to Clay's hand wrapped around her right shoulder, then up to his face. Tuck held his stare for a few heartbeats, a silent warning there as his eyes narrowed slightly. *You hurt my cousin, I'll kill you.*

Clay kept Zoe right where she was and met that stare head-on, acknowledging and accepting his actions. He knew he was being territorial and over-protective but he didn't care. On top of already being concerned about what she'd landed herself in with her volunteer work, seeing Zoe knocked to the floor had triggered something primal inside him. He didn't want to examine it too closely, he just knew that no one else was touching her or offering her comfort when she had him here.

Tuck pushed out a breath and headed over to where Evers was still talking with Phillips and Wallace. They were laughing at something one of them had said, but Evers's eyes widened when he took in their grim expressions and the mark on Zoe's face.

"Whoa," he said, bending to put his mostly finished to-go cup of beer on the ground, then rose. "Did I miss some fun in there?"

"Yeah, *fun*," Schroder muttered, scowling as he crossed his arms.

Evers looked at Tuck. "What the hell happened?"

"Just some assholes trying to start some shit," Tuck said with a careless wave of his hand.

Evers's gaze shifted to behind them. "That them?"

Tuck swung around, grunted. "Yeah."

"They look pretty pissed off. Think they're gonna follow you?"

"If they're stupid, maybe."

Clay wanted to get Zoe out of here and back home. He didn't think those guys would try anything, but you never knew and they could be carrying knives or guns. "We'll keep an eye out."

"We're heading back to Biloxi. You coming with us or staying here?" Tuck asked Evers.

"Wallace volunteered to bunk with Phillips and give us his room at the hotel for the night so I can meet up with some of the guys tomorrow. You guys are welcome to crash with me if you want, save yourselves the drive back to Biloxi," Evers said.

"Or y'all could stay with me," Zoe offered. "I've got a couch and a king-size bed, so I can fit at least three of you at my place if I take the daybed out on the patio."

"You're not sleeping on your patio," Clay said, an edge to his tone.

"Thanks, but I can't stay anyway, I've got a meeting in Biloxi first thing," Tuck said. He looked at Schroder. "What about you?"

"I'll stay with Evers. Bed sounds a lot better right now than a ninety minute drive."

"Fine. Bauer and I'll walk Zoe home. I'll text y'all in the morning, let you know what the plan is."

"Sounds good," Evers answered. His eyes cut behind them again. "They're still there, but just glaring. You guys watch your backs."

"Will do," Tuck said, though he didn't seem too worried about the possibility of a continuation of the fight.

They split up, the others heading down St. Phillip to go back to their hotel, and Clay and Tuck heading back up Bourbon with Zoe. She stayed in the circle of his arm as they walked, making all of Clay's protective instincts flare as they moved down the crowded sidewalk. She didn't seem to notice all the men checking her out as she passed by, but she was too quiet and he had a feeling everything that had happened tonight had rattled her more than she let on.

A block up the street, a group of young twenty-somethings spilled out of another bar in front of them. The lead guy stumbled toward them, lurched to a stop three steps away and Clay jerked Zoe behind him just as the guy bent over and started puking all over the sidewalk.

Clay sidestepped, keeping Zoe on his left side this

time, away from the mess. Clay shook his head. "I hate people," he muttered under his breath.

Zoe made a strangled sound and Clay glanced down to see her fighting a laugh. "Not *all* people," she pressed, poking him in the ribs with a black-painted fingernail.

One side of his mouth turned upward. "No. Not all." What he felt for her was pretty much the opposite, actually. Would've been a helluva lot easier if it wasn't.

By the time they reached her place she looked tired, and the mark on her cheek had taken on a faint bluish tinge that meant she was going to wake up to a lovely bruise there in the morning. She pulled the bicycle chain lock free of her gate. "You guys coming up for a while?"

"We gotta hit the road, hon," Tuck said.

Her hand froze around the top of the gate. "Oh. Okay." Clay didn't miss the disappointment in her voice, and when her big, golden eyes flashed from her cousin to him, it felt like invisible fingers had closed around his heart.

She didn't want to be alone. But she wasn't going to say it. And Clay could tell she also wanted him to be the one to stay.

"I can stay," he heard himself say. In the split second of silence that followed he was aware of both of them gawking at him, but he only cared what Zoe thought about his announcement and when she smiled in relief he knew he'd made the right call. "I don't have any meetings or anything in the morning and I'm free tomorrow anyhow." He could feel Tuck's eyes boring into him as he spoke, and ignored him.

"I'm glad," Zoe said, then asked her cousin, "Will you be coming back tomorrow, then?"

Clay glanced over in time to catch Tuck's subtle glare, saw his jaw flex before he looked at Zoe and softened his expression. "Sure. Soon as I can," he added, shooting another hard look at Clay. "Can I talk to you for a second, Zo?"

She hesitated, then dispersed the gathering tension with a bright, "Sure." She looked up at Clay. "Go on in. I'll just be a sec." She swung the gate open for him and stepped out of view.

Clay knew exactly what Tuck was about to say, and even though it pissed him off somewhat, he understood. As he walked through the entryway and into the courtyard alone, he was suddenly hit with the enormity of what he'd just done. He'd just agreed to spend the night alone at her place, with no one else around until at least tomorrow afternoon.

No wonder Tuck had glared daggers at him.

The thought of being alone with her for that long simultaneously thrilled and terrified him. He wanted Zoe, badly, but he no longer trusted his instincts when it came to women. And he'd just all but publicly claimed her.

Tuck, Evers and Schroder had just seen him go all territorial with her, and everyone at that bar, too. Strangely, he didn't regret it. He couldn't turn off his protective feelings toward her, and didn't want to. The only other woman he'd ever reacted this strongly to was Eve.

And look how that turned out for you.

The derisive voice in his head annoyed him. Zoe couldn't be more different from his ex. He'd learned a lot since then. He wasn't naïve, he wouldn't be fooled like that again. And there were none of the red flags with Zoe that had been there with Eve. Tuck and Celida loved Zoe to death, and Clay trusted their judgment, even if he didn't trust his own.

Except his brain was shouting that he'd be a freaking idiot to pass up the opportunity of going for it with Zoe.

He pushed out a breath and ran a hand over his

closely-shorn hair. Tuck was out there warning her off him right now. How the hell he was going to make it through the night without acting on his newly intensified feelings for her, he didn't know.

Chapter Seven

Zoe's stomach buzzed with unease as she followed her cousin a few paces down the street, away from the entrance to her place and out of Clay's earshot. She was pretty sure she already knew what he was going to say, and wasn't surprised at the disapproving look on his face when he turned to confront her.

Hands on hips, he stared down at her in the light of the streetlamp behind her. "You sure you know what you're doing?"

"I'm just letting him stay over." She didn't want to be alone in her place tonight and she wanted to spend more time with him. Which was plain stupid. His earlier rejection had sounded pretty final and Clay was hard enough to stand by his word no matter how much he wanted her. But she still wasn't ready to concede defeat.

Tuck's gaze hardened. "You know what I mean."

She crossed her arms. "Yeah, and I'm a big girl, so while I appreciate you watching out for me, you don't need to in this case. Besides, he already turned me down earlier."

A flare of surprise flashed across his face, but then he frowned. "And now he's staying the night."

"He's not interested in getting me into bed, Tuck. He already made that clear."

Tuck watched her for a long moment, as though contemplating what he wanted to say next. "He's a good guy," he said finally. "He is. But he's not the same as he used to be. He's...I dunno. Damaged."

"Because of his ex."

"His ex," he allowed with a nod, "and...other shit that comes with going to war and being in our line of work."

She nodded. "I understand." She didn't need Tuck to explain that Clay was world-weary and distrustful. But there was so much more to him than that, and as a man and Clay's friend, Tuck would never see what she did.

She suspected Clay's choice to distance himself emotionally from the rest of the world actually came from a deep-rooted self-doubt. And that he secretly longed for far more than he'd ever let anyone know. His ex and whatever had happened between them had wounded him deeply, in ways he'd never admit to. The experience had shaken him. She understood all that perfectly. To a point. Her divorce had been painful enough and she hadn't suffered what he had, yet she was willing to risk her heart again.

"Do you?" Tuck studied her. "I love the guy like a brother, Zo, but I've known you forever and I know how you are, how hard you'll keep trying in a relationship when you see good in other people. He's never going to let you in the way you want him to. I don't even think he's capable of it now."

She tilted her head. "So he's a lost cause, as far as women are concerned?"

"Right now? Yes. And I don't want to see you get hurt, least of all by one of my friends. Because he would hurt you, even if he didn't mean to."

Wait. "You think he'd actually hurt me? Physically?" She was outraged that Tuck would even infer that.

To her surprise, her cousin's gaze hardened. "No. Never. And whatever you've heard about him on that front is bullshit."

Zoe relaxed. Nobody had told her what had happened between Clay and his ex, but from certain comments made by Tuck and Celida, she knew something big had gone down. She wanted to know what it was, but this wasn't the time to ask, and she'd rather hear it from Clay anyhow. "Okay, then, what? You're worried he'll love me and leave me?"

"That's exactly what he'd do, yeah."

She lowered her head, covering a wince as the words hit home. Tuck knew her better than anyone except maybe Celida. He rarely ever gave his opinion about her personal life and she'd be stupid not to listen to him. He'd always given her sound advice, always been there for her, especially through the decline of her marriage and subsequent divorce. "All right. I hear you."

Tuck watched her carefully for another moment, then sighed and hauled her into his arms for a hug. "You're gonna do what you're gonna do, I know. Just be careful, yeah?"

"Yeah. See you tomorrow?"

"You bet. Celida said to say hi. She's going to call you, maybe later tonight."

"Okay." It'd been a few days since they'd spoken last.

Tuck released her and eased back. A broad smile spread across his face. "I'm gonna ask her to marry me, Zo."

Zoe gasped, both hands flying to her mouth. She blinked against the sudden sting of tears. "For real?"

He nodded. "Saw a ring in a shop window on Royal

Street earlier. I'm gonna buy it tomorrow and pop the question the week I get back to Virginia."

Oh, damn, now she was crying. She wiped at the tears spilling down her cheeks, smiled up at the man who'd been like her big brother her entire life. "Do you know how you're gonna do it? It has to be romantic, and you have to get down on your knee when you ask her. She'll blush like crazy and probably mutter something about how stupid you look, but she'll love it."

Tuck grinned. "Yeah, I think she will too."

"You need any ideas? Want me to brainstorm about some possible locations? In a park, maybe. Or on a boat. Ooh! Take her rock climbing and propose at the top of the mountain—"

He laughed. "I got this, Zo, but thanks."

Zoe set both hands on top of his broad shoulders and squeezed. "I'm so happy for you. I can't wait until I get the call."

"Just don't blow the surprise when you talk to her next."

She snorted, feigning insult. "If you didn't trust me to keep the secret, you never would have said anything."

He tweaked the end of her nose. "I know. Now go on, go keep Bauer's cranky ass company." He kissed the top of her head and walked away, toward the parking garage where he'd left his vehicle.

Zoe stared after him, conflicting emotions swirling inside her. Joy that her cousin and best friend were about to take the next step in their relationship—because she had no doubt that Celida would say yes when Tuck asked her—and a surprisingly painful ache of something resembling...loss. Which was weird, because she hadn't been looking for anything permanent with Clay, and yet the reality of there not being even a possibility of something between them, hurt a lot more than she would have imagined.

The bump on her cheek throbbed in time with her heartbeat as she walked back down the sidewalk, entered her gate and locked it behind her. She found Clay waiting in the courtyard, standing beside the cobalt-blue door, and the sight of him there with his muscled arms folded across his wide chest hit her like a punch to the diaphragm, taking her breath away. He had a magnetic pull on her, his quiet yet commanding presence impossible to ignore.

He frowned when she stepped into the light of the lantern hanging above them on a wall of the courtyard. "What happened?"

"What? Oh," she said, touching one hand to the wetness on her face. She wiped the last of her tears away. "Happy news. It's all good." She wasn't going to explain, but she'd be surprised if Tuck hadn't already mentioned something to Clay about his plans, since they worked and lived together.

Those vivid blue eyes searched hers as she approached. "You sure you want me to stay? I can still catch up with Tuck if you've changed your mind."

It was little, unexpected glimpses of care and consideration like that from him that made it near impossible for her to merely be his acquaintance. After the time they'd spent together just before and after he was injured and the occasional e-mail since, she considered him a friend, but she wasn't sure he saw her that way. "No, of course not. I'm sure."

Except she wasn't sure at all anymore. Not about what she wanted with or even from him at this point, nor whether she could pull back emotionally when she'd been so set on becoming lovers, maybe more.

Who are you kidding? You definitely wanted more.

Yeah, she did. That's why Tuck's words were hitting her so hard.

Clay didn't say anything more as she unlocked the

door and punched her code into the alarm keypad. She was keenly aware of him behind her as she led the way up the old, creaky stairs to the main level, and conscious of the buzz of nervous anticipation squirmed in her belly. She could almost feel his eyes on her bare nape and shoulders, lingering on her ass as she moved. More tingles flowed through her, heating her insides. He was a powerful, outrageously sexy man. Pretending she didn't want him was going to be an exhausting effort.

As she reached the top of the stairs Tuck's warning echoed in her mind but the stubborn part of her refused to abandon all hope. She *knew* something had changed between her and Clay tonight. She'd felt it in the cab when he'd gone with her to meet Leticia. She'd seen it when he'd picked her up off the floor at the bar and she'd caught the concern in his eyes. He'd been so comforting and protective, in his own quiet, alpha male way. Her shoulder tingled as she remembered the feel of his hand where it had curled around her, the warmth and hardness of his arm as it rested across her upper back.

He'd have been protective of any woman in that situation. It doesn't mean anything.

She desperately wanted it to though.

Blowing out a breath, she hooked her purse on the newel post and headed for the kitchen. "You want anything to drink?"

"No thanks, don't worry about me. You should put some ice on that before it swells up."

She stopped and put a hand to her cheek as she turned back to him. "Is it that bad?" It hurt, but the back of the guy's skull had hit her cheekbone, so no big surprise. Her eye socket didn't feel swollen though, and the bump on her head didn't hurt much at all anymore.

His blue eyes dropped to her where her fingers covered the spot. "I'd say it's gonna leave a mark," he said with a matter-of-fact shrug.

She turned back to the kitchen. "I'll just take some ibuprofen." She opened the cupboard next to the sink and took out a tablet, downed it with some water and wondered what the hell to do next. Normally she was just fine on her own, but with everything that had happened tonight, his offer to stay had filled her with relief at the thought of having someone here with her.

But maybe this wasn't a good idea. If she couldn't have him, then the best thing for her right now was some distance from him. She opened the dishwasher. "It's late and I'm sure after your training you're even more tired than I am. You can take my room, I just changed the sheets on the bed this morning in case you guys decided to crash here."

"I'm not taking your bed." He hadn't moved from his position in the living room.

She rolled her eyes at his adamant tone and put the glass in the dishwasher, avoiding looking at him. "You're six-four. You take the king-size bed, I'll be fine in the guest room."

"I'm fine on the couch." His words had that ring of finality she was becoming all too familiar with. But if he expected her to give in just by being bossy, he was going to be disappointed.

"Clay. Stop. You're taking my room." She strode down the short hallway to what served as the master bedroom and turned on the light as his footsteps approached behind her. "We have to share the bathroom though. It's just across the hall from the guest room." She sounded so damn lame. And this wasn't at all how she'd envisioned a night alone with him would go.

Before she could turn around a big hand planted itself on the doorframe next to her head. She swiveled her head to look up into his face—not something she was used to doing at five-foot-ten—and found him close, so close she could see the dark blue ring around his irises.

The breath halted in her throat as his scent teased her, a clean, citrusy scent you had to be near him to notice. His body heat reached out to her, warming her spine, making her aware on a cellular level of just how big and powerful he was. Of all that strength at her back, all that raw sexuality seething just beneath his cool exterior.

He stared at her for a long moment before glancing over at the king-size four-poster, done up in a red velvet coverlet with black mosquito netting hanging from the canopy. A wave of desire slammed into her as images popped into her head of what he'd do to her in her sumptuous bed with those hands, that long, hard body.

"I can't take your—"

She reached up to lay her fingertips against his lips, tried to ignore the little shockwave that sizzled up her arm, or the need to slide her thumb across his lower lip, savor the only soft spot in that hard face. "Stop. I told you what I want, and I'm not taking no for an answer." The second she said it she realized what an epic Freudian slip it was. Her subconscious knew exactly how badly she wanted him and wasn't about to let her forget.

Something dark and intense kindled in his eyes. His hand came away from the doorframe, reached up to slowly wrap around her wrist. The feel of those strong fingers twining around that fragile part of her sent a shiver of longing through her. She knew he'd be unlike any lover she'd ever had. Authoritative, forceful even. The thought of those strong hands holding her wrists above her head as he pinned her to the bed nearly weakened her knees.

Her pulse spiked at the unmistakable heat she saw in his eyes but she forced herself to pull her hand free and look away. "If the air-conditioning's too cold there are quilts in the trunk over there," she told him, trying to ignore how breathless she sounded as she walked to the wooden blanket chest she'd placed at the foot of the bed and tapped it.

In her peripheral vision she could see Clay shift his stance to lean one muscled shoulder against the jamb as he watched her. "We could share."

She stilled and looked over at him. "Not into torture, thanks."

He blinked at her. "Sleeping with me would be torture?"

His teasing tone warmed her but she wasn't letting him make light of this. "You told me no once already. So I'm respecting that and the only way to continue to do so is for me to sleep in a different room. I don't play games and I know you hate them too."

He sobered and inclined his head in acknowledgement, but that cynical expression was back in his eyes. The one that said *come on, all women play games*. The one she wanted to wipe from his face forever by making him realize once and for all that she was nothing like his ex, or anyone else he'd been with. "So what did Tuck say to you?" he asked.

"Pretty sure you can figure it out."

He stood there, unmoving, and studied her for a long moment. "He's right."

She turned to face him fully, curious. "About what?"

"That I'm no good for you."

"You don't think so either?"

A muscle flexed in his square jaw. "No."

"Well then, disaster averted. We'll just forget the rest and go back to the way things were between us before you got here." Though she had no idea how in hell she was going to do that. She had strong feelings for him and if he didn't reciprocate them, then it was best that she pull back now.

He didn't answer, kept staring at her for such a long time that she had to fight the urge to fidget. When he spoke at last his voice was pitched lower than normal. "Can you forget the rest?"

"Can you?" she countered, arching a brow.

"No," he finally admitted, and for a second she was sure she hadn't heard him right. "And trust me, if you were anyone but Tuck's cousin, I'd...."

You'd what? she wanted to shout, dying to know. *Walk across this floor, grab me and kiss me until I can't breathe? Rip my clothes off and take me right now on my bed?*

He shook his head, the movement tight, his posture rigid. "You should listen to Tuck. I don't want you to get hurt either."

She folded her arms. "Because you're so sure you would have hurt me?"

He straightened and looked away. "I wouldn't mean to, but...I don't know." He ran a hand over his buzzed hair, the move making his biceps and triceps flex in a way that made her mouth go dry.

Then it hit her. It wasn't just women he didn't trust. He no longer trusted *himself* when it came to judging someone's character. And that damn near broke her heart. Though she was still shocked that he'd opened up this much. Pushing for answers now might risk him shutting down again but she had a feeling that if she didn't ask now, she'd never get the chance again. "I need to ask you something really personal."

His eyes shot to hers and he straightened even more, as if he was getting ready to take a blow. "Okay."

She licked her lips, considered her words. But really, was there any way of putting this delicately? "I know something bad happened at the end with your ex, but Tuck's never told me."

Clay looked away again, stared out the window overlooking the street as he gave a thoughtful nod. At least he wasn't leaving. "You want to know what it was." His tone was flat, almost lifeless. He was already disengaging, pulling back from her when she wanted the exact opposite.

She forced herself to hold her ground rather than let it go, because this was too important. Whatever had happened, it was the crux of why he was so jaded now. "I do."

He took a deep inhalation, released it slowly, and when his gaze came back to her she saw both pain and defiance there. He was ready for her to judge him for whatever he was about to say. Expecting it, even. "I was charged with domestic assault and thrown in jail."

Though she'd vowed to keep her expression impassive, she felt her eyes widen at the admission, made so matter-of-factly. "You were?" She just couldn't picture him harming a woman.

He nodded, his jaw flexing once. "We were fighting. I lost my temper, grabbed her hard enough to leave marks. That was all she needed to have me arrested."

Zoe studied him for a long moment. Something didn't ring true there. He was leaving something important out, and she had a feeling she knew what it was. "Did she assault you first?"

Another terse nod.

"And they arrested her too, right?"

"Yes."

Zoe stared back at him, waiting for more, but he didn't say anything else. Clay was one of the most controlled people she'd ever met. Right up there with Tuck, whom she measured every other man against. She tried to imagine what Eve could have done to make someone as remote as Clay lose his cool enough to react physically without thinking. Everything she came up with was ugly. There was no way he'd lost control without serious provocation first. Not someone with his elite military background and training.

"So she provoked the incident and pushed you until you broke." No easy feat, she was sure.

His lips curved in a cynical smile that hurt her heart. "Doesn't matter what she did, I'm still the one who marked her and got locked up for it. If not for Tuck and our CO, my career would have been over then and there."

True. "Well, I'm glad they were there to defend you and stop that from happening."

The fierce way she said it seemed to take him off guard. His bitter smile vanished and a slight frown appeared between his dark eyebrows. "I shouldn't have touched her like that," he said, as if Zoe didn't understand his part in the incident.

"No, you shouldn't have," she agreed, not about to absolve him of his share of the blame, "but that instance doesn't automatically mean you're dangerous to all women. I've handled enough domestic abuse cases in my time to know the difference." She also knew Clay well enough to realize that whatever had precipitated the event, Eve had likely manipulated it carefully. Tuck had told her many times what sort of a person Eve was. Thank god Clay had finally ended the marriage.

He didn't look away. "I'm dangerous to you."

The quietly spoken words sent a shiver through her, the sexual undercurrent in them unmistakable. "I already told you, I like dark. And you don't scare me one bit."

Desire flared to life in his eyes, and this time when his mouth curved up on one side it was with amusement. "How the hell did you go through a divorce and come out the other side like this?" He nodded at her, his gaze raking over the length of her body and back up, leaving tingles in its wake.

"You mean my fondness for Victorian Goth?"

The smile grew, both sides of his mouth lifting now. "No. I mean, how did you come through it and still be so…alive."

Alive. The word resonated inside her. He'd just expressed exactly what he felt was missing inside him and she wasn't even sure that he realized it. She considered her response. "I guess I decided at the start of it all that I wasn't going to let it change who I was. And it sounds like my divorce was much more civilized than yours, so that helped." No epic battles or physical confrontations or calling the cops.

She paused to consider her next words, wondering how to explain it. "I've known exactly who I am since middle school, and I wasn't going to let my ex or anyone else change me. No matter how many snide or hurtful comments he made toward the end of our marriage about the way I dressed or a million other things about my personality that he hated, I stayed true to who I was.

"It took me a long time to see how his negative comments and neglect was affecting me, and to recognize it for what it was. Abuse. That's when I knew I had to get out. I vowed then and there that I'd be a better person after, that I'd live life to the fullest and not be afraid to give my heart again."

She knew that Clay was afraid to open himself up to that kind of pain again, and she didn't blame him one bit. "Even though the thought of being emotionally vulnerable to anyone again is scary, I know that not every guy is like Mark. Just like not every woman is the same as Eve. And if I closed myself off from everyone to protect myself against the threat of ever being hurt that way again, then I let him beat me. And God knows, I hate to lose," she added wryly.

Clay gazed back at her in silence for a long, intense

moment before nodding once, the gesture loaded with respect. "I think that's amazingly brave, but it doesn't surprise me that you came through it so well. You're strong. One of the strongest people I've ever known, actually."

Her cheeks heated at the compliment, especially coming from a man who'd made it through hell to become a SEAL. Feeling awkward, she waved his praise away. "You might want to take a look in the mirror sometime, then."

He snorted. "Physical strength has nothing to do with it. You're half my size, but you just managed to make me look like a pussy with that speech."

She laughed and turned back to the bed to straighten a corner that didn't need fixing, calling herself a hypocrite. Being turned down by him earlier made her want to step back and protect herself from him now. Didn't that go against everything she'd just said? "Well, I already told you how I see you, and it's pretty heroic, so just think about that the next time you're giving yourself a mental beating."

He didn't respond and when she turned back to him she saw that he was standing inside her room. The expression on his face tangled her into knots because it was so unguarded. She could clearly see the admiration for her in his eyes, the longing to reach for what he wanted.

But despite her brave speech about not being afraid to open up her heart to another man after her divorce, she had a feeling that Clay could inflict far more damage to her heart than Mark ever had. And worse, he'd do it without even trying. He'd just said as much.

No. If he wanted anything more than friendship from her, he'd have to make the next move.

"So you'll take my bed?" she asked, needing some space now.

"Yeah," he said with a nod, and again she saw that quiet respect in his eyes. "Thanks."

"Sleep tight, then. See you in the morning."

As she started to walk past him he stopped her with a hand on her upper arm. Zoe froze, braced herself and looked up into his eyes, her pulse thudding in her throat.

Staring down at her, Clay lifted a hand and gently stroked a fingertip over the bruise on her cheek. "Sleep well, raven."

The unique endearment, meant just for her, his unexpected touch, blindsided her. When he lowered his hand she managed to walk past him and out into the hall to shut the door behind her. As soon as it closed she bowed her head and closed her eyes, battling for strength.

Sleep well? Not a chance, with him stretched out in her bed and her lying in the next room. She'd be lucky if she got any sleep at all tonight.

****

Carlos jerked awake when his cell phone shrilled from the nightstand. Sitting up in his empty bed, he grabbed it, pushing down the surge of excitement and hope when he saw it was Gill. "Hey. You find something?"

"Got a name for that number you wanted. Zoe Renard. Lived in Mid-City and is now in the Quarter."

The name wasn't familiar to him. Leticia had never mentioned anyone named Zoe before. A new friend maybe? "What's she do?"

"I'm not sure what she does now, but she was a practicing lawyer until a little over a year ago. Goth chick. I'll send you a picture."

Carlos's muscles went rigid at the first part. "What kind of lawyer?"

"Family. She went to Tulane, then worked at a firm

up in Shreveport."

That bitch. That bitch was giving Leticia legal advice, probably had been the one to tell her to leave him.

He grabbed the phone records again, counted the number of calls to and from Zoe in the past month. Thirteen times.

Alarm bells started going off in his head. The calls had started right around the time when things had gotten really rocky between him and Leticia, when she'd suddenly grown a backbone and fought him at every turn. He'd initially thought Leticia was just suffering from a case of cold feet but now he wondered if this Zoe had influenced her. Maybe fed her some bullshit story about how Leticia could do better, how she should get out and never go back. The paper crunched in his fingers as his hand curled into a fist.

"Where in the Quarter is she?" It was only a little after one in the morning. He had plenty of time to act on this.

"Um, I didn't look. I'll have to get back to you."

"Forget it. I'll find her myself." He disconnected and immediately called another contact, this one through the agency.

"I'm in the middle of a job. Got a suspect I'm looking at and I need an address. I know it's late, but can you help me out?"

"I wouldn't do it for just anyone, but for you, sure," the woman said, the invitation clear in her voice.

Carlos smiled. "Thanks, you're a doll."

"I know." The clicking of keys on the other end told him she was already working her magic on the keyboard, looking in the agency database. "You in town?"

He wanted to lie but she'd likely trace his call once they hung up. "Yeah."

"Maybe we could meet up next week. Been a while

since I've seen you."

"Sure, sounds good." He'd fucked her for information before, and he'd fuck her again if it helped him find Leticia. But the whole time he had her under him, instead of blond hair and blue eyes, he'd imagine Leticia's thick, honey-streaked, deep brown hair, sea green eyes and flawless, pale-brown skin.

"Okay, got the address." As she recited it he mentally zeroed in on the exact spot in his mind. He knew the Quarter by heart, practically every inch of it. He knew *exactly* where Zoe Renard lived.

And he was going there to get answers.

Chapter Eight

Clay opened his eyes in the darkness and lay still, trying to discern the sound that had woken him. Not from a deep sleep, since he'd only been dozing off and on for the past few hours. Kinda tough to sleep with a hard-on that refused to go away because his subconscious wouldn't let him forget that the woman he wanted so much he could hardly think straight was sleeping in the next room.

Out in the street below he heard a street sweeper working. Inside, there was the occasional quiet groan of old pipes. Then came quiet footsteps in the hall, just beyond his door, heading in the opposite direction. A moment later he heard a soft snick and then a slider opening.

He sat up and dragged his jeans on over his boxer briefs. Silence greeted him when he stepped out into the hallway, broken only by the tick of a clock somewhere in the family room and the hum of the refrigerator in the kitchen. His bare feet were silent on the wood floors. Beyond the sliding door that led to the patio, he could see Zoe's silhouette illuminated by the glow of her laptop screen.

He was glad he wasn't the only one who couldn't

sleep, but seeing her working out there, he had to wonder what she was typing. The idea that it might be another one of those insanely hot sex scenes he'd read before made his erection so hard it hurt. Standing back from the slider, hidden in shadow, he watched her fingers fly over the keyboard.

He'd thought a lot about what she'd said earlier. About how she'd refused to let her ex win and had consciously chosen *not* to close herself off.

He'd done the exact opposite and that's why he'd meant it when he'd said that Zoe was one of the strongest people he'd ever known. And that comment about not every woman being like Eve had resonated with him too.

Zoe was Eve's opposite in every way. Edgy and dark compared to his ex-wife's sugary blonde appearance. Strong and grounded compared to the deep-rooted insecurity he hadn't recognized in Eve until they were married. The signs had been there, he'd just chosen not to pay attention. Zoe was loyal and kind-hearted compared to Eve's narcissistic and conniving ways.

The woman had dropped everything and gone off to meet a woman in need in the middle of the night, would have gone off on her own with only a can of pepper spray to defend herself, and right after she'd witnessed a mugging. That was something so far out of Eve's comprehension, it was laughable.

So yeah, maybe it was time he pulled his head out of his ass and admit that Zoe was nothing like Eve. That she was nothing like any woman he'd ever met. He couldn't deny he had growing feelings for her, even if he didn't want to name them yet. The pull he felt toward her was powerful, undeniable. And each minute he spent in her company, he only wanted her more.

Zoe shifted the laptop and swung around on the daybed so that her profile was to him. This time the glow from the screen gave him a perfect view of her face. Was her cheek still hurting? Her hair was loose around her shoulders and she was wearing something shiny and purple, some kind of robe. His fingers curled into his palms as he imagined tugging the halves of it apart to finally see what he'd been fantasizing about for so long.

In that moment the reasons he'd given for keeping his distance seemed insignificant. Yeah she was Tuck's cousin, but Clay respected her and her decisions, so if she still wanted him, why the hell should he say no? They both wanted each other, they were both consenting adults, and they were alone for the rest of the night.

He wanted to kiss her so badly, touch her naked body and stroke her until she trembled, make her cry out his name. He was dying to find out if she'd like the rough edges of his sexuality that he'd never let anyone see. Clay wanted Zoe to *see* him. The real him, nothing held back. His gut told him they'd be explosive together in bed, in the best way possible.

Handling explosives was one of his specialties.

Decision made, he crossed to the slider and gripped the handle. Zoe's head jerked up when he began to slide it open. She shut the laptop and set it aside as he stepped out. It only took a moment for his eyes to adjust to the darkness, broken by the faint glow of a streetlamp across from her building. Now he heard the quiet sounds of jazz floating from down the block, people talking as they passed by on the sidewalk beneath her balcony.

"Couldn't sleep, or did I wake you up?" she whispered, scooting aside to make room for him.

Clay lowered himself onto the daybed beside her, momentarily distracted when the hem of the robe rode up her thighs as she bent her legs and tucked her feet beneath her. *Can't sleep because I want to be buried inside you.*

"What are you doing working at this time of night?"

he asked instead, reaching out to tuck a lock of silky hair behind her ear. His fingers slid through the strands in a caress far gentler than he was feeling at the moment, when all he wanted was to pin her flat on this bed and devour her, inch by inch. Another scene from one of her books popped into his head. The one where the hero had surprised the heroine from behind one night, pinning her down and taking her right there out on the lawn, where anyone might see them.

The balcony wasn't a lawn, but the scene was hot and gave him ideas. Zoe pinned beneath him on the daybed, naked and wet for him, fighting to stay quiet while he made her come. He was rock hard at the thought.

Zoe stilled at the contact and stared at him questioningly. Thunder rolled faintly in the distance, the air suddenly feeling heavier. "Couldn't sleep, and I like working in the middle of the night anyway. It's quiet, the moon's out and there's something magical and sensual about sitting out here creating worlds and characters while jazz music floats up from down the street."

There was something magical and sensual going on here, yeah, but it had nothing to do with the city or its music.

He let his fingertips trail along the side of her face, careful of her bruised cheek as he lowered his hand. Her skin was so soft, just touching her like that made him hard all over. He caught her quiet indrawn breath, noted the way her nipples hardened against the satiny fabric of the robe and knew she was naked underneath.

Clay looked up into her eyes, saw the pupils expand in the faint lamplight. In the sudden stillness, the air around them seemed to crackle with latent energy.

Clay gripped the edge of the quilt she'd spread onto the bed to keep from touching her again. "Tell me no, Zoe." His voice was deeper than normal, raspy, but he couldn't control it any more than he could the desire streaking through him.

She licked her lips, leaving them shiny in the soft light, making him want to taste those tempting curves. "Why? Because you turned me down earlier?"

He deserved a fucking medal for that. "Because you're supposed to be off limits."

Her chin came up, a defiant expression on her face that only made the desire flare hotter. He loved that she didn't back down from his direct challenge. He got the feeling Zoe didn't back down from anything. "Says who?"

"People who care about you." Tuck, for one, and that should be enough. Clay was sure Celida would have said something to warn her off him too.

Zoe studied him for a moment while the heat built inside him, wanting to be unleashed. "What about you? Do you care about me?" she asked softly.

He did. More than he'd ever expected to. "Yeah." And even though that meant he should get up and walk away, he couldn't help but reach out a hand to touch the stubborn point of her chin, rub his thumb lightly across her full lower lip. "And so you need to tell me no, right now, before I do something you might regret later."

She inched closer, leaning forward at the waist, and the combined lust and anticipation in her gaze made him bite back a groan. Her whisper was seductive as hell. "I'm not going to regret it."

Clay's control snapped.

He slid his hand to the back of her head, plunging his fingers deep into the thick, cool fall of her hair to pull her head back as he brought his mouth down on hers. He caught her gasp with his lips, tasted her husky moan as his tongue delved inside.

Her hands went to his shoulders, fingers digging into him in the exact opposite of a *stop* signal. Clay shifted to one knee and leaned over her, forcing her back against the mattress.

She went willingly, parting her legs to make room for him, her hands now pulling at him. He kept one hand wound in her hair to hold her where he wanted her and set the other beside her head as he leaned over her and settled his hips between her open thighs. And Jesus, he could feel her heat through his jeans.

Twining his tongue with hers, he rocked his hips, rubbing the aching bulge of his cock against her. Zoe cried out softly, wrapping her arms and legs around him. It wasn't enough. He wanted to see her face. Drink in her expression as he took control and drove her out of her mind.

Clay lifted his head to look down at her. They were both breathing hard. Her lips were wet and swollen, her pupils so wide they all but swallowed the whiskey-colored irises. His gaze zeroed in on the pulse point fluttering rapidly at the side of her throat. Keeping hold of her hair, he arched her neck and set his mouth there, flicking his tongue over the sensitive spot, giving her the edge of his teeth.

She gasped and tipped her head back farther, offering more. Wanting it.

He moved his mouth down the slender column of her neck, breathing in that heady, exotic scent that clung to her skin as he worked his way down to where the lapels of the robe made a deep V. Zoe shifted restlessly against him, her hands wandering over his back and shoulders as he pushed aside the edges of the satin to expose even silkier flesh beneath it.

He bit back a growl at the sight of her breasts bared to him. Pale and round and firm, the nipples pink and tight. Cupping one in his free hand he lowered his mouth and closed his lips around a rigid peak. Zoe arched like a bow and let out a husky moan that made him shudder as her hands flew up to clutch at his head.

He'd fantasized about this way too often, but the reality was a million times better. She was like liquid fire in his arms, scorching him with her heat.

But he was determined to make her go up in flames.

He sucked again, rubbing his tongue along the tip of the taut flesh and the moan she let out this time was needy, breathless. "Shh," he whispered, his entire body throbbing at the feel and taste of her, her unbelievably erotic response. If a little foreplay got her this hot, what would happen when he buried his cock inside her?

Even as he thought it, he dismissed the idea, ignoring the painful pressure in his groin. She'd already been warned about who he was. He'd been a mostly selfish lover since the end of his marriage. This was his chance to prove otherwise to her—and himself.

When he moved to her other nipple and closed his mouth around it, sucking hard, her shocked cry sliced through the quiet like a blade. Clay reacted instantly.

Releasing her hair, he brought his palm down over her mouth to silence her, rolling off her and turning her onto her side, facing away from him, and threw one leg over hers to hold her down.

Zoe went still against him, her hands blindly gripping his wrist, the round curves of her ass pushing against his fly. Leaning close until his mouth brushed her ear, he whispered, "I'm going to make you come, right here, right now. And I don't want anyone to hear the sexy sounds you make but me."

Zoe's heart pounded against her ribs at the feel of that hard hand across her mouth. Her fingers dug into his thick wrist, her body fighting a flood of desire more intense than she'd ever known, along with a dark thrill of fear. The throb in her bruised cheek didn't even register right now. She could feel every inch of his powerful frame pressed up against the back of her, knew she'd never be able to break his grip. But she knew he'd never hurt her and she desperately longed to see this dark side of his desire for her.

Her breathing sounded overly loud in the stifled quiet. The pressure of his hand was firm, unyielding, but not painful and he was giving her plenty of room to pull air in through her nose. She shivered at the feel of his warm breath tickling her ear, the side of her neck as his words slid through her, part promise, part threat. She honestly didn't know which turned her on more. None of the men she'd been with were even remotely like Clay.

Her thoughts fractured like a glass shattering on a tile floor when his other hand yanked the lower edges of the robe apart. The satin halves split apart and slid down to pool around her body, leaving her exposed to the sultry night air. His low groan of approval sent a shiver racing through her.

Keeping his hand firmly in place across her mouth, he used the other to torment her nipples some more. Each time he squeezed and rolled the sensitive peaks between his skilled fingers it sent a hot stab of sensation down to the pit of her belly and between her thighs where she was already wet and aching for him. Being held captive like this, out in the open with the balcony and her plants providing them the illusion of privacy, his touch was a thousand times more erotic.

She writhed in his grip, his arms holding her so tightly that she couldn't move more than a couple inches, but the pleasure was so great she couldn't hold still and the feel of those steely muscles caging her only made the whole experience hotter.

His teeth closed around a tendon at the side of her neck, startling a gasp from her that was cut off by his hard hand, then his lips closed over her skin and he sucked. Zoe's eyes slid closed and she nipped at his palm, earning a low, rough chuckle from him.

The hand at her breast slid lower, trailing ever so slowly over her ribs, her stomach. Zoe wriggled her hips, trying to part her legs for him but his thigh trapped her, pinning her down. She was held in a warm, immovable vise and she didn't want to escape.

Those long, maddening fingers burned a path across her belly, over the rise of her hip, before traveling back toward the apex of her thighs. Her sex throbbed, aching for his touch, needing and trusting him to relieve her.

The pads of his fingers delved lower, stroked across the top of her mound. And stopped. He'd gone still behind her. His breath halted for a moment, then released on a rush of warm air that was half groan, half sigh against the side of her neck. "Oh, god, so smooth," he whispered, stroking the soft skin she'd just had waxed the day before.

Zoe trembled in his arms and didn't bother trying to reply, since she couldn't talk at the moment. The rich approval in his voice told her all she needed to know. But she was so damn wet and needy she thought she'd die if he didn't slide his fingers into her folds.

A second later, he did, and the sudden rush of heat made it feel like flames were racing over her skin. She sucked in a breath and moaned as he traced every flushed, swollen fold, desperate for more.

"You're fucking drenched for me," he murmured, satisfaction lacing every word.

She nodded and pulled in another breath, fighting to stay still while every muscle in her body drew taut, her toes curling in anticipation.

He drew his nose up the side of her neck, sucked at the spot just below her ear that made her see stars. "Gonna make you come, raven."

A whimper escaped her when he pressed two

fingers inside her and stroked, igniting hidden nerve endings that flared to life beneath his touch. His soft groan was muffled against her neck as he drew her moisture up her folds to rub the throbbing bud at the top of her sex. She let out a choked cry and threw her head back against his hard shoulder, her fingers gripping his wrist like it was a lifeline.

He didn't tease. His clever fingers rubbed her clit in a tight circle, upping the pressure slightly only when she made an incoherent sound of need and pressed her mound into his hand. She could feel the orgasm rising already, building deep in her belly.

The breath sawed in and out of her lungs. He plunged two fingers back inside her, rubbed against that amazing spot before withdrawing to caress her clit. Back and forth he pleasured her, alternating between those beautiful penetrations and gentle circles on her most sensitive spot until she was quivering in his arms.

Clay made a deep sound of approval and mouthed the side of her neck, his tongue caressing softly, then plunged his fingers back into her. She mewled as he squeezed his palm around her sex, the heel of his hand making contact with her swollen clit.

"Ride my hand," he commanded in a low voice.

Lost, helpless in the grasp of the lightning gathering inside her, Zoe did. She used the few inches of leverage she had and rubbed herself shamelessly against his hard palm. He kept the pressure steady, letting her set the movement and rhythm, his body an immoveable force surrounding her.

The feel of his fingers buried inside her, the thought of what the thick cock pressed against her would feel like in their place, knowing he was in full control, sent her over the edge. Her inner muscles clamped down on his fingers, her thighs tightened around his hand, and the orgasm broke. Her muffled shriek of ecstasy was trapped by his palm as she exploded in pulse after pulse of exquisite pleasure.

He kept his hand tight against her while the waves faded. Her muscles gradually relaxed and her hands slid from his wrist, her body too sated to expend even that much energy.

She might be a writer, but there were no words. No words whatsoever to describe what he'd just done to her, or the burgeoning feelings he'd awakened inside her.

The pressure of Clay's hand lessened over her mouth. Releasing her, he stroked the side of her face with his knuckles, then slowly eased his other hand from between her thighs. Zoe moaned softly in protest and wriggled back toward him, seeking more contact.

Her eyelids were too heavy to force open, her body too weak to move. Totally relaxed, at least for the moment. As soon as she recovered enough to remember her own name, she was going to take this sexy man for the ride of his life and give him the same pleasure he'd just shown her. In just a few minutes, so she could savor this delicious feeling of safety and contentment of being in his arms as she relaxed.

She was vaguely aware of the light weight of the quilt sliding up her body, Clay's heat as he wrapped a thick arm around her waist and pulled her tight into him. A moment later she felt the brush of his fingertips along the side of her face, then the warm press of his lips against her temple and let herself tumble headlong into sleep.

Chapter Nine

Carlos kept the brim of his ball cap pulled low over his forehead as he turned up the sidewalk and headed north on St. Peter's Street. The Quarter was never empty, even at this late hour, but the streets were quiet. As long as he looked confident and unassuming, no one should be suspicious of him walking around alone.

He hitched the backpack up higher on his shoulder as he walked. It held his tools, lockpick kit, pistol and extra magazines, just in case. Not that he expected to run into any trouble. Zoe Renard lived alone in this rental apartment, and she was divorced. Nothing in her social media accounts mentioned a boyfriend or any other sort of significant other. Should be easy to sneak into her place, get her, and leave. Even if she had a gun somewhere inside, he still had to risk it.

He hadn't decided whether he was going to kill her or not though. If she told him what he wanted to know and it led him to Leticia, he might let her live.

A group of about eight or so people were walking toward him on the same side of the street. He stepped off the sidewalk and onto the road to give them room, got a nod and a raised to-go cup by way of thanks, and stepped back up when he'd passed them. Zoe's building was on the left, a two-story brick building with a private entrance. He'd scoped it out a couple hours ago to check out what kind of locks and security she had, and she hadn't been home.

Coming closer to the building, he caught a glimpse of someone out on the balcony and from the height and build he knew it was her. He quickly ducked into the shadows beneath the wrought iron structure and into the alcove at the entry.

Setting his backpack down at his feet, he quickly put on gloves and withdrew the bolt cutters he'd brought. As far as locks went, the one on the gate was pathetic but good news for him. Any security system in the building itself he'd have to deal with.

Time was critical. The more headway Leticia had, the farther she could run from him. He wiped away the film of sweat that had gathered on his forehead with the shoulder of his T-shirt.

The possibility of losing Leticia made his hands shake. His breathing was harsh to his own ears. He hadn't slept much the past two days, couldn't eat, and no amount of alcohol could numb the panic that was slowly engulfing him. Carlos needed to find out where she was, *now*.

Just as he lifted the bolt cutters toward the bicycle chain, he heard the slider to the balcony open and someone else stepped outside. Carlos froze and tipped his head back, straining to hear what was going on. He could barely hear them, but there was no mistaking the deep timbre of a man's voice.

He pressed his lips together, hesitating. He didn't have time to deal with the complication that came with subduing another person, and he had no idea who this guy was. If he had to kill him to get what he wanted from Zoe, it would be that much harder to hide the evidence and clear himself if he was ever questioned about it.

Dammit to fucking *hell*.

Compelled by the sense that Leticia was slipping away from him with each passing second, Carlos put the cutters in position and sliced through the chain holding the gate shut. He quickly reached out to catch the loose ends, wincing as one of the ends clanged against the wrought iron. He stilled and listened intently, and this time an unmistakable female moan of surprised pleasure floated down to him.

The sound jolted through him, making him hard as he remembered all the times Leticia had made a sound just like that for him. A wave of anger and desperation rose up and he lowered the cutters. He unwound the chain, reached for the latch, and the burner phone buzzed in his pocket, startling him.

Shit!

He put the cutters away and grabbed the phone, knowing it could only be Gill, and that it was important.

She's close to her cousin. Sealed military record, listed as FBI agent but can't find details. Flight records show he's in town right now though. Thought you'd want to know.

The security conference.

Even as he thought it, sweat broke out all over his body. Top people from every important agency in the U.S. and a dozen other friendly countries were here to meet about things like global and homegrown terrorism, the war on drugs and the illegal immigration problem currently plaguing the country. Carlos knew some of the attendees personally.

Another moan came from the balcony, muffled this time.

He mentally cursed. He was pretty sure Zoe wasn't fucking her cousin up there right now, but this entire situation was way more complicated than he'd originally thought. This added worry about her cousin—whoever he was, a sealed military record meant he was likely Spec Ops trained—no, he'd have to come back. Get her when she was alone.

Coming here had been risky. Sure as hell that guy upstairs with her right now wouldn't be leaving for a long while, if at all. He had to abort the op.

Shoving the phone back into his pocket, he peeled off his gloves and zipped his backpack shut, then hurried back down the street, choosing a different route. Halfway up the street he paused to look back at the balcony. He couldn't see anyone and there was no light up there, but he had no doubt Zoe was still getting busy with her nocturnal visitor.

That bitch had cost him the love of his life.

His fingers clenched around the strap of the backpack as he turned away and walked to the end of the block. He would make her pay for what she'd done. And if Leticia escaped because of this lost time, he'd kill Zoe for it.

He'd give it one more day. This time he'd have her followed or do it himself, grab her when she was alone and vulnerable, probably once it was dark. Then he'd get everything out of her and make her suffer for everything she'd cost him.

****

Zoe woke to find herself alone in her bed, noticed the light seeping through the edges of the blackout blinds and immediately rolled over to look at the clock. Almost seven. She vaguely recalled waking when Clay got up from the daybed. Without a word he'd gathered her up, quilt and all, and carried her into her room. She'd been too sleepy to appreciate it fully at the time, but now the ultra-romantic gesture made her smile.

He'd even lain beside her in the dark and she'd slid back to sleep, still having every intention of waking him up with her hands and mouth exploring that delectable body. Unfortunately he wasn't here.

She sat up, pushing the hair out of her face, a slight throb in her cheek. "Clay?"

No answer.

The purple robe she'd had on last night was still loosely draped around her body. She got up and tied the sash securely around her waist before leaving her room. The bathroom and guestroom doors stood open and she didn't hear any sound from the kitchen. She stopped in the hallway, a sense of disappointment washing over her. He hadn't just up and left, had he? After last night?

She checked the kitchen just in case, but there was no note. He wasn't out on the balcony, either. Snagging her purse from the newel post, she took out her phone. No texts.

Pushing aside the growing annoyance, she headed to the bathroom. She had to get ready and go to the shelter to meet with Leticia. She'd just have to worry about Clay later.

She was in the middle of stripping when she heard his voice call out.

"Zoe?"

Her heart leapt. "In the bathroom. Be out in a sec." Fumbling to get the robe back on, she hastily ran her hands over her hair before cracking the door open, all the while berating herself for being so excited that he was still here.

She opened the door to find him standing in front of her wearing his jeans, and nothing else.

Her mouth went dry, her toes curling into the hardwood floor as she took in the sight of that magnificent torso displayed before her in all its naked glory, gilded by the morning light streaming in through the sliders leading to the balcony.

The muscles in his arms, chest and abdomen were taut and delineated, marred only by the five or six inch incision bisecting his lower abs where the surgeons had gone in to repair his ruined discs back in June. A gorgeous black-inked tribal tat marked the left side of his chest, flowing over his pec in a series of intricate lines and swirls. She wanted to trace every line with her tongue. She'd felt that body up against her last night, and those arms had caged her so tight as he'd rocked her world with nothing but his fingers and a few hot words.

Managing to drag her gaze back to his face, she found her voice. "Where'd you go?"

He didn't seem the least bit embarrassed by her blatant perusal of his body. But why should he, when he looked like that? "Was gonna grab us something to eat from the diner I saw down the street. But then I found this." He raised his hand and for the first time she noticed the T-shirt in his grip, and her bicycle chain wrapped up in it. "Someone cut it in half last night. I used the shirt to keep from contaminating any prints on it."

Frowning, she stepped forward to take the bundle from him. The cut edges of the chain looked clean, telling her it had to have been some kind of tool. She looked back up into Clay's face and rubbed her hands over her upper arms to ward off the sudden chill. "Did they come into the courtyard and try to get in the house?" It alarmed her that somebody had tried to break in last night while she'd been home.

He took the shirt and chain back, set it on the kitchen counter. "Don't think so, it was still wrapped around the gate. Ever had anything like this happen before?"

"No, but I've only been here a couple months." And suddenly she felt a lot less safe here alone.

He folded his arms, muscles shifting in a display of latent power. "Kind of coincidental that someone would randomly try to break in last night, right after you helped that woman, don't you think?"

"I…don't know. He couldn't have followed us. You were there and you didn't see anyone."

"No," he allowed. "But if he's as connected as the woman says, he could have traced you through your phone."

Zoe had pondered that for a minute yesterday before dismissing it as something dreamed up by her overactive author's imagination. Now that Clay seemed to be concerned too, she realized she might be in more danger than she'd thought.

"I'll get a new one today." And she was never going out again without her pepper spray. She might even have to carry the pistol locked in the gun safe in her closet. Tuck had insisted she get it years ago and had taught her how to use it. She hadn't been to the range in forever and now she regretted the lapse.

He nodded. "Good. And what about the woman?"

"I'm supposed to meet her at the shelter this morning. Try to help her figure out what to do from here." She ran a hand through her hair. "I tried to convince her to let me get Celida to help her, but she's too scared to trust anyone."

His eyes searched hers, and she saw a warmth that hadn't been there before. "You're not going to let this go, are you?"

"I can't just abandon her and her son. Not now. I'll make her see reason today, explain the near break-in and get her in contact with Celida. Trust me, I don't want trouble any more than she does."

Clay nodded. "And we'll get Celida to find someone who can tap into the CCTVs in the area. See if we can find out who cut the lock."

"Good idea." Man, usually she wrote this kind of stuff, not experienced it firsthand.

"And I'm going with you to the shelter." She opened her mouth to argue but he held up a hand. "I won't go to the house itself, but I'm not letting you go there by yourself, especially now."

She wasn't about to argue with that. "Okay. Thanks, I really appreciate it."

He surprised her by reaching out and sliding his thumb across her lower lip, setting off an explosion of heat deep in her abdomen. "No need to thank me for that, raven." Before she could respond or even part her lips to lick at his thumb, he dropped his hand and indicated the bathroom with a terse nod. "Get ready and I'll take you over."

After scrubbing herself in the shower and wishing they had time for Clay to join her there, she dressed in a black, halter-style dress with a sequined skull on the front of it and did her hair up in a French knot at the back of her head. Teeth brushed, makeup on, she exited the bathroom to find Clay at the kitchen sink, drinking a glass of juice. He'd put his shirt back on, much to her chagrin.

"You're phone rang a couple times while you were in the shower," he said, and downed the last of the juice.

She hurried over to her purse and checked her phone, saw the owner of the shelter had called. Not good. Zoe called her back and asked what was going on.

"She's gone," Diane said simply. "We convinced her to stay long enough for her and Xander to eat breakfast, then she took off. Something about her ex being close, that she could feel it, and nothing we did or said would change her mind. She left a sealed envelope for you though. I opened it," she added in an apologetic tone, "but only because those two need protection, *now*."

Zoe agreed. "What does it say?"

"Okay, there are four lines. First one says C, B, period. Then K, A, A, E, A, L."

"Hang on," Zoe said, rushing to the kitchen to grab a pen and paper and write it down. What kind of code was this?

"Second one starts with what looks like a minus sign, then E, L, period. Next is L, K, O, C, L, A."

"Got it. Third?"

"B, E, vertical slash, L, H."

This didn't make any sense at all. "And the fourth?"

"B, O, colon, B, B. That's it. Do you know what it means?"

"I don't have a freaking clue," Zoe muttered, rubbing her forehead. It looked like total gibberish. She stared at it for a long moment. Was it initials in there somewhere? The boyfriend's maybe? She felt Clay come up beside her, and turned the pad she was using so he could see the letters as well as the ideas she had scribbled down and crossed out as she dismissed them.

"I think it's Black Horse," he said in a low voice.

Zoe lowered the phone and looked up at him in astonishment. Black Horse? "What?"

"Black Horse. It's a code sometimes used by the military, dating back to Vietnam, and each letter in the words signifies a number between zero and nine. Usually to give map coordinates. So this first line reads three, zero, period. Four, two, three, one, two, four."

He paused, studied the letters a moment longer and nodded in certainty. "They're map coordinates, but in decimal form. In the military we used the Military Grid Reference System. I'll need to convert these into degrees, minutes and seconds. Hang on." He punched something into his phone, brought up a website and entered the numbers.

"I think her dad was in the Air Force." He or somebody like him must have taught Leticia this. Zoe was impressed, and really freaking worried. Secret codes? Map coordinates? This situation was obviously far more dangerous than she'd imagined, and she'd already imagined it was bad.

Clay nodded as he did the conversion, eyes fixed on the phone. "There we go. So the first number is latitude and the second is longitude. She's gotta still be pretty close to New Orleans, which means the latitude is north thirty degrees, twenty-five minutes, twenty-two-point-five-one-four-three seconds. Longitude is west ninety-one degrees, eight minutes, forty-six-point-seven-two-two-three seconds." He wrote them down in degrees, minutes and seconds for her.

"Holy crap," she mused as Clay opened some sort of navigation ap. "Where is that?" Those were some pretty damn precise coordinates.

She raised her phone back to her ear as he punched the numbers into the program and showed her where the point for the coordinates was on the map. "Nairn Park in Baton Rouge," she said in disbelief, to herself as much as Diane. "It's right off I-10 and my...my parents live close to there." Oh god, her *parents*, she thought with a sinking sensation in her gut.

"Third line must be a date, and the fourth looks like a time," Clay said before she could say anything more, writing down the numbers from the rest of the message. "September fifteenth, oh-six hundred hours."

"She wants me to meet her there, tomorrow at six am," Zoe murmured, astonished. How the hell had Leticia come up with this idea? What if Zoe hadn't had Clay or one of the others here to help her figure out what the message said?

"Do you know why she'd go there?" Diane asked.

Zoe swallowed, a heavy weight settling in her stomach. Obligation and responsibility. And guilt. It had been stupid of her to share such personal information with Leticia, but she'd never expected it to come back and bite her in the ass like this. Lesson learned.

God, she felt stupid having to admit this to Clay and Diane. "She knows my family's there, and that my father was a former DA. That's one of the reasons I was able to earn her trust in the first place. She was obviously scared that her ex was getting close to her and Xander, and wanted to get out of town immediately." Could there be another reason why Leticia had chosen Baton Rouge though? She'd never mentioned any relatives or friends living there to Zoe.

She voiced her suspicion. "Maybe she wants to meet me and stay at my parents' place for a couple days, because she'd feel safe there?"

"You really think she'd ask that of you?" Diane asked, her voice taut with disapproval.

The usual professional boundaries between volunteers at the shelter and the women they dealt with had been blurred a long time ago with Leticia in an effort to gain her trust, and it was Zoe's own doing, so she couldn't be upset about the liberties Leticia was taking now. "I don't know what to think right now, except she's clearly desperate and believes she and her son are in imminent danger."

"So will you go?"

She looked up at Clay again and found him watching her, then swallowed. "I don't want to stand her up and leave her waiting out there alone with her son at six in the morning, and she begged me not to go to the cops with this, so…" She raised her eyebrows at Clay, looking for his input. This was partially her fault, by not maintaining clear boundaries with Leticia before. What choice did she have now but to go?

"I'll come with you," he said. "And Tuck. But when we meet her, this all ends. We have to turn this over to someone in law enforcement, even if she doesn't like it.

Enough's enough. We need to find out who this guy terrorizing her is, and bring him in."

Convincing Leticia to trust anyone in law enforcement was going to be a challenge, but maybe if she met Clay and Tuck in person she'd relent. And Clay was right, this was getting dangerous and had to end before things escalated or Zoe got involved any further. She nodded. "Okay."

But now she was worried about how Leticia and Xander were doing, out there all on their own, being hunted by a man so dangerous that Leticia had fled town and left a desperate coded message for Zoe. Had she actually expected Zoe to drive to Baton Rouge and meet her at the park all alone tomorrow morning? It had to be because she'd hoped Zoe would take her and Xander to her parents'. It was the only explanation Zoe could come up with.

"Thank you," Diane said, sounding relieved. "Please keep me updated. I'm worried about her, Xander, *and* you."

Zoe wasn't feeling too great about the situation either. "I will, and thanks for calling. Bye." She ended the call and put her phone on the counter.

"You sure you're up for this?" Clay asked, watching her with that intense, penetrating gaze. She was surprised he wasn't putting the kibosh on the whole thing immediately, but he must have seen how important this was and that a woman and boy's lives were in danger. Deep down he wasn't nearly as much of a hard-ass as he'd like the rest of the world to believe.

Zoe nodded, bit her lip. If she had him and Tuck with her tomorrow morning, she'd be fine. "Even if I wanted to go to the police for help with this, I have nothing to give them except the info she's given me. No name, no physical description or address for the guy. And for all I know, he might be a cop."

He grunted. "Call your parents while we have Celida check the local cameras, mention what's going on and we'll go from there. If you're facing a credible threat, we're going to take some serious precautions. And then I want you to come with me and meet Tuck and the others at the hotel."

That last part made her stomach knot. "Why, you think we need to bring everyone in on this?" She needed a team that size for backup tomorrow morning?

"Not sure yet, although we'll have to tell Tuck, but that's not why." He shrugged. "I just want you to come with me."

Two months ago that display of nonchalance would have fooled her. But now she knew him well enough to realize that despite his remoteness, that nonchalance was feigned. Because he *did* care.

And he wanted to spend more time with her enough to ask. The thought sent a wave of warmth through her. "Should I change then?" She'd never been to a security conference before. Was it all professional attire? "I can do corporate Goth like I used to back when I worked at the law firm. Black skirt suit, ruffled blouse, skull pin on the lapel and my coffin briefcase."

"Corporate Goth." His lips twitched and his gaze traveled the length of her, stalling on her breasts and legs. "But no need to change. You look great just like that."

She felt a blush working its way up her cheeks, his approval touching her deeply. "Thanks."

For whatever reason, at the end of their marriage her ex had suddenly become embarrassed of her style and the way she dressed, especially when he was trying so hard to impress his conservative friends at his law firm. Hoping for a big promotion that had never materialized. It hadn't shaken her confidence to the point of making her question her identity, but it had hurt and she wasn't wasting her time on another guy who didn't like who she was.

Apparently Clay had no problem with any of that, and no problem taking her to meet his professional colleagues as she was.

In giving her that compliment and the respect that came with it, he'd stolen yet another little chunk of her heart. At this rate, he was going to hold more of it than she did.

And she didn't even want to think about what the implications of that were yet.

Chapter Ten

Supervisory Special Agent Matt DeLuca ordered himself a plate of shrimp and grits while he waited for the man he was meeting with. The guy was somewhat of a legend in the intelligence community and Matt had heard a lot about him, but they'd never spoken before. There were a few priority cases they'd worked on in conjunction with the NSA recently, though never with any direct contact with Rycroft, and a few new ones on their radar to discuss. The conference here in New Orleans provided the perfect opportunity to meet.

The waitress brought him his meal and he paid for it in cash before taking a bite as he turned from the counter to survey the room. The conference hotel was a wet dream for any terrorist looking to put a serious dent in the US effort to win the War on Terror. Agents and other personnel from half a dozen different agencies were there to discuss the hot topics of the day, trying to stay one step ahead of the enemy.

Which was why Matt was meeting his contact at a quiet diner on the other side of town.

His focus sharpened on the doorway as a man stepped inside, directly across from where Matt was sitting. He was around six feet tall, graying hair, and carried himself like a seasoned operator in his dress pants and pinstriped button-down shirt. There were plenty of men who matched that description at the conference right now, but something about this man's demeanor told him instantly that it was the NSA's Alex Rycroft.

Rycroft scanned the diner, his gaze locking on Matt instantly, and headed over. Matt set his fork down and stood. "Rycroft?"

"DeLuca," Rycroft said, shaking his hand in a firm grip. "Good to meet you."

"You too." The guy was in his early fifties but still did fieldwork sometimes and Matt could already tell that middle age hadn't affected his operational edge any.

Rycroft took the stool beside him and ordered a coffee. "So, how are your boys? Heard a few of them got pretty banged up a couple weeks back," he said while they waited for the waitress to get the coffee.

He meant during the op at the federal bank in June, when a veteran who was an explosives expert had taken hostages and threatened to blow the building. It hadn't taken long for DeLuca and the rest of the FBI team to figure out what Ken Spivey really wanted.

Revenge. A misguided effort to avenge his son's and wife's death years before, when they'd been killed in the crossfire during a similar HRT op in a bank hostage taking.

Matt had been forced to make the call and approve the breach, knowing he was sending his guys into a possible death trap. Three of them had been badly injured on the attempt, Bauer the worst of them. Even though he knew he'd made the right call that day, Matt still felt responsible for what had happened to his guys.

"They're all back to active duty status, except for one, and he'll be there shortly too. Their team's on training cycle right now." Bauer was technically on limited duty until he had the all-clear from his docs, though he'd been participating in this latest training in Biloxi with the DEA guys. He'd made it back much faster than the doctors had anticipated, but that didn't surprise Matt or anyone who knew him. Once a SEAL, always a SEAL. Those guys didn't take well to lying around, even during recuperation from a serious back injury.

"Glad to hear it." The waitress set the coffee mug on the counter. Rycroft picked it up and looked at Matt. "Should we sit someplace a little more private for this?"

It wasn't a question, and Matt heartily agreed on the change of location, away from any potential eavesdroppers. He got up and followed Rycroft to an empty table at the back of the restaurant with four upholstered chairs surrounding it, set into a quieter corner. They wouldn't be talking about anything classified out here in the open, obviously, but it was a good chance to at least get on the same page about a few things and having now met Rycroft in person, it would only help in future operations.

"So," the NSA agent said, easing back into his chair. "You were Corps, right?"

"Yep. Eleven years."

"Scout Sniper first, before you moved into FORECON?"

Matt was pretty sure the man had read up on him and already knew everything about his background, but he didn't mind playing along while they felt each other out a bit. "That's right." The Marine Corp's Scout Sniper School was one of the toughest things he'd ever done. He still wore his HOG's tooth—the 7.62 mm round given to him upon graduation—around his neck. He also had a badass tat on his right shoulder blade.

Rycroft nodded. He'd chosen a table against the wall, leaving Matt to take one across from him. Matt didn't like having his back exposed to a room like this but he knew Rycroft was vigilant. It was in the way his gaze rarely stayed still. For guys like them who'd spent their lives on the front lines in harm's way to defend their country, it was second nature. He knew Rycroft had spent nearly his entire career in the Army in SF.

"One of the Titanium guys I've worked closely with over the past year was FORECON."

Matt nodded. "Sean Dunphy. I know the name, but we never met. Heard he got hit by an IED in eastern Afghanistan and it was pretty bad."

"Killed the other guys in the SUV with him, and temporarily paralyzed him from the waist down. But he's walking now." Rycroft's cool gray eyes warmed a fraction with something close to pride. "In fact, he just got married in the spring."

"Glad to hear that. I heard you got married recently, too. Congratulations."

He smiled a bit. "Thanks." He glanced down at the gold band on Matt's ring finger. "I'm sorry for your loss."

Matt nodded and took another sip of his beer to cover the all too familiar pang he still felt whenever someone mentioned Lisa. Four years after her death and it was only now becoming easier to think about her without feeling suffocated by the loss, and being able to remember her as she'd once been. Before that horrific Fourth of July holiday that had shattered his entire world.

He set the beer aside. "Thanks. She was an amazing lady." He wished he'd told her that more often.

Well, he wished he'd done a lot of things differently.

"Evers tells me your better half is pretty great too," he added, for something else to say and to turn the conversation away from his dead wife.

A real smile softened that hard face for a moment. "She is. The women in our lives have to be, to put up with us."

"True enough," he said with a laugh. He leaned back and stretched his legs out, deciding to switch topics and get straight to it. "I hear we might have a few current interests in common."

Rycroft's smile disappeared and he was all business again. "That we do. You'll be getting more intel on this in the coming weeks but I wanted you to hear it from me first. That cell you and your boys tangled with back in April?"

The Uyghur Islamic cell, based out of Xinxiang, China. That entire situation had been more than personal for Matt's team. Evers's girl, Rachel Granger, had been taken and held hostage by them. Tuck's girl, Celida Morales, had been badly injured during the kidnapping. "What about it?"

"They've got more operatives here than we realized, and have activated more, including linking with another group in Juarez."

Mexico. "Seriously? They're doing that kind of networking now?"

Rycroft nodded. "Intelligence says they're planning to target something in D.C. or New York. We think maybe subway systems."

They discussed a few more details then talked about an upcoming raid on a suspected financier's place. The man was rich and heavily guarded, so the HRT was going to be serving the warrant.

Rycroft paused when his phone rang. He pulled it from the holder on his hip, frowned at whatever the message read, then said, "Excuse me a second." He dialed someone, his voice taut as Matt listened to the one-sided conversation. "I'm on my way. Meet me in the lobby in fifteen." He put the phone back and stood.

"Come on. Got a situation at the hotel."

Matt pushed to his feet, frowning. "What kind of situation?"

"Security breach."

Dammit. He'd known that the conference being held this close to September eleventh was a bad idea. What the hell had the organizers been thinking? "Some of my guys are there." More were meeting him there later.

"Not to worry," Rycroft said as he headed for the door. "It's been taken care of."

From his flat tone Matt had a pretty good idea what that meant, but the breach was a definite concern. There could be others. He jogged with Rycroft to the nearest streetcar stop and hopped on. He had a lot of questions but couldn't ask them in public so he took a deep breath and tamped down his impatience while they rode to the hotel.

As the streetcar began to slow at their stop Matt could already see the emergency vehicles parked along the curb out front of the hotel. He followed Rycroft through the police perimeter and into the lobby.

A wall of noise hit him, generated by hundreds of conversations going on at once. Groups of people stood around talking on the polished marble floor and in the adjoining lounge. A few were watching the cops proceedings with interest, but from everyone's relaxed body language Matt got the sense that nobody knew what was going on. His muscles loosened.

Beside him, Rycroft scanned the lobby, and his eyes locked on something—or someone—across the room. The NSA agent stilled.

Matt turned his head in time to see a young woman wearing a black skirt suit standing near the elevators. She was staring straight at Rycroft.

"Will you excuse me for a minute?" Rycroft said.

Matt watched as Rycroft walked to the woman. He stopped close to her, bent his head when she leaned up to whisper something to him. He drew back, frowned, said something, and the brunette answered. Whatever she said, Rycroft didn't like it.

Mouth pressed into a thin line, the NSA officer took the woman by the arm and led her back across the lobby toward Matt. It was clear from her stiff posture that she wasn't thrilled about coming over, but Rycroft wasn't giving her a choice.

Matt watched her as they approached. She appeared to be in her mid or maybe late twenties, and she was a knockout. Too young for him, but he could still appreciate a beautiful woman when he saw one. She had dark caramel skin, deep brown eyes and near-black hair that fell to the middle of her back in gentle waves that curled at the ends. When she and Rycroft stopped in front of him he started to offer his hand then changed his mind at the last second when he saw the expression in her eyes.

A flicker of wariness and mistrust before she went back to being a blank slate. The eyes of someone who'd experienced a lot of bad shit, up close and personal. It made him even more curious about her, and her connection to Rycroft. Then he noticed the way her gaze cut over to Rycroft, and Matt clearly read the earnestness in her posture. Whatever she'd told him, it was urgent and she wanted to act.

The other man was grim, all business. "Wait here for a few minutes. I'll be right back," he said to her, leaving her standing stiffly before Matt as he walked away at a brisk pace toward the elevators and disappeared inside one.

Matt intended to find out what the hell was going on, but for now the woman was clearly uncomfortable and he wanted to put her at ease. "I'm Matt," he said.

She nodded, the motion stiff as she scanned the room. On edge, as though she was looking for another threat. Or maybe expecting one. "B."

Okay, so not very talkative. Matt followed her gaze, searching the lobby, but nothing tripped his internal radar. He didn't like it, because he knew damn well there was something big going on behind the scenes that he was unaware of. "B as in the name Bea? Or as in the initial?"

Those espresso brown eyes met his for a moment, not a hint of warmth or humor there. "Just B."

Alrighty then. Not very friendly, either. "So what's going on?"

"Nothing," she answered, her tone crisp. Nothing about her radiated concern or fear, but he could tell she was still on alert. Matt wanted to know why.

He studied her face, trying to figure out what mix of heritages made up her features but couldn't say for sure and there was no discernable trace of an accent in her voice. She sounded pure American, could have been born and raised anywhere in the heartland. Where were her parents from? From her looks it could have been anywhere from Pakistan or India to maybe Fiji.

A long, tense silence spread between them. He tried to come up with something to say to fill the void, not one of his specialties but he wanted to see how much information she'd give him. Although he could already guess. "So you work with Alex?"

She looked at him again, her gaze so intense it probably intimidated most men. Unfortunately for her, he and most of the others at this conference didn't fall under the pussy umbrella. "No."

He bit back a chuckle at her brusqueness and opened his mouth to say something else, just to see what she'd do, but her phone rang. She checked the message, her mouth flattening into a thin line of what could only be distaste.

"I'm supposed to take you up to the tenth floor to meet Alex," she said to him, sounding none too happy about it.

"Good, let's go." He was anxious to get answers. He followed her to the elevators, endured more resolute silence from her as they rode to the tenth floor. Agents from various agencies filled the alcove where the elevators were. They checked Matt's ID but not hers, which he found interesting, and let them through.

"This way," B said to him, not bothering to look back as she turned left and marched down the hallway that was also manned by armed agents. "Down there," she finished, pointing to the third room on the left where the door stood open, guarded by more agents.

Matt passed her and headed for the room, arriving just as Rycroft stepped out and acknowledged him with a nod. "What's up?" Matt asked. Whatever had happened in that room, it was a big deal.

Rather than answer, Rycroft tilted his head toward the room and stepped aside to let Matt see inside. He was shocked to see a whole FBI forensics team there, gathering evidence. A young man of Hispanic descent was lying on the floor staring at the ceiling, a single bullet hole gracing the center of his forehead, and Matt suddenly understood why Rycroft had wanted him up here.

He whipped his head around to glance over at the NSA agent, who was on his phone to someone. "Part of the Juarez cell?" he guessed.

Rycroft nodded and went back to his conversation. A few seconds later he put his phone away and faced B, who was waiting a few yards down the hallway. She had her arms folded across her chest, standing absolutely still, her expression blank as a clean whiteboard. Was she staying at a distance so she wouldn't have to put up with more small talk from him? Or maybe the dead body bothered her, but he didn't think so. Her eyes had told him she was no stranger to seeing death.

Rycroft nodded to her once, the gesture almost one of approval. "It's taken care of."

She stared at him for a long moment, opened her mouth like she wanted to say something, then closed it and relented with a nod. Uncrossing her arms, she brushed her hands down the front of her skirt, smoothing the fabric in a gesture that seemed like an afterthought. "You'll be in touch?" she asked him.

"Yes."

She glanced at Matt, looked at him for less than a heartbeat, then walked away, her high heels soundless in the carpeted hallway.

Matt watched her walk away, his gaze sticking on her mile-long legs before he looked back at Rycroft. "Who was that?"

The man gave him a hard smile. "I could tell you, but then she'd have to kill you."

Under the circumstances Matt didn't know whether to laugh or not, but it didn't seem like the guy was joking, so he let it drop. "Gonna tell me what happened?"

Rycroft's gaze cut back to the body on the floor. "He was one of the militants directly financed by the man we talked about earlier. Managed to get past the security measures in place under a false identity, and somebody helped him smuggle a small arsenal of automatic weapons and explosives into his room. From what we can tell, he and his pals were going to try to pull off a Mumbai-style attack and blow up the hotel." He shrugged. "There'd been some recent chatter that the cell might try and pull off some kind of an attack here, so we came prepared."

They sure as hell had come prepared—they had an

FBI team on standby, already doing their thing.

Matt nodded, finding the idea of the attack alarming, but not surprising. In his experience, terrorists weren't afraid of dying, and the man growing cold in there right now must have known he wouldn't walk away from whatever he'd planned here. Not with this kind of crowd in attendance. Security at the hotel was tight, and thankfully the attendees were staying at various hotels in the area so they weren't all lumped together in one big, juicy target.

The sheer ballsyness of the plan was cause for concern though. "Any more intel about further attacks?"

"Nope. All taken care of now." He nodded toward the body. "He was the leader of the group. It'll take the others too long to reorganize for them to be able to pull off the attack now."

"Who took him out?"

"Can't tell you."

Matt frowned. He had top security clearance. If Rycroft couldn't—or wouldn't—tell him, then only a few people within the intelligence community knew about the hit. Matt glanced down the hallway to look for B, but she was already gone. "So B, or whatever her name is. She's an agent?"

Rycroft half-smirked. "Something like that. But not one of mine," he said evasively.

That left a whole slew of possibilities, each more intriguing than the last. There was a helluva lot more to her than met the eye, that was for sure, Matt thought as he walked with Rycroft back toward the elevators. Whatever the truth about her was, he had a feeling it would surprise the hell out of him.

Chapter Eleven

C lay stepped out of the shadows of the arched brick entryway and onto the sidewalk, casting a cursory look around before Zoe joined him. The foot traffic on the street was relatively quiet right now. A few couples and small groups were strolling along but he didn't see anything suspicious.

He heard Zoe's quiet footfalls on the brick behind him, then the squeak of the gate. She stepped up beside him, her soft floral-and-musk scent teasing him. That dress hugged every sexy curve she had, the dark fabric stark against her pale skin. Her purple-streaked, black hair was pulled up on top into two little pigtails while the rest was left free to stream down her back. Her lush, full lips were covered in a deep red gloss that made them all shiny and made him want a taste. The darkening bruise on her face made him want to kiss it away.

Last night hadn't been nearly enough. Not for either of them, he hoped. He could still hear the sexy sounds she'd made for him as she'd rocked against his fingers in a desperate struggle for release. A release he wanted to witness again, only next time, while he was buried deep inside her.

With effort, he mentally switched gears back to the

present. "Did you reach her?" he asked. She'd said she would call Celida about the local CCTV footage right after talking to her parents, and he'd stepped outside to give her some privacy.

"No. She'll call me back when she gets my text." She took a look around at the street, and while he was glad she was taking extra care to be aware of her surroundings, he hated that she was feeling nervous because some asshole had tried to get into her place this morning. He wanted to put her at ease, make her feel secure again.

And anyone thinking of targeting her was going to have to get through him first.

Wanting to touch her, reassure her, Clay wrapped an arm around her shoulders and drew her close to his side. She glanced up at him in surprise at the gesture, then flashed him a sweet smile that hit him straight in the center of his chest and slid her arm around his waist. "I like this," she murmured.

He liked it too. Too much. She was already further under his skin than he'd let any woman since Eve. Yet even with her he'd held part of himself back. With Zoe, he felt like he could truly be himself. And if he didn't get them moving, he was going to drag her back around the corner into her courtyard, pin her to the rough brick wall and put his hands and mouth all over her until she was desperate to have him inside her.

Damn. "Come on."

The September sun shone bright in the clear blue sky, its heat reflecting off the sidewalk. A slight breeze stirred the air, bringing with it the scents of chicory coffee and pastries from the bakery down the street. They stopped in and grabbed a bite to eat. Zoe convinced him to buy a beignet, a square French donut coated in powdered sugar.

"These aren't the same as the ones at Café du

Monde, but I actually think they're better because they're less greasy and not as messy to eat." She dug one out of the white paper bag and held it out for him to taste.

He leaned down and took a bite of the still-warm pastry. Her eyes went all smoky when he slowly closed his teeth around the edge of it, holding her gaze. He nipped off a piece and straightened, the sugary confection bursting on his tongue.

"Good?" she asked, her voice husky.

He hummed in agreement and licked the residual sugar from his lips, stilling when she slid her tongue across her lower lip as though she wanted to do the licking for him. The thought of that glossy red mouth beneath his, moving down his naked chest and stomach, her kneeling in front of him to unzip his pants while he threaded his hands in her hair and drew her toward his straining cock…

It felt like every drop of blood in his body had just diverted to his groin. Now he was sporting the mother of all erections and had no way to hide it. They were in the middle of the bakery, for godsake. "Let's go," he said, more gruffly than he'd intended.

Zoe didn't seem bothered by his tone. She reached into the bag for her own beignet, contentedly sipping her coffee as they exited the shop. On the sidewalk he kept her to the inside, away from the street. She slipped up close to his side again, her shoulder brushing his chest, and offered a little smile of encouragement. Biting back a chuckle at the adorable request for physical contact, he slid an arm around her shoulders once again.

"Ever been inside the cathedral?" she asked as they neared Jackson Square. A jazz band was performing out front for the crowd assembled next to the impressive church. The ring of a trumpet blended with the deeper notes of a tuba, rising into the clear air.

"No."

"I'll have to take you in later. The interior's really something. Gorgeous stained glass windows, marble floors, beautiful murals."

He looked down at her in surprise. "I didn't take you for the church-going type."

"Well, not now, no. But I was born and raised a Catholic and I can still appreciate the beauty of a building like that. I just rebelled harder than most girls in my teens," she finished, fluttering her lashes at him.

"I bet you were always a rebel." He couldn't see her ever being any other way.

"I guess to a certain extent," she said with a shrug. "I think my parents would say I've always been known for standing my ground and saying what I think."

He'd met her parents briefly at Tuck's dad's funeral in June. Seemed like good people. "Don't I know it," he muttered, earning a light jab in the ribs with a black-painted fingernail. He'd never forget that dig about him having a bug up his ass.

"What about you?" she asked, peering up at him. "Were you always kind of...rigid?"

His lips twitched at her choice of adjective. As a writer, she'd have plenty in her vocabulary arsenal to choose from, so he knew she was being polite. For him, the world was nearly always black and white and he wasn't embarrassed by his sometimes-rough edges. "I was raised in a conservative family, so I guess I've always been pretty set in my views." And he made no apologies for that.

"Ah. You were always on the straight and narrow, then? Apple of your parents' eye? Bet that drove your sister nuts."

His stomach grabbed slightly as he thought of Pam, who was two years older than him and had once been the golden child of their family. Honor roll throughout all of school, head cheerleader in high school, valedictorian, captain of her softball team at college. One car wreck had destroyed everything.

Zoe tilted her head. "What's wrong?"

"Nothing. I was just thinking…" He drew a deep breath, let it out slowly. "About my sister."

"Tuck's told me a bit about her. Is she any better?"

He hid a flinch. "No." And the sad truth was, she was never *going* to get better. The car accident at age twenty-six had screwed up her back, but the prescription painkillers had begun the endless downward spiral that had ruined her life.

"I'm sorry."

He nodded, jaw tight. "It's all right." He'd long ago accepted that there was nothing he or anyone in his family could do to save her, not from the drugs, certainly not from herself. "She's addicted to the point that no one can help her. She's been in and out of rehab more times than I could count. Can never stay clean. I think the longest stretch was eleven days."

Zoe winced. "What kind of drugs?"

"OxyContin's her drug of choice, but she'll take whatever she can find to stay high. She's done crack, meth and heroin too." It was like she couldn't stand to face what her life had become and needed the drugs to stay numb so she wouldn't have to deal with it.

"God." She glanced up at him as they walked, her eyes full of understanding. "Is that why you were so dead set against using painkillers in the hospital?"

"Yeah. I figure if it could happen to her, then it could happen to anyone, and I didn't want to tempt fate just in case, you know?"

She nodded. "Where is your sister now?"

"With my parents, back in Pennsylvania. I talked to my mom a couple days ago." He hesitated before continuing, part of him relieved to be talking about it.

Zoe made him feel like he could tell her anything and she wouldn't judge him. He felt more comfortable with her than he did some of his teammates, guys he entrusted his life to in the line of duty. "They'd just found her on the street again."

Zoe leaned into him and squeezed her arm around his waist. "Sorry to hear that. Did she go back into treatment?"

"No. My mom is afraid to let her out of her sight, so she keeps her with them and gives her regular doses of OxyContin to keep her there. It's twisted as fuck, but that's how it is, and at least the dosages are controlled that way so she won't overdose. It's one of the reasons I left to join the Navy. I couldn't stand watching that cycle anymore. I don't understand it and I don't condone it. My mom and I have gone twenty rounds about it. She always says I don't understand and won't until I'm a parent. My dad buries his head in the sand and lets her enable Pam. They'd both rather keep her addicted and at home with them because they're afraid she'd die otherwise."

"I understand. And it also explains why you turned out the way you did."

He raised an eyebrow at her. "How did I turn out?"

"Honorable, focused and dependable. And also a big-time control freak. Which, considering your background, makes total sense and I don't blame you for it."

"I guess I am, yeah." He slowed as they reached the square, met her gaze. "Especially in one notable area." The statement hung in the air between them, heavy with promise. He'd already shown her last night that he wasn't conventional in bed. And judging by her reaction, she'd loved it as much as he had.

Her golden eyes widened a fraction as his meaning sank in. Blowing out a breath, she shot him a mock glare. "You're such a tease, saying that out here in public when you know I can't get another demonstration."

Reaching out a hand, he cupped the edge of her jaw and brushed the pad of his thumb across her lower lip. "I don't recall teasing last night, raven."

Her pupils dilated. He felt goose bumps rise on her bare shoulder. "No, I guess you didn't. You sure took me by surprise though."

His thumb rubbed across her lower lip more firmly, testing the resilience of that soft flesh. "In a good way?"

She nodded. "In a *very* good way. I wanted to return the favor but when I woke up you were gone."

Part of him wished he'd been there when she'd woken up, but the other part knew if he'd stayed, he would have woken her in a way that left her pinned, helpless and writhing. As much as he loved that idea, he knew things would get intense between them from here on out and he wanted to make sure she was ready for it.

He glanced down to find her hardened nipples standing out against the stretchy fabric of her dress. Given the temperature was currently in the mid-seventies and rising, it made him smile. Any satisfaction he felt in that moment evaporated the second she parted her lips and let her tongue dart out to lick his skin. His gaze flashed to hers, a jolt of lust slicing through him when she closed her lips ever so slowly around his thumb and sucked.

He pulled in a sharp breath, his dick throbbing at the blatant caress meant to mimic her sucking something much more enjoyable. *Fuck.*

"Now who's teasing?" he murmured, his vigilance shot all to hell. They were standing in the open, totally exposed, and he couldn't have said how many people were behind them or on either side of them, let alone have any clue if a threat was coming. It was so unlike him to lose focus, it shocked him. *Shit. Get your head on straight, man.*

With a knowing smirk, Zoe released his thumb just as slowly as she'd taken it in, dragging the edges of her white teeth over it. "Believe me, when I start teasing you, you'll know."

Oh, he'd show her the true meaning of teasing later when they got back to her place. That couldn't come soon enough for his liking.

Wrapping his arm around the curve of her waist, he regained his vigilance and guided her around the spectators enjoying the free music. If he hadn't promised to meet Tuck and DeLuca in the hotel lobby ten minutes from now, he'd have hustled her straight back to her place that instant and shown her exactly what he'd been fantasizing about doing to her these past few months.

They walked up Chartres Street, past the shops and restaurants, and when the hotel's side entrance came into view, Clay immediately noticed the increased security presence outside. A half dozen government vehicles were parked around the perimeter, along with several NOPD cars and an ambulance.

Zoe must have picked up on his sudden tension because she looked up at him uncertainly. "Is everything okay?"

"Not sure." He kept her close as they approached the perimeter and he spoke to one of the uniformed cops. In the covered parking area next to the side entrance, another vehicle was pulled up to the door with its rear doors open. Men were loading a stretcher into it, and Clay caught a glimpse of a black coroner's bag before it disappeared into the back of the vehicle.

From the amount and type of security here, this was no simple case of finding a dead body. Had to be a homicide. He tightened his grip on Zoe and turned his body to keep her from seeing the body bag. "What's the story?" he asked the cop, showing him his FBI badge and ID.

"We received word about ten minutes ago that everything's secure."

"Thanks." Clay walked Zoe over to the wall of the hotel and dialed Tuck, who picked up on the second ring. "I'm outside with Zoe. What's going on?"

"We were just getting briefed on that," Tuck said, voice tense. "We're in the lounge. Bring Zo in for a minute if you want."

"Will do. We've got something to tell you, too."

He kept a hand on the small of Zoe's back as they showed their ID once more to the men guarding the side entrance. Men and women stopped and stared at her as they made their way through the lobby, but Zoe didn't seem to notice or care and he found that confidence extremely sexy.

"Whoa, Schroder looks a little green around the gills," she said over the buzz of background conversation filling the lobby.

Seated at the table with Tuck, Evers and DeLuca, their medic was sprawled in a chair with his head resting in one hand, eyes half closed, his face looking pale beneath his red-brown stubble. "That he does."

Everyone looked up at them when they entered the lounge. There was no alarm on any of the men's faces, and Clay relaxed a little. Tuck's and Schroder's eyes bounced from where Clay's hand was planted against Zoe's back, then up to his face. DeLuca pushed up the brim of his San Diego Chargers ball cap and grinned, appearing amused at seeing them together.

"Looks like you need a hair of the dog," Clay said to Schroder.

The guy grimaced and squirmed in his seat, placing one hand on his stomach. "No thanks. Pretty sure I've got an entire fur coat in me already."

"Spent half the night on the bathroom floor," DeLuca said with a shake of his head, settling back into his chair and crossing his arms. "Evers was nice enough to throw him a pillow before shutting the door."

"Yeah, I appreciated it," Schroder muttered, rubbing a hand over his face.

"So what's the deal with all the security?" Clay asked. He didn't mention the body bag. Zoe might have a fascination with the darker side of things, but she wouldn't like knowing someone had just died here a little while ago.

The guys glanced at each other before looking at him, and Clay understood that whatever had happened, it wasn't something they could say in front of Zoe. "Tell you later," Tuck said. He aimed a smile at his cousin. "You hungry?"

"No, we already ate," she answered. "Have you spoken to Celida this morning?"

"Not since around six. Why?"

She licked her lips, shifted her weight. "Can we talk to you for a sec?"

Frowning, Tuck's gaze went from her to Clay and back. "Sure." He rose from the table and followed them a short distance away to give them some privacy.

Clay was prepared to give him a rundown but Zoe told him what had happened. Tuck's expression grew increasingly darker with each piece she revealed. "What do you mean, you're going there tomorrow morning?" he finally demanded.

"I have to. It'll be okay though, because Clay's coming. I was hoping you would, too."

Tuck sighed and ran a hand over his face. "Well, shit, I can't let you go there without—"

The sound of the Adams Family theme song came from Zoe's purse.

She dug out her phone, already knowing who it was

because of the specific ringtone. "It's Celida."

Walking a few steps away from the guys as they continued to talk about her security situation, Zoe plugged her other ear and answered. "Hey, bébé. You get my message?"

"Yeah, and I've had one of our guys pull some footage from the cameras in your neighborhood. The perp was wearing a ball cap and hoodie, so we can't get a good look at his face, but he was carrying a backpack that could have had a bolt cutter inside it."

"Okay. Anything else?"

"Nothing besides his obvious physical description. Looks like he's in his thirties. Can't tell from the shots we have because there are lots of shadows, but he's either dark-haired or has a shaved head. Big guy, over six feet, and he looks pretty built."

Zoe swallowed as a shiver crept up her spine. If this wasn't random, then it might be Leticia's ex, and based on that description, it wasn't hard to imagine why Leticia would be afraid of him.

"I'm sorry I don't have anything more concrete for you, but we'll keep working on it. I've got another tech lined up to take a look once she finishes something else for me. Not that you're not a priority for me."

"I understand. Thanks."

Celida snorted. "Don't you dare thank me for that. And by the way, what's this about Bauer staying the night at your place last night?"

Tuck must have told her. Zoe smothered a smile at the blatant interest in her best friend's voice. "What about it?"

Celida made a huffing sound. "You guys were alone?"

"Yeah."

"*And*? Come on, Tuck was all in a twist this morning when I talked to him, all protective big brother.

It was adorable. He told me he said his piece to you before leaving last night."

"He did, and I love him for it. But I'm a big girl. I can take care of myself and make my own decisions."

"I'm well aware of that, hon, and you're preaching to the choir anyway. Now tell me what I want to know before you make my head explode. You two together, or what?"

"Um…" Not exactly. "I'm not sure what we are."

Celida gasped. "So something happened?"

Zoe couldn't help but smile. "Yep. And if I'm not mistaken, a whole lot more's gonna happen later today." It would if she had anything to say about it.

"Get outta here! You and Bauer?" She sounded both fascinated and aghast.

"Don't read too much into it." Zoe didn't know what would happen between them after today, let alone once he left the city. "I'm just taking this one day at a time, and I plan to enjoy him while I can."

"I want details," Celida insisted. "Full disclosure, specific details. But not to the level of what you write in your books," she added hastily. "This is Bauer we're talking about. I'd never be able to look at him again without wanting to scrub my brain with bleach."

Zoe laughed. "Got it. I'll give you the G-rated version."

"R-rated is fine. Nothing over that though. Just don't say his name when you tell me."

Clay and Tuck were watching her now, obviously wondering what news Celida had shared. "I gotta go fill the boys in, bébé. Talk to you soon, okay?"

"Sure, hon. Be safe. And… God, I can't believe I'm saying this about Bauer, but I would support your decision with any other guy you chose, so…enjoy."

"Thanks. I will." She hung up and walked back to the guys to fill them in on the dead end with the CCTVs.

Tuck stared at her for a long moment, hands on hips, that familiar expression on his face that told her he was weighing options. "Clay's gonna take you back home, and then I want you to stay there. If this guy's targeted you, then you need to lie low. Keep your alarm on. You've still got the nine-mill I bought you, right?"

"Yes." God, he was making her more nervous by bringing that up. The thought of using that on someone to defend herself wasn't one she relished.

Her answer seemed to satisfy him. "Either me or Bauer or both of us will stay with you tonight, and Bauer will stay tomorrow because I've got more meetings here. Speaking of which…" His gaze shifted to Clay. "The rest of us need to fill you in on a couple developments."

Zoe knew it had to be about whatever security situation had just happened, and didn't protest.

Clay nodded. "I'll take her home then head back here." He looked at her. "Ready?"

She wasn't about to argue. "Yeah." With Clay at her back she was as safe as she was going to get. Normally she loved solitude and her own company, but suddenly the thought of being left alone at her place filled her with dread.

Chapter Twelve

Carlos exited the bathroom and bought another to-go cup of coffee on his way out of the café. His fifth of the day, and it wasn't yet nine-thirty. The caffeine helped clear away the cobwebs clouding his brain, but it was making him even more twitchy. He needed another hit, either of coke or another upper, just to keep him going.

All his senses were heightened as he stepped out onto the sidewalk, his awareness of the time passing so acute he could almost hear a clock ticking in his head. His weapon dug into his lower back with each step, the feel of it reassuring. He had a full mag and two spares in his backpack, and he was fully prepared to use every round to clear a path to get to Zoe.

This was all Leticia's fault. She'd pushed him into a corner and this was his only way out. When he got his hands on that bitch he'd make her regret ever walking out on him.

Sipping the steaming hot brew, he headed east until he reached Zoe's street. He'd seen her leave almost forty-five minutes ago, with the guy he assumed she'd been with last night. Big fucker, and from the way he moved and kept checking their surroundings, Carlos knew he was trained. And not just any regular military or law enforcement training. The guy had an edge to him Carlos had recognized immediately.

Which meant he had a big fucking problem on his hands.

How was he going to get to her now? He'd considered breaking into her place while she was gone to wait there for her, but there was a chance he wouldn't be able to disable the alarm system and he was pretty sure that guy would come back with her. He was prepared to take the man down to get to Zoe, though he'd have to capitalize on the element of surprise and a guy like that would be hard to catch unawares.

He slipped in behind a small crowd of people gathered to watch a brass band playing in the middle of the intersection, where he could keep watch for Zoe to return. He sipped at his coffee, not even tasting it, and jammed his other hand into the front pocket of his jeans. His right foot tapped an anxious beat along with the drummer, every note the band played scraping over his tautly stretched nerves like the jagged edge of a rusty knife.

Two days since he'd lost tabs on Leticia and he was already losing his mind. What if he didn't find her? What if she managed to get out of the city and evade him forever?

The thought pushed his agitation to a whole new level. It was all he could do to stand still and wait while his heart pounded and panic swirled inside him so strong it made sweat break out over his body. Still no trace of her. Not even with all his resources and contacts, both in law enforcement and the criminal underworld.

How could she do this to him? There was no way she didn't know how much he loved her, but she also knew he wouldn't tolerate her up and walking out on him. He'd made that crystal clear when they'd first gotten together.

He smothered a yawn, mentally shook himself. Sleep deprivation was starting to take its toll, dulling his mind. He couldn't afford that. To pull this off he had to be sharp, at the top of his game. He wanted Leticia back, wanted her tied to his bed until he took his fill of her and punished her for the fear and humiliation she'd caused him by running.

Zoe Renard was his only chance of finding her now. No more waiting. It had to be today, whether Zoe's lover was with her or not. He couldn't spend another day without Leticia. She'd be afraid of him at first, but the punishment she had coming was necessary.

He tuned out the people around him, mostly tourists wearing those stupid plastic Mardi Gras beads—even though it was the middle of September, many recording or snapping pictures of the band with their phones. The music faded away as he stared down the length of Zoe's block and thought of Leticia, her perfect pale-brown skin.

A cab turned the corner at the far end of the block and parked alongside the curb. The back of his neck tingled as the rear doors opened and Zoe stepped out with her lover. Wearing wraparound shades, the guy looked around and reached back to take her hand. As they turned and walked across the street toward her building, Carlos could see a faint bulge beneath the back of the guy's shirt at waist level. Definitely carrying. Clearly not an easy target, even if he managed to get a drop on him. Which he doubted he would.

A nervous buzzing began in the pit of his stomach. Could he really take the man down in order to get to Zoe? If it came down to it, he'd take him out and anyone else who stood in his way.

He pushed away from the brick wall he'd been leaning against, was halfway down the block without even realizing what he was doing when something stopped him. He blinked, came out of the fog he'd been in.

Fuck, he was losing it. Attacking now, in broad daylight when she had that kind of backup? Practically suicide. His instincts had never let him down yet, so he obeyed and stayed where he was, each second its own separate torment as he chose another hiding location in an alcove five doors down from Zoe's place. His heart hammered and his breathing was erratic. He could feel his hands shaking.

Get a grip. You have to calm down. Think! This is your only chance to find Leticia. Don't fuck it up.

He'd have to wait and hope the guy left. Fucking sucked, but that was his only option at the moment.

With his gaze pinned to the building entrance where Zoe and the man disappeared from view, he stayed put. If her lover left her alone, even for a minute, Carlos would attack.

****

They'd taken a cab back to her place to save time, and already Zoe regretted that her time alone with him was coming to an end. On the walk to the hotel she'd felt like they'd bonded a little. He'd opened up to her about things she'd never expected him to. That had to mean something, because she knew Clay didn't open up to many people.

"Can I sneak into the bathroom before you grab your shower?" she asked him as she led the way up the creaky old stairs.

"Sure, yeah." He slung the garment bag over one broad shoulder and moved to the living room.

She freshened up in the bathroom, splashing water on her face and spritzing on some perfume before walking out. Only to stop dead at the sight before her.

Gilded by the bright light streaming through the sliding glass doors leading onto the patio, Clay was on the floor of her living room, doing pushups. He was facing away from her, moving up and down in a steady rhythm, every muscle in his back flexing beneath that thin gray T-shirt.

Oh my gawd...

She must have made a sound because he whipped his head around and caught her staring. Well, okay, devouring him with her eyes, if she was being honest. "What are you doing?" she managed, making use of the two remaining brain cells that were still functioning.

"PT," he answered, doing another pushup. "My physio has me on a strict routine of core exercises to keep everything in my lower back and stomach strong while I finish all my rehab."

"God bless her," Zoe murmured.

Clay stopped, slung his head around to look at her and let out a short laugh. She started at the sound, stared as the smile he gave her completely transformed his hard features. If she'd thought she was having trouble breathing while watching him do the pushups, that smile made it feel like all the oxygen had been suddenly sucked from the room.

Then it faded, replaced by growing sexual interest and he shifted as though he was going to get up.

"No, don't stop." She was suddenly inspired.

Walking toward him in her best prowl, she held his stare as she knelt at his head, then lay down on her back and shimmied underneath him. He watched her without moving. "I thought maybe I could help you finish up your exercises," she whispered, reaching out to trail her forefinger down his scruffy cheek. "You know, be your spotter. Exercising's more fun when you do it with a partner."

His blue eyes heated, turning molten as he stayed

braced over her, unmoving, all his weight propped up on his hands. Zoe took the opportunity to run her hands along his shoulders and down his chest, savoring the feel of all that steely strength. "Can we lose this?" she asked, plucking at the soft cotton.

"Yeah." His voice was guttural. He got to his knees long enough to reach for the bottom of the shirt and peeled it up over his head, flinging it behind him.

Zoe had no idea where it landed and didn't care—she was too spellbound by the sight of his naked torso and his sexy tribal tat to think straight. She'd spent a lot of time thinking about his body, especially after she'd seen him getting out of the hot tub that night at his and Tuck's place. But as he reassumed his original position, all those muscles in his arms and chest bunching to hold his weight, she felt the hedonistic need to savor him bit by bit until she'd explored every inch of his body.

His eyes searched hers, a knowing gleam in them. "Ready? I got nine more to go in this set."

She moistened her lips, dragging her gaze from the striated muscles in his chest and shoulders, up the column of his throat where the dark stubble covered his jaw, cheeks and upper lip. Her palms trailed ever so lightly over his back, awed by the heat of him, the feel of those muscles shifting beneath her touch. "I'm ready." So ready she was wet and aching for him. No man had ever affected her like this.

Holding her gaze, he slowly bent his arms and lowered his weight until his chest brushed hers. Even through her bra and dress she felt that contact against her erect nipples and gasped, her hands tightening on his wide shoulders.

His hips settled between her splayed thighs, his erection pressing against her throbbing sex with a tantalizing pressure that sent a torrent of heat through her. She gasped, bit her lip and returned the pressure, lifting into him, but he merely smirked and pushed up on his hands once more, aware of exactly what he was doing to her.

"Nine," he murmured, his low, intimate tone making her insides quiver.

It was sex, while fully clothed. Mind-blowingly hot.

He repeated the motion, just as slow, a demonstration of smooth, controlled power as he slowly drove her out of her mind with want. "Eight."

Oh my god, she was never going to make it to the end of the set without either dying of heart failure or sexual frustration. The snug dress she'd thought was so sexy when she'd put it on this morning was now hampering her ability to wind her legs around his hips and get more friction where she needed it.

She wanted to feel him moving against her naked skin. Impatient, she ran her hands down his ribs to the waistband of his jeans and reached for the buckle of his belt.

He grabbed one of her hands in his, drew it upward and gently pressed the back of it against the floor beside her head in a silent command. Then he raised an eyebrow and dipped again, this time on one arm, the show of coordination and strength doing ridiculous things to her already revved libido. "Seven."

As he bottomed out this time, Zoe grabbed the back of his neck with her free hand and locked her mouth with his. He kissed her back for a moment, then gave a low chuckle and lightly sucked at her lower lip before pushing back up to starting position. "Bad girl, trying to distract me like that. That's six."

"I want you naked." Her voice was low and breathless and she saw the answering desire ignite in his eyes.

"Sure you could handle me naked, raven?"

Oh yeah. "I'd give it my best."

His mouth curved up on one side in a crooked smile that made her heart flutter, and he released her wrist. Immediately she took his face in her hands and when he lowered his weight this time, he rubbed against her in a full body caress calculated to make her go cross-eyed before covering her lips with his. Slow, lingering pressure, a tender bit of suction that curled her toes.

Zoe moaned and twined her tongue with his, struggling to hook her feet around the backs of his thighs. Clay lowered himself even further, taking his weight on his elbows as he kissed her, slow and deep and thorough. His big hands slid into her hair as his mouth cruised over her chin, down her throat, giving little flicks of his tongue that set her nerve endings on fire.

He inhaled deeply when he reached her cleavage, easing aside the stretchy fabric to nuzzle the curve of one breast, encased by black lace. Needing his mouth on her, wanting to move things along, she dragged the thin straps of her dress down her arms and shimmed until the fabric pooled at her hips.

Clay's gaze seared her as he stared at the sheer lace cups. Then he bent and licked across her straining nipple, slow and lazy. Her hand went to the back of his head, fingers digging in to pull him closer. His mouth closed around her and she saw stars, the fabric making the wet glide of his tongue an erotic torment.

When she arched up with a gasp he slid a hand beneath her and unhooked her bra. Zoe impatiently shrugged it off, a sound of pure need exploding from her when he sucked her into his mouth. She floated in a sea of bliss as he tugged the dress past her hips and over her legs, rising on his knees to look down at her.

Zoe's breath caught at the sight of him. His nostrils were flared, eyes raking over the length of her body as he took in her belly ring and landed between her legs to stare at her waxed mound. His big hands slid up her calves and outer thighs, curving around them as he bent her legs at the knee and pushed them toward her. She lay still, letting him position her, a delicious thrill rocketing through her at being so exposed to this insanely sexy man.

His fingers flexed, his gaze moving from between her legs up to meet her eyes. "Stay still." His voice was a deep rasp.

Zoe watched him, unmoving, her muscles knotted with anticipation. Clay kept a firm grip on her thighs as he knelt and lowered his head to kiss her navel, sliding his tongue into it in a way that made her gasp, and shudder. Her clit throbbed, her slick sex open and aching. His mouth was hot against her skin, layering nibbles and kisses over her abdomen, his stubble scratching in stark counterpoint to the smooth caress of his tongue.

She raised her head to watch him, not wanting to miss the moment when his mouth touched the aching bundle of nerves at the top of her sex. Those big hands held her where he wanted her as he kissed the top of her mound, looking up the length of her body, staring into her eyes as he opened his mouth and touched his tongue to her swollen clit.

Zoe's muscles contracted, a moan tearing free from her throat as pure pleasure sizzled along her nerve endings. He did it again, slower this time, lingering as he stroked his tongue across the straining knot of flesh, then dipped down to slide it into her body.

Her head fell back and she closed her eyes, letting herself get lost in the sensations. His grip was firm, his mouth wickedly patient as he took her to the edge of orgasm in a matter of seconds.

Her hands blindly dug into his head, her hips moving restlessly, his commanding hold and her helplessness only driving her arousal higher. Soft, wet suction on her clit, and the hot, smooth penetration of his tongue. Over and over he alternated the two until she was quivering and straining in his arms, whimpering for release.

His hands relaxed and his mouth disappeared from between her legs. Desperate, Zoe snapped her eyes open and automatically sat up to reach for him, but he was already hauling her into his arms and striding for her bedroom.

She was going to burn him alive.

Clay had never been this turned on in his life. Not to the point where his hands shook and it felt like his heart might burst out of his chest.

The feel of Zoe naked in his arms, her hot little mouth sucking and licking at the side of his neck, his jaw, made it nearly impossible for him to walk. He hurried into her room and set her down on her back, ignoring the slight twinge in his lower back as he did so. Pleasing her, finally getting inside her, was worth any pain.

She lay spread out before him on that crushed red velvet bedspread, her multi-color hair spread around her and her golden eyes heavy-lidded with desire. Her small, round breasts were topped with dark pink nipples, still erect and shiny from his mouth. And between her legs, her bare mound framed wet, swollen folds he couldn't wait to taste again.

Without a word he took out his wallet and removed a condom, then undid his jeans and shoved them and his boxer briefs down his legs. She bit her lip as his erect cock sprang free, swollen and dark. Zoe's little noise of pleasure and approval made his hands shake as he rolled the condom on and turned back to her.

She looked like a fucking pagan offering, splayed out there before him, and he couldn't wait to drive into her, feel her pussy contract around him. Before she could move, he was on her, one hand wound in her hair, his mouth devouring hers as he lowered his weight on top of her and growled at the pleasure of the skin-on-skin contact.

Zoe sighed into his mouth and wound her arms and legs around him, his straining dick rubbing against her abdomen. God, he wanted to fuck her. Hold her down, plunge into all that heat waiting for him and give her the ride of her life, until he'd imprinted himself on her forever.

Drowning in her taste, knowing she was tasting her own arousal on his tongue, he groaned when she slid one delicate hand between them to wrap around his cock. Her grip tightened and he felt her smile form against his lips.

"I want to suck your cock," she whispered, finishing with a playful little nip that nearly destroyed what little control he had left.

Clay squeezed his eyes shut and gritted his teeth as his dick flexed. Oh, fuck, he wanted that. To straddle her chest right now and ease his cock between her lips so he could watch her mouth close around the swollen head, those sultry golden eyes gazing up at him the whole time. But he knew if she wrapped her lips around him right now, even with the condom he would come in a matter of seconds and he didn't want that.

Rearing back on his haunches, he seized both her wrists and yanked them beneath her, shifting to grip them both with one hand, locking them at the small of her back. She gasped, her eyes widening at the sudden loss of control, but then she relaxed slightly, her golden eyes smoldering up at him with a combination of anticipation and trust that made him feel fucking invincible.

She was wet and ready for him and he couldn't wait another second. Holding her hands beneath her, he lifted her right leg over his shoulder, then the left, watching her eyes the whole time. Zoe shifted slightly and licked her lips, the pulse in her throat beating fast. A tiny edge of fear, an acknowledgement of his size and her helplessness.

Clay smoothed his free hand down her thigh, up the midline of her body to cup her face, his reassurance rewarded with an easing of the tension in her muscles and a gentle sigh. Rubbing his thumb over her cheekbone he whispered, "Relax for me, raven."

With another soft sigh, she did, her fingers flexing restlessly in his grip.

He was so hard he didn't even have to guide himself into position. He lined himself up and moved his hips back and forth, rubbing his cock along her wetness. Her gasp was electric, tingling across his skin. His fingers tightened on the edge of her jaw and he pressed inward. Hot, wet heat enveloped him.

Zoe sucked in a sharp breath and arched her back, a soft cry spilling from her lips. She was panting, her inner muscles clamping down on him to pull him deeper. He pushed forward, groaning at the friction until he was buried balls deep. She curved her lower back more, tried to move her hips but with her legs over his shoulders she had no leverage.

God, he loved seeing her this way. Lost in pleasure, helpless with it.

Bending, he settled his weight on his knees and kissed her, the change in angle burying him impossibly deep. Zoe whimpered into his mouth and squirmed, her body quivering beneath his.

Trailing his tongue across her parted lips, he eased back enough to look into her eyes and eased his open palm down her throat, over her shoulder, down her ribs and hip to her thigh, and back up. A slow, almost possessive caress meant to reassure her that this was more than just sex, that she meant something to him.

He cared about her, admired and trusted her. He didn't know what the future had in store for them, if anything, but he knew what he felt for her was real and if there was a shot of something more with her, he would take it. Words weren't his comfort zone, so he infused his touch with the intention that he meant to worship and adore her in this bed, in a way he'd never done with another woman.

She answered with a grateful smile that wrapped around his heart and squeezed like a fist, and tightened her inner muscles. Now it was his turn to suck in a breath.

Hiding a smile, he tangled the fingers of his free hand in her hair and began to move. Zoe cried out as he surged forward, the position allowing him to hit both her G-spot with his cock and her clit with his body. She felt fucking amazing, so tight and hot, his cock making wet sounds as it slid in and out of her. Her cries took on a desperate edge as she neared her release.

He pushed back the sharp rise in pleasure rocketing up his own spine, focused on making her come for him. Pulling his hand free of her hair, he slid it between them to glide his thumb across her clit.

"Ah! *Clay...*"

Yeah, raven. He pumped slowly and firmly, caressing her taut bud. Her head twisted to one side, her eyes squeezed shut as he pushed her to the peak and over. Zoe's wail of pleasure echoed around the room as her sex contracted around him.

Breathing hard, he pulled out and released her hands. She opened pleasure-glazed eyes to stare up at him but he reached for her shoulders and turned her, burying his mouth in the side of her neck, reveling in the shiver he dragged from her. "Hands and knees," he rasped out, needing to come so badly his muscles trembled.

Zoe rolled over without a word and peered over her shoulder at him, hair disheveled, eyes heavy-lidded, lips swollen from his kisses, that luscious, round ass on display for him. He stilled when he saw the tattoo spreading across the small of her back. Two black, feathered wings, delicate and beautiful. So detailed he half expected them to feel real when he stroked his fingertips across them.

Raven's wings.

A territorial, primal growl started up in his chest but he locked it down. His gaze landed on her purple robe, draped across one corner of the bed.

Grabbing it, he pulled the belt through the loops and used it to tie her wrists together. Her excited breathing rasped over his senses as he planted them above her head on the mattress and pressed down in a silent order to keep them there.

Seizing her hips, he hauled her back to meet him, then took a fistful of her hair and pulled her head down to the bed. Zoe didn't resist, merely rested her cheek on the velvet and looked back at him with such adoration and trust that his throat tightened.

Needing to claim her, he squeezed her hip and plunged into her. He groaned at the sensation of being enveloped by her heat, holding her in place as he single-mindedly went after his own orgasm. Before had been for both of them, with the intent to make her come. This was for him, his most primal side finally exposed, and he fucking loved that she trusted him enough to surrender to him this way.

He rode her hard and deep, the pleasure rising fast, taking him under. Through the fog of sensation he heard her whimper, felt her squirm against him and realized she was close to coming again. Immediately he slipped a hand around to cup her smooth, bare mound, stroking her clit with his fingertips.

She quivered against him, her shallow breaths and soft cries telling him she was almost there. Clenching his jaw against the pleasure, he allowed himself to look down, enjoy the sight of her purple-and-black hair wound around his fist, the expression of ecstasy on her face and his cock all slick and shiny as he fucked her from behind.

Her shattered moan of release reached him, mixed with the pleasure spiraling out of control until it shorted out his brain. Heaving a deep groan, he let the orgasm take him, the pulses so intense he was gasping for breath when they faded. He peeled his eyelids open to find Zoe curled up on her knees, flushed cheek pressed into the bedding, her eyes closed.

Inhaling her scent, he bent and pressed gentle kisses along the smooth skin of her upper back and shoulders. Her lips tugged up into a smile and she moved languorously beneath him. He eased his grip on her hip and dragged the fingers in her hair over her scalp, earning a soft sigh of contentment from her. Then he reached up and undid her wrists, rubbed them gently.

In the quiet of the room reality crept back, and he glanced at the clock. Shit. Only twenty-six minutes until the meeting. Though he would have liked to stay and stroke her bare back, cover her soft skin with more kisses and caresses while she recovered, he had to go.

Withdrawing from her body gently, he smoothed a hand down her spine as she stretched out onto her stomach and pillowed her head on her hands with another sigh. Rising from the bed, he drank in the sight of her like that, couldn't resist leaning over her to kiss her temple, her cheek, the corner of her mouth.

"Wish you could stay," she whispered, pressing her lips to his in a tender kiss.

"Me too." He stroked a strand of hair away from her face, ran his fingers through the length of it. "Don't get up. I'm gonna grab a shower. You made me all sweaty."

Another grin. "I regret nothing."

Chuckling, he rose and headed into the bathroom. After the shower he put on his dress slacks and shirt, was debating whether or not to wear the fucking tie when Zoe stepped into the open doorway. Wearing that shiny purple robe from last night, she folded her arms and leaned a shoulder against the jamb. Her eyes traveled the length of his body and back up, her interest and approval clear.

He grinned at the look on her face. "What?"

She shook her head. "You are insanely hot in that."

"In this?" Wasn't a tux or a fancy suit most women seemed to love men in, but still, not his preferred wardrobe of jeans or cargo pants and a T-shirt either.

Her eyes took on a decidedly wicked gleam. "Oh yeah. I've always had this fantasy about you wearing something like that."

His fingers stilled on the last button, his full attention on her now. He fucking loved that she'd fantasized about him. "Really. And what am I doing to you in this fantasy?"

She gave him an enigmatic smile that made him crave to get inside her head, unlock her deepest, darkest desires. "You're making me do things to you. Very hot, delicious and naughty things. I'm on my knees. Naked. While you wear that outfit." She gave a mock shiver. "You know, suit porn."

No, he didn't know, but it sounded fucking hot and it was making him hard all over again. "Suit porn."

"Mmhmm," she murmured. "You like?"

Was that some kind of trick question? "Yeah." Hell, he'd better quit thinking about getting her naked and get his ass to the meeting. He cupped the side of her face. "You can tell me more about that fantasy later." And all the others, too. He couldn't wait to find out what that dirty little mind had come up with about the two of them.

She smiled against his mouth and kissed him. "You coming back after?"

"As soon as I can. But I'll probably have Tuck and another couple guys in tow." Dammit. He wanted to explore her body again, watch her eyes dilate as he made her come a dozen different ways.

"That's okay. They can't stay forever, and I can be really quiet, especially with you there to muffle any sounds I make."

Christ, this better be a really fucking important and enlightening meeting. He straightened, dropped his hand and grabbed his tie. "Don't forget what Tuck said earlier," he said, heading for the stairs. She followed. "Set the alarm once I leave, and don't leave the house just in case. I shouldn't be more than a couple hours." *I hope.* "I'll have my phone with me so if anything comes up, shoot me a text."

"Okay, but don't worry about me, I'll be fine." Taking him by surprise, she cradled his face in her hands and leaned up to press a sweet, soft kiss on his mouth. "See you soon."

He nodded, couldn't help but take another taste of those tempting lips. "You can count on it, raven."

Chapter Thirteen

Carlos nearly dropped his drink when Zoe's lover suddenly appeared on the sidewalk in front of her building. Ducking his head, he pretended to be interested in the cold dregs of his coffee while watching the man out of the corner of his eye.

The big bastard paused to look around, up and down the street. His gaze landed on Carlos and held, as if he somehow instinctively sensed that he might be a threat.

Every muscle in his body went rigid, the paper cup crinkling under the pressure of his hand. His pulse thudded in his ears, more perspiration breaking out across his skin. The cotton T-shirt was sticking to his back and chest and the band of his ball cap was soaked with sweat. Carlos didn't want to have to engage this guy out in the open in broad daylight, but if that's what it took to get to Zoe, he'd do it.

He was getting Leticia back *today*.

Excitement bubbled in his gut. He was juiced, ready to act, his free hand resting behind his back against the wall, the pose casual but it also put his hand mere inches from the weapon tucked into his waistband. Part of him hoped the man would walk toward him and make a move.

Whatever it takes. Zoe's the key.

The man stood there for what felt like an eternity before looking the other way. Apparently satisfied everything was as it should be, he began walking away from Carlos to the end of the street and soon disappeared from view around the corner.

Carlos released a slow breath of relief but didn't dare move for long minutes in case the guy came back to double check. He waited another tortuous few minutes, every so often checking to his three and nine o'clock to ensure the man hadn't doubled back around the block to sneak up on him.

But he didn't come back, and Carlos didn't dare linger here any longer. He'd stayed in this location for too long already, and who the hell knew how many CCTVs or security cameras had already captured his image in the Quarter today, no matter how careful he'd been to keep his face averted.

This is it.

Heart pounding, Carlos pulled out his phone and texted his accomplice. A low-level gang member who owed him a few favors and was driving the getaway car for this initial stage of his plan. *Going in. Pull up now and wait for me.* Because this wasn't going to take long.

The *OK* reply came a second later.

Pushing away from the wall, a rush of excitement flooded his veins as he headed for Zoe's building, his boots making quiet thudding sounds on the cracked sidewalk. Blood roared in his ears, his heart pounding an erratic rhythm against his ribs as he broke into a jog.

He barely felt the backpack bumping against his spine. All his senses were suddenly sharpened, the way they always were during an op. He was pure instinct and training now. The sound of his breathing was rough and ragged, his vision narrowed on the opening to Zoe's building, mere yards ahead in the red brick wall.

Two people turned the corner at the far end of the street and started up the sidewalk toward him. A man and a woman, in their sixties. No threat to him.

They froze and stepped back in alarm when they saw him coming, the apprehension on their faces no doubt due to the fierce look on his own. He didn't care. Couldn't give a shit about who was watching him or who had seen him now. Mentally he was already past the point of no return. He was dragging Zoe out of this building, one way or another.

Carlos rushed past the startled couple without bothering to see if they'd follow, picking up speed as the adrenaline rush spiked, roaring through his system. Zoe was inside, alone, unguarded and had no idea he was coming for her.

It was perfect.

The gate was closed, but they hadn't been able to replace the lock yet. He wrenched it open with one hand and ran through the vestibule into the courtyard.

His eyes quickly adjusted to the dimness and he stared at the dark blue door barring his way, taking everything in within a few heartbeats. Brass knob, simple lock, but there was no way she'd live here alone and not have a solid lock in place. But he was experienced with kicking in doors and he had tools if his boot didn't do it.

She didn't have a weapon registered to her name, he'd already checked. His only real problem now was her possibly having an alarm system. If she did and it was set right now, he was going to have less than a minute before it went off. Would still give him plenty of time. He could feel the shape of the syringe in his back pocket. The ketamine would make it easy for him to get her to the car.

You're mine. The hairs on his forearms stood up

and his nape prickled.

Stepping back to give himself some room, he drew his weapon from his waistband and reared his right foot back, ready to smash his boot into the lock.

****

After Clay left, Zoe set the alarm to stay mode and took a quick shower to rinse off, trying not to get her hair wet. It was so thick it took forever to dry, even with a blow-dryer. She kept the water temperature on the cool side, sighing at the feel of it on her skin. Her hot, still-sensitive skin that tingled even now from the memory of Clay's hands and mouth.

A satisfied smile curved her mouth. She'd known they'd be off the charts together in bed, but my god, the way the man took control and gave so much pleasure was better than her hottest fantasy of him. Suit porn notwithstanding.

Less than five minutes later she was toweled off and wearing the dress Clay had peeled off her earlier. It had been two days since she'd written any new words in her latest manuscript, and after the amazing sex she'd just had, she was feeling energized and inspired to do some word count damage. She didn't mind being told not to leave her house because she loved being here anyway, the alarm made her feel secure and she enjoyed spending time on her own.

On her way through the living room she picked up her laptop from the coffee table, where Clay must have placed it last night after carrying her to bed. She grinned to herself at the memory of all those muscles flexing against her as he moved, already looking forward to what would happen when they were alone next. He'd been more than generous this morning, with a knee-melting combination of authority and tenderness she had no experience with or defense against. Zoe couldn't wait

HUNTED

for more. But next time, she wanted to focus on pleasuring him.

And stupid though it might be, she sincerely hoped there would be more for them than just a weekend of great sex, because she was seriously falling for him. For a few moments there she'd felt him open up to her emotionally, had felt that gut-deep connection between them as he seated himself fully inside her and stared down into her eyes.

It was a huge step for him, letting her in that far, and she wondered whether he'd recognized it for what it was. She knew he'd felt it; the question was whether or not he was ready to face it and be honest with himself about it.

Out on the balcony, ensconced on the daybed with her Sleepy Hollow pillow behind her back, she opened her laptop, accessed the file she needed and scrolled to where she'd left off. An intense scene where the heroine was fighting for her life against a sadistic serial killer.

All her heroines were strong and smart—if there was one thing she couldn't stand in romance, it was wimpy heroines—and this one was currently hunting around the old mansion's living room for a weapon to use against her would-be assailant. Heavy brass candlesticks and an antique paperweight she could bash in his skull with.

Zoe could see the scene in her mind, as vivid as any movie on a big screen. Her heroine scrambling for a place to hide, grabbing the paperweight and flinging it with all her might, a sickening, bone-cracking thud as it slammed into the side of his head. The words came easily today, and she credited the renewed creative energy to all the endorphins still rushing through her bloodstream.

Getting into the zone wasn't always easy for her, but she was there now and lost track of everything but the words she typed onto the screen, totally immersed in the world she'd created. She jumped when a loud bang suddenly came from downstairs, freezing her in place.

A second later came another one, as though someone was slamming something into her door.

She shoved the laptop aside, rose and stepped through the sliding glass door, every sense on alert. Clay had only left a few minutes ago and there was no way he'd be banging on her door like that—

The sound of the door smashing into the wall downstairs sent her heart rocketing into her throat. Her entire body flashed hot, then cold.

There was no time to grab her phone from her purse on the other side of the room. She turned and raced for her bedroom, terror knifing through her, making her knees weak.

Flinging the door shut she twisted the lock home, then dove for her nightstand and accessed the gun safe in the bottom of it. She always left it in there, had never taken it out except when Tuck dragged her to the gun range with him.

Heavy footsteps raced up the stairs. Her heart pounded sickeningly. *Hurry, hurry...*

"Zoe," a male voice shouted.

"*Shit*," she whispered, her hands shaking as she turned the combination dial. Right to the first number. Left to the next.

"Zoe!" A roar this time, the rage and menace in that voice sending panic streaking through her.

Third number. Why the fuck were there so many numbers in this damn combo?

Finally she got it unlocked and yanked out the gun. As an added safety precaution she never left it loaded. She slammed the magazine into the bottom of the grip just as her alarm system went off. The electronic shriek sent chills snaking down her spine as she fumbled with the switch to turn the safety off.

Something smashed against her bedroom door and it flew open, slamming into the wall. Zoe caught a blur of movement as she turned on one knee and raised the pistol—

A brutal hand grabbed her wrist, twisting it viciously as he wrenched her arm up and out. Zoe screamed in rage and terror as the gun fell to the floor. She made a desperate grab for it with her free hand but the man flattened her on the floor with his weight.

Enraged, terrified, she bared her teeth and shoved with all her might. He seized the hand she was going for his eyes with and dragged it over her head with the other.

No! Instinct took over.

She lashed out with her knees, her head, tried to sink her teeth into his arm but he avoided her every move with an ease that scared her even more. It was obvious he had more training than the average street thug.

Bucking and twisting, she finally looked up into his face. It was almost worse that he wasn't ugly. He was younger than her, maybe in his late twenties, light bronze skin, dark eyes. Strong, lean build, the ropey muscles in his arms corded as he held her despite every effort to break his hold. He stared down at her with blatant rage that chilled her to the core.

Before she could move he leaned in until their noses almost touched, the fury and leashed violence in him making her tremble. He would kill her. She saw it in his eyes.

"Where *is* she?" he snarled, eyes narrowed, nostrils flared. The tendons in his neck stood out in sharp relief, his breathing harsh and unsteady.

Zoe was too far gone with fear and shock to even contemplate faking like she didn't know who he was talking about. "Get off me, motherfucker!" she screamed, managed to sink her teeth into his forearm. He hissed, transferred both her wrists into one hand and slammed her head into the floor hard enough to make her see stars.

"Where. Is. She!" He bit out each word, his anger palpable.

Zoe refused to give in. She thrashed in his hold, tried to ram her head into his face but he whipped aside just in time and cracked his open palm against the side of her face. The force of it snapped her head around. She gasped, cringing as pain flared out across her cheek, her jaw.

He gave her a rough shake. "*Where is she?*" he shouted into her face.

"Go to hell," she shot back, watering eyes closed, unable to summon the guts to look him in the eye when she said it.

With an inarticulate sound of rage, the man she knew had to be Carl grabbed her by the hair and wrenched upward. Zoe cried out and locked a hand around his wrist to keep him from ripping her hair out, automatically rising to her knees to lessen the pain.

He yanked harder until she stumbled to her feet, and before she could move he had her bent over the bed, face crushed into the bedding. Her struggles this time were useless.

He clamped her hands together at the small of her back and cinched something hard and tight around them. She tossed her head and lashed out with her feet, but she had no leverage and her bare feet hit his hard thighs without enough force to even budge him.

She was pinned, cuffed, helpless. Even if nobody heard her over the alarm, she had to try. Drawing as much air into her starving lungs as possible, she opened her mouth and screamed the only word she knew might help, as loud as she could.

"Fiiiiiire! Fiiiiiire!"

Carl clapped a hand over her mouth and nose, cutting off her air. "Shut the fuck up!"

Zoe shrieked behind his hand, tried everything she knew of to throw his hand off, but he was too strong. Panic seized her, shorting out her brain.

Her body flopped and thrashed around in a desperate struggle for air. Her lungs burned until she thought they'd burst and her eyes began to bulge. Black spots danced in front of her eyes, then a gray haze began to descend.

He tore his hand away. Zoe heaved in a ragged breath, then another, her body limp and trembling. But he wasn't done. He flipped her over, set a hand around her throat and stared down at her with cold, murderous eyes. "Gonna tell me now?"

She was so far gone with fear and shock she couldn't have told him even if she'd wanted to.

His face tightened and he pulled something from his pocket. A syringe.

Zoe made a sound of protest and tried to roll away as he uncapped it, and then the sting of a needle burned in her outer thigh. "Now you're gonna be sorry," he muttered, tossing the empty syringe aside.

What had he injected her with? She started to shake, felt the drug take hold of her and drag her into a surreal place where she could hear and think but couldn't move. She was paralyzed.

The shriek of the alarm mixed with the roar of blood swirling in her ears as he hauled her upright and slung her over his shoulder. "You're gonna tell me where she is," he threatened, rushing back through her living room to the top of the stairs.

Her stomach sank. He was taking her somewhere. The police would never get here in time.

"You're gonna tell me *exactly* where she is," he repeated as he hit the stairs and grabbed her purse from the newel post, "or I'll make you suffer so bad you'll beg me to kill you."

Zoe's throat constricted as nausea crawled around in her gut. She hung limp over his shoulder as he descended the stairs. She had a vague impression of light and shadow.

"What are you doing?" a male voice said, filled with outrage and shock.

"Get the fuck out of my way," Carl snarled at him.

"Put her down!"

Carl's muscles shifted as he raised his arm and two shots shattered the air. She heard the man fall, could hear him gasping for air. Carl took off, leaving her neighbor, Mr. Yeager, bleeding on her courtyard floor.

Zoe tried to cry out but she couldn't make her lips move, and then she had to squeeze her eyes shut to block out the blinding sunlight as he hit the sidewalk. She heard the sound of a car door opening. He tossed her inside on the backseat, climbed in after her and slammed the door shut.

"Go!" he barked.

The driver hit the gas and the car shot away from the curb with a squeal of its tires, taking her where no one would find her.

Chapter Fourteen

Clay shifted in the chair and tried to get comfortable. He was seated at the middle of a long board table in a meeting room with DeLuca, Tuck, Evers, Schroder, and three of the DEA guys they'd been training with in Biloxi. They'd already been talking—well, Tuck, DeLuca and the DEA guys had been—about ongoing security issues along the Gulf Coast and the threat of Islamic jihadists smuggling across the border from Mexico.

Tugging at the thighs of his pants, he tried stretching his legs out a bit to relieve the pressure in his lower back.

"Bauer. Go grab us all some coffee," DeLuca said.

Clay looked at him. Yeah, his CO knew exactly what was happening and was giving him an out. He opened his mouth to argue, but he had nothing to add to the conversation thus far and getting up to walk around for a bit would definitely ease the ache in his spine. He took drink orders from everyone and tried not to scowl, then headed down to the lobby and stood in line at Starbucks.

While he waited he texted Zoe. He was anxious to get back to her, and even more anxious for it to be nighttime so the others would leave and he'd get to be alone with her again.

He felt happier than he had in years, lighter, and it had everything to do with Zoe. Tuck had given him a hard look when he'd arrived for the meeting but Clay wasn't worried. His friend would get over it, and Clay planned to make it clear she meant way more to him than just a fuck buddy.

He ordered the drinks and checked his phone while he waited against the wall near the bar. No answer. Probably either taking a nap or working. He really liked the thought of her curled up in her bed, tired and sated from what they'd done together.

And the suit porn thing. He so wanted to try it, see how worked up he could get her. They definitely clicked on many levels, but he'd be lying if he said the sexual piece of the puzzle wasn't huge for him. He'd held that part of him back for so long, being able to finally express it had been a liberating experience.

He wanted more, and plenty of time to explore all the facets that made up Zoe. She was the most fascinating woman he'd ever met and he wasn't about to let what happened with his ex fuck up the chance with someone like Zoe.

Still no answer from her when the drinks were ready so he loaded up two cardboard carry trays and took them back up to the conference room. He turned the corner in the hallway when he saw an unfamiliar woman standing beside the meeting room door, raising her hand as if she was going to knock on it. She glanced back at him, doing a split-second up-and-down appraisal. Not sexual, but definitely sizing him up.

"Can I help you?" he asked, an edge to his tone as he sized her up in turn and came nearer. Late twenties, if he had to guess.

Long dark brown hair, bronze skin, sharp features.

Slender build, maybe five six and one thirty or so. He couldn't see any weapons tucked into the waistband of her cargo pants or beneath the black T-shirt, but her stillness and her unreadable eyes told him she was trained. Clay wasn't ready to drop his guard. She could have a blade strapped to her somewhere.

Her dark gaze held his, unflinching, her expression giving away no trace of emotion. "I need to talk to Commander DeLuca."

Clay mentally raised an eyebrow. *Do you?* "About what?" Whoever she was, she had to have high security clearance to get through security and up here. Clay still didn't trust her.

No reaction. Not so much as a flicker of emotion in those deep brown eyes. "I've got a message from a mutual acquaintance."

That was way too cryptic for his liking. "A mutual acquaintance."

She folded her arms across her chest. "That's right."

He held her stare for another few moments, trying to get a read on her. Finally deciding she wasn't a threat to DeLuca and the rest of them, he relented with a nod. He'd stick around long enough to make sure his CO was cool with this and ensure there was no security threat. "Hold on and I'll get him for you." He let himself in and shut the door in her face, already wondering who she was and how the hell she'd known about this supposedly secret meeting.

Everyone looked up at him as he set the drinks down, but he sought DeLuca's gaze. "Woman outside to see you," he said to him. "Says she's got a message from a mutual acquaintance."

DeLuca frowned. "Excuse me," he murmured and rose from the table. He tried to skirt past Clay but that wasn't happening. Until Clay knew she meant no harm to DeLuca or anyone else in the room, he wasn't leaving anything to chance.

He opened the door and blocked the doorway with his body while he verified that the woman wasn't holding a weapon. She was standing right where he'd left her, arms still folded across her chest. He could see there was nothing in her hands, although something told him this woman's hands—hell, her entire body—were weapons themselves.

This time she dropped the blank slate façade and raised an almost mocking eyebrow at him. Stepping aside, faint surprise registered on DeLuca's face when he saw the woman. They knew each other, that much was obvious.

Clay spoke to him while looking straight at her. "You good here?"

"All good," DeLuca confirmed. Clay nodded and stepped back into the room to let them talk in private. Tuck and the others were watching him.

"What's up?" Tuck asked.

"Dunno." But it was weird, and had to be important if the message had to be delivered in person during this meeting.

He pulled his chair out from the table, intending to take a seat, when the door suddenly opened and DeLuca's gaze shot straight to him, his expression grim. "Need to talk to you." He looked over at Tuck. "Both of you."

Clay felt his stomach drop. This wasn't good.

He and Tuck stepped out of the room. DeLuca faltered for a second, staring down the empty hallway in surprise. The woman was gone.

"What's going on?" Tuck asked, frowning as he shut the door behind them.

DeLuca turned to face them, hands on hips. "There was an incident in the Quarter about half an hour ago." His eyes flicked to Clay.

And just like that, Clay knew.

Zoe.

Something had happened to Zoe. His heart seemed to seize in his chest.

"Witnesses say a man broke into your cousin's place. He shot her neighbor twice on the way out and put her into the back of a car."

Tuck's face went white and Clay felt his own blanch at the news. "What—" He shook his head. "You sure?"

DeLuca nodded, met Clay's gaze. "I'm sorry."

Clay put both hands over his nose and mouth, dragged them down his face as his blood congealed in his veins. "She had the alarm on. I heard her set it."

"It's what alerted the neighbors. NOPD are on scene."

Tuck didn't bother listening to whatever else DeLuca had to say. He whipped open the door and said, "We've got a situation. Everybody move."

Everyone rushed out and DeLuca filled them all in on their way to the elevator. Clay's heart banged against his ribs, his mind racing at a million miles per hour. "Was she hurt?" He couldn't take hearing she was dead. Just…couldn't fucking deal with that possibility.

"Witnesses said she appeared to be unconscious and the guy carried her out over his shoulder."

Clay closed his eyes.

Fuck. Me.

He shouldn't have left her. He should have stayed and then this never would have happened. God*damn* it.

He couldn't even look at Tuck. The only positive was that she was still alive. The fucker must need to keep her that way otherwise he'd just have killed her already.

Clay was sick with fear as they all raced to the parking garage, piled into two SUVs and roared the short distance to Zoe's place. On the way there Tuck told DeLuca about the situation Zoe had gotten involved in with Leticia and her son. They arrived to find the cops had already cordoned off the area, forcing them to park half a block away.

Everyone else hung back from the building as Clay, Tuck and DeLuca showed their ID and entered Zoe's courtyard. A forensics team was already there collecting evidence and documenting the blood spatters on the brick floor and wall.

Clay's heart plummeted at the sight.

Tuck was on his phone, speaking to Celida. He ended the call and spoke to Clay, rage burning in his brown eyes. "Celida's on it. She's helping get an agency taskforce together and they'll be on the next flight down."

"Okay," he said. But it wasn't okay. None of this was fucking *remotely* okay. Clay dragged a hand down his face. The only thing they had going for them at the moment was that it made no sense for the kidnapper to kill Zoe. At least not until the guy found Leticia.

A detective walked over and introduced himself to them before talking about the attacker. "Shot the neighbor nearly point blank in the chest, twice," he said to Tuck. "He coded as they were loading him into the ambulance. Don't think he'll make it."

Not Zoe's blood. The neighbor's.

His heart started beating again.

Clay stepped around the officers crowding the vestibule and courtyard, steeling himself when he saw the wooden cobalt door sagging on its hinges. The fucker had smashed it in and gone after her in fucking broad daylight. There was no way this was random, it had all the hallmarks of a targeted kidnapping. Had to be Leticia's ex, or someone working for him. He'd kill Zoe.

No, Clay told himself with a mental headshake. Zoe

was smart. Clay knew she'd understand that her life hinged on her not giving the kidnapper the information Leticia had left in that note this morning.

Upstairs more cops were gathering evidence. He showed his ID to the lead detective and explained who he was. The guy waved him toward the back, then into Zoe's room. Like the lower door, the one to her bedroom was also askew, the wood around the lock shattered.

Taking that in, and looking at the bed where they'd shared something so intense and beautiful less than two hours ago, it made him sick to think of her being attacked here in her own private sanctuary. On the far side of the bed, a tech was bagging a pistol.

"Found it lying on the floor," the detective told him. "It's a twenty-two, has her prints on it. Gun safe was open and the safety was off. Looks like she was getting ready to fire it when he came through the door and disarmed her."

So she'd barricaded herself in here and tried to defend herself but hadn't had time to get a shot off. He could see it unfolding all too clearly in his mind, imagined her mad scramble to her room, locking the door and going for her weapon. The sick sensation in his gut worsened. If he'd been here, Clay would've dropped the bastard with two shots to the chest the instant he breached the lower door.

Tuck came up behind him. "I gave it to her over a year ago when she moved down from Shreveport," he said, his voice hollow, the same way Clay's chest felt right now.

"I know."

"I took her to the range a few times. She was getting good."

Clay wished she'd had the chance to use her skills.

"The good news is, there's no blood spatter. But we did find this." The detective waved another tech over and took a clear plastic evidence bag from her. He held it up and Clay saw the uncapped syringe in it. A jagged bolt of fear shot through him.

"What is it?" His voice was raspy. What the fuck had he injected her with?

"From the initial analysis of what was in the syringe, ketamine. We don't know how much was in here, but presumably enough to incapacitate her."

Because it would make it easier for the asshole to drag her out to the getaway car if she couldn't fight back. Clay's hands curled into fists. Even at a low dose the ketamine would leave her helpless and cause hallucinations for up to an hour.

Whoever this bastard was, he wanted him dead, but Clay wanted him to suffer first. Preferably at his hand.

Tuck set a hand on his shoulder. "Witnesses got a partial plate on the getaway car. Cops are running a search now."

He managed a nod, still staring at the empty syringe.

"Bauer. Tuck."

They both turned at the sound of DeLuca's voice and headed out of the room. He was standing in the living room near the top of the stairs with one of the DEA agents, his face somber.

Clay's stomach plummeted at that look. God, she couldn't be dead. Just couldn't.

"Whoa, no, we haven't heard anything more about her," DeLuca said when he saw Clay's face. "Richter thinks he might know about another connection though."

Clay pulled in a deep breath to calm his racing pulse and focused on the DEA agent, former SF, a couple years older than him. "A connection with Zoe?" Every cell in his body was screaming at him to start looking for her, *now*. They had to find her.

Richter nodded and put his hands on his hips. "Tuck

already knows some of this, but we've had problems recently with one of our own. He's been deep undercover for us the past eighteen months, working on cracking a major drug cartel smuggling into Louisiana and Mississippi via the Gulf. Couple of times over the past few months he's missed check-ins with his handler, even gone off grid completely once before and it almost got him canned, but this time he's definitely gone off the reservation." His blue eyes cut to Tuck. "DeLuca told me about what's been going on with your cousin, and I'm starting to think this guy might be involved. No one's seen or heard from him in three days."

Clay felt Tuck's attention sharpen. "Involved in what way?" his buddy demanded.

"He's got ins with the local gang scene, as well as plenty of cops and other law enforcement agents in the Gulf region. Word is, while he's been undercover the lifestyle proved too much of a temptation and he's been dealing on the side. Internal Affairs just confirmed with us this morning that they've been building a case against him. They couldn't move too soon but now they've discovered that he's been playing for both teams, using one side against the other.

"They reported that he got involved with a woman about a year ago, and apparently he's obsessed with her. Like, way over the top, according to IA's sources." His eyes met Clay's. "Word is she took off on him two days ago and he's been pulling every resource he has to find her. And the description of the kidnapper given by the witnesses today matches our guy."

Clay braced himself, all his muscles tensing. He wanted to hunt this fucker down and get Zoe back. "Who?"

"Carlos Ruiz." Richter held up his phone, kept talking but Clay's whole being was focused on the image of the Hispanic man on the screen.

Wherever he was, Carlos Ruiz's days as a free man were numbered. And if he harmed Zoe, he was a dead man walking.

Chapter Fifteen

Zoe fought her way up through the endless twilight she was suspended in, swimming back toward consciousness. She became aware of two men talking close by. A bitter, metallic taste filled her mouth. Her head pounded.

It took all her effort just to force her heavy eyelids open a crack. She didn't know how long she'd been out of it but it must have been a while. She was on her back, her hands still bound behind her on something cool and smooth, likely linoleum. He'd tied her wrists so tightly her hands were numb.

She didn't feel any movement so they weren't in a vehicle now. The two men had been talking off and on in the car but she couldn't remember anything they'd said.

Weird images and almost flashbacks had kept hitting her. At one point she'd been certain Clay was there, sitting next to her in the backseat. She'd tried to reach for him, beg him for help. He'd held a finger to his lips in a silent command for her to be quiet, then vanished before her eyes. A hallucination, caused by whatever drug she'd been injected with. The outside of her left thigh felt like someone had kicked it with a steel-toed boot.

A rustling sound came from somewhere close by. "She's coming out of it."

Carl. Had to be him. He'd jammed the needle into her.

Quiet footfalls approached and through her cracked-open eyelids she made out a pair of combat boots and dark jeans in front of her face. He hunkered down next to her, grabbed her jaw none too gently and twisted her face up.

She struggled to keep her eyes open, tried to focus on his face, then wished she hadn't. Anger burned in his eyes, banked now, not that terrifying rage he'd demonstrated before. They were bloodshot, with deep shadows beneath, as if he hadn't slept in a long time.

"I've disabled your phone so nobody can track you here. No one's coming for you. You gonna tell me where Leticia is now?" he demanded.

Her tongue was thick in her mouth, clumsy. Preventing her from getting out the *fuck you* sitting on the tip of it.

His fingers and thumb squeezed, biting into her jaw in a painful grip. "Is this where she is?" He held up something and it took her a long moment to focus on what was in his fingers and realize it was the coordinates she'd written down. Her purse. He must have taken it and found it in there. God, why hadn't she destroyed the damn paper?

His jaw flexed once, his nostrils flaring. Something about his manner was off. He looked manic, those bloodshot eyes wide, his muscles twitching. She'd seen enough addicts in her time to know he'd been using something, but she didn't see any needle tracks on his forearms. "I'm only gonna ask you one more time," he said in a menacing tone.

"Hey, man, she's still too out of it to be questioning her. How much did you give her, anyway? She's been like that for almost two hours," the other man said from behind him, out of Zoe's view.

Two hours. She fought back a rush of grief and fear. Did anyone even know she was missing yet? Carl had shot her elderly neighbor. The wounds had been severe. Someone must have heard the shots and come to investigate, or maybe call the cops. But Clay and Tuck might still be in meetings and have no idea anything had happened to her. The longer it took for them to start looking, the less chance she had of being found, let alone rescued.

"Shut up, Gill," Carl snapped, then turned back to her. He yanked her chin up, peered down into her eyes. Whatever he saw there must have disappointed him because he cursed and released her face with a rough little shove that knocked the back of her head against the floor. "Her fucking pupils are still dilated," he said in disgust, and got up.

Zoe lay very still as he stomped away and she tried to gather as much information as possible about what was happening. From what she could see they appeared to be in a small house. The room was dim, the only light a small lamp set into one corner. A strong musty smell invaded her nose. She swallowed, fought back the waves of nausea that kept hitting her. Carl wanted Leticia. He had the coordinates, and therefore no longer needed Zoe.

She had to think of something that would make her useful to him. Otherwise there was no reason for him to keep her alive.

Her muscles jerked at the thought, a full-body tremor snaking through her. She ordered herself to remain still, but as the minutes ticked past the pain in her shoulders and arms increased until she couldn't keep from shifting to ease the pressure on her joints.

Carl noticed her tiny movements. He stopped talking to the other man and stalked toward her again, each thud of his boots on the floor making her want to squeeze her eyes shut in terror.

He walked over and nudged her hard in the ribs with the toe of his boot. "You ready to talk yet?" When she didn't respond he jabbed the same spot. She gritted her teeth. "Hey. Enough fucking around. I need answers and if you don't start talking, you'll be sorry."

She couldn't avoid this much longer, and she'd like to keep her ribs and other bones intact. Battling through the lingering mental fog from whatever he'd injected her with, she slowly shifted to her side and made herself look up at him. He had her bound, drugged and on the floor.

But he still hadn't beaten her, and if he thought she was going to be cowed in his presence, he was in for a surprise. She was going to use every remaining asset available to her to survive, beginning with her brain.

He braced his feet apart and set his hands on his hips, staring down at her with what he likely thought was an intimidating stance. All she saw was a pathetic excuse for a man who got off on threatening and abusing women so he could feel powerful.

Carl pulled the piece of paper from his pocket, unfolded it and held it out. "These are coordinates. Why do you have them, along with a date and time? Is this about Leticia, or the guy you're fucking?"

He knew about Clay.

A chill swept through her. He'd been watching her. Them. That's how he'd known she was alone in her place, and why he'd chosen to attack when he had.

Done with waiting, he dropped to one knee beside her and seized a handful of her hair, wrenching her head back, forcing her to look at him. "Talk, bitch!" He shook her once, the sharp jolt making her stomach roll.

"Leticia," she managed, her head bent back at an awkward angle.

He leaned closer, until she could smell him. Sweat. A hint of soap. And the stench of desperation. "It's in Baton Rouge. That's where she is?"

"Yes," Zoe whispered.

His eyes flared with triumph. Hope. "She's there now? When did she send you this?"

She tried to shake her head, couldn't because of the iron grip he had on her hair. "This morning."

"So is she still there? Why did she give these to you?" His voice practically vibrated with emotion.

"I'm supposed to meet her," Zoe pushed out past the lump in her throat.

Carl's focus sharpened even more. "This location at six tomorrow morning?"

There was no way around it. He knew the code and had understood everything she'd written down, so lying was plain stupid. She had to make him think she was still necessary to him. "Yes."

"What about the kid?"

"I don't know." Though Zoe couldn't see Leticia leaving her son.

Carl snorted. "There's no way she'd leave that little shit behind." He lowered the paper, seemed to be mulling something over as he watched her, the grip on her hair never easing. "So what's her plan? Why you? Were you the one who told her to run from me?" He yanked sharply on her hair, wrenching a gasp out of her as it felt like he was going to rip the handful right out of the scalp.

Tears stung her eyes at the painful burn but she refused to let him see. She hated him. Hated everything he stood for. And if she got the chance, she'd make him pay for all of this.

"You did, didn't you? You stupid bitch, you told her to leave me!"

It took everything Zoe had not to cringe away from

the rage she saw burning in his eyes. He yanked her head back farther, her neck bent at a near impossible angle, and bent down to snarl in her face. "Is that why she wants to meet you? So you could help her get away?"

Don't let him see you're scared. He'll feed off it. You have to stay in control. Her heart thudded sickeningly against her chest wall. Admitting the reason for the meeting—for Zoe to put Leticia in contact with the FBI—would be suicide.

Make it clear he still needs you for this. Somehow she found her voice. "She insisted on me being there. Alone. If she sees anyone else she'll run." Her voice shook slightly, a product of her fear and the awkward angle of her neck.

His lips thinned, deep furrows creasing his brow as he stared at her, weighing the truth of her words. "So you'll have to show up then, won't you?"

God yes. It would at least buy her another twelve-plus hours. Time for Clay, Tuck and the cops to find her. "Yes. It's the only way."

Carl yanked her head forward this time, his gaze boring into hers. "If you're playing me, if she doesn't show, I'll kill you."

Zoe suppressed a shiver at his cold tone, his even colder eyes. "It's the truth."

Apparently satisfied, he flung her head backward. The back of her skull bounced off the linoleum with a nauseating thud that made her see stars for a second. Before she could regain her wits he'd already grabbed her feet and put another plastic zip tie around them. Then he rose.

"We'll leave before first light. The cops will know you're missing by then and your boyfriend will be looking for you. He military?"

She shook her head. It wasn't a lie, not really. Clay had been out of the Navy for years now.

Carl grunted. "He's no civilian, I know that much. Does he know about the meeting location or the coordinates?"

"No." She kept her voice low, devoid of emotion, hoping he wouldn't know she was lying.

He paused, turned his head to speak to the other man, still waiting over in the dingy kitchen Zoe could see into. "Find out what chatter's going on in the local law enforcement scene about her." He nodded to Zoe. "If they know about the meeting, they'll be waiting. I'm not walking into a trap." He turned back to her, his dark eyes narrowing to slits. "Remember what I said."

With that he turned and stalked back into the kitchen, speaking to his accomplice. "We leave at oh-four-hundred." He pulled a gun from the back of his waistband. "If she tries to escape, shoot her," he said, setting the weapon on the table next to the laptop.

Casting her one last look of utter loathing, he took off in the opposite direction, down a narrow hallway and disappeared from view, leaving Zoe lying helpless on the floor.

****

It felt like days instead of hours before the taskforce was finally assembled together at the local FBI office. Clay stood against the wall at the head of the conference table while DeLuca and the local agent-in-charge gave the briefing, and it wasn't because his back was bothering him.

It was because if he was forced to sit on his ass right now with Zoe missing, he might explode.

The room was packed with cops and agents from various law enforcement groups, including several of the DEA guys they'd been working with, and Clay's entire team. Their sniper teams were still in Biloxi on standby, and could be called in with an hour's notice in case of an op.

Everyone was quiet as the lead DEA agent detailed everything about the case so far. Carlos Ruiz's picture was up on the main screen for everyone to see, along with his service record and what the IA people had compiled against him to this point.

It wasn't good news for Zoe.

Drug trafficking. Weapons smuggling. Three possible recent murders of people he'd used as sources during his undercover work.

Clay's fingers dug into his palms, his hands fisting tight as he stayed in position with his arms folded across his chest. The thought of Zoe being taken by this piece of shit, imagining what might have happened or might be happening to her at this very moment while everyone stood around analyzing the case was slowly driving him batshit crazy. He ached for the chance to see her, touch her, hold her again. He was terrified it might not happen.

"NOPD found the getaway car ditched on an access road six miles out of town, not far off I-10." He glanced at Clay, then Tuck. "No bloodstains found anywhere inside it and they got a few prints that confirm the kidnapper was Ruiz."

That was good news, but it didn't mean she wasn't bleeding now. God, he felt sick with worry. This entire time in NOLA so far had been a serious wake-up call where Zoe was concerned. Her being taken was a giant kick in the nuts and made him vividly aware of how much he cared. She brought color and warmth into his stark, cold world. She made him feel like the man he'd always wanted to be.

He'd give anything to get her back and have the chance to tell her so.

"Ruiz's known residence is empty and so is Leticia Harland's. They're both being watched but Ruiz won't go near either of them. There are no known friends or relatives in the area and right now the team has no other leads as to where the cops should start looking," the DEA agent continued.

Clay kept listening while he scanned the room. His guys were seated at the back. Schroder, Blackwell, Cruz, Evers, Vance. Tuck stood behind them, also leaning against the wall, chomping on a piece of gum. He looked over and met Clay's gaze, and Clay knew he and his buddy were thinking the exact same thing. They were both praying for a tip that would lead them to Ruiz, give them a chance to execute an op to bring the fucker down and free Zoe.

Barring that, he'd take anything that got Zoe back alive and unharmed.

Once the briefing was over he found himself in the totally foreign position of not being able to do anything. During ops cycle, after a briefing he'd usually get his gear together, do a weapons check or some PT to burn off steam.

Right now there was no op to plan, no gear to gather and he sure as shit didn't feel like hitting the gym. He waited against the wall while all the cops and other agents left the room, leaving just him, his teammates, a couple of local Feds and the DEA crew. "So what's the plan?" he asked Tuck, deferring to him because he was team leader.

"Celida just texted me a few minutes ago, she and her team are on the way in from the airport. She's been trying to track Zoe and the other woman."

They knew the location and time of the meeting, and wanted to find Zoe before then. Clay hated sitting around doing nothing. He wanted to jump into a vehicle and start searching, be on the move when a good tip came in. It made more sense to wait until they had more intel though.

Resigned, he stayed where he was and half-listened

to the rest of the guys as they talked. He wasn't social at the best of times but right now he was incapable of carrying on a conversation with anyone. He kept remembering the way Zoe had smiled at him in the bathroom as he'd dressed this morning, her golden eyes alight with pleasure and pride. Pride in *him*.

It'd been a long time since he'd truly felt proud of himself. When Zoe looked at him he felt like a good man, like he could do anything. Facing the prospect of a world without her, of her being snatched from his life like this…it opened up a giant hole in his chest.

He stood that way, apart from everyone else while the acid burned in his stomach, until the conference room door opened and Special Agent Celida Morales swept in. Agent Greg Travers was with her, along with two other agents Clay didn't recognize.

Tuck went over immediately and hugged her close, murmured something to her, but when they parted a few moments later there were no tears in Celida's eyes. Her best friend might be missing, kidnapped by a rogue DEA agent, but one look at Celida and it was clear she had her game face on. And judging by that determined expression, she planned on hunting down Ruiz no matter how long it took. It gave Clay hope to know that for at least a few people involved in Zoe's case, it was personal. They had a vested interest in solving this case, and in making sure Zoe was found alive.

Celida nodded at Clay and got right to the point, the scar on her cheek moving as she spoke. "Nothing yet. The local agents and us have feelers out to a list of Ruiz's contacts in the area. He's used a couple different burner phones here in the city but nothing since he took Zoe. We know he's going to use her to get Leticia, so at some point Zoe will have to give him the coordinates and time, if she hasn't already. Right now it's his only way of finding Leticia, and our only way of finding him.

Unless we get a credible tip in the next few hours, our best shot is planning to take him at the meeting point tomorrow morning. It's all we've got at the moment, unfortunately." She looked at Tuck and DeLuca. "What've you guys got so far?"

It went without saying that the local Feds and cops had jurisdiction, and that Clay and his teammates would only be called in if Ruiz barricaded himself with hostages or a hostage extraction was deemed necessary. And even then, only if they were cleared to do so.

Clay came away from the wall and gathered around the table with everyone else as they went over maps and satellite images of Nairn Park and the surrounding area. The park itself was a flat, grassy area next to what looked like a construction site of some sort. DeLuca reviewed everything, made some suggestions, then Tuck tweaked them.

"Sniper teams deployed here and here," Tuck said, touching two spots on the map where the screen of trees and brush around the park provided good camouflage and the guys would have good sightlines of the area. Then he looked at the local FBI agent-in-charge, Ames. "Where do you want to position on the highway?"

The park was right off I-10, so they needed to cut off any and all exits if Ruiz managed to evade the trap and attempt an escape.

"We'll have agents and officers covering all entry and exit points, including this access road running parallel to the park," Ames said, his deep voice carrying around the room with ease. He was a former Army Master Sergeant, and Clay liked the way he ran things. Calmly and efficiently. His word was law with his people, but he wasn't an asshole about it and seemed to be open to suggestions if anyone voiced one.

Clay followed everything closely, studying the map, trying to think like Ruiz. If he was that focused on getting Leticia back and Zoe had given him the meeting time and location, there was no way he wouldn't show up tomorrow morning. He had to know the cops and Feds were coming for him, but to a man like Ruiz, it wouldn't matter.

He could send someone else to the meeting place, but Clay doubted he would. Not with this much at stake. The man was willing to throw away his career and face life in prison for the chance to be reunited with his woman. No, he'd be there in person.

DeLuca, Tuck and Ames discussed several more points, backup plans, exfil plans Ruiz might have in mind. He'd have to come in by vehicle, and the only other option for getting away was to go on foot through the brush and head toward the river. There was no way he'd be able to make it far, even if he managed to somehow evade all the law enforcement officers the area would be crawling with.

Tuck fell silent, looked around the table. "Anything else?"

Everyone shook their heads, including Clay. At this point there was nothing more to plan and their team wasn't even officially on standby. He looked at DeLuca. "So what now?"

His CO took off his Chargers cap and ran a hand over his short hair. "I'll call the sniper teams in, have them bring in everyone's weapons and kit. If we get the nod, we'll be ready."

Feeling helpless didn't sit well with Clay, but he had no choice. This was the best they could do for the moment and he was gonna have to find a way to live with it.

He fucking hated it though. It felt too much like when he'd been forced to step back and watch his sister self-destruct, only this time Zoe's life hung in the balance and right now it was in someone else's hands.

Straightening, he looked at Tuck, who lifted his arm for Celida and wrapped it around her shoulders. Clay wanted to be able to do that with Zoe so bad right now his muscles cramped. "I'm gonna take off," he told them. He needed to get the hell out of here, walk, do something to burn off the excess energy thrumming through him.

Maybe he'd walk back to Zoe's and wait. Being in her place, surrounded by her eclectic collection of bats and skeletons and crows, breathing in the scent of her perfume... He needed to feel close to her right now and that was the only way it was going to happen. He could deal with her insurance company for her, have her doors fixed for her, get everything cleaned up for when she came home.

Because she *was* coming home. He refused to believe anything else. And when she did, he was going to make it clear what she meant to him and that he wanted her in his life going forward.

He couldn't imagine his life without her in it. He'd lived in darkness for too long. She was his light and he wasn't letting her go.

"You'll call me?" he asked them, aware that his voice was rough but not giving a shit that it betrayed his worry.

Celida gave him a sad smile and nodded, while Tuck answered. "'Course, man. Soon as we hear anything."

With a weary nod, Clay turned and strode from the room.

Chapter Sixteen

The sun was a faint glow on the edge of the horizon when they left the house the next morning. Carl, or Carlos as the other man had called him, had hauled her up off the floor where she'd stayed all night and freed her hands only long enough for her to use the bathroom. She'd searched frantically for a weapon but the cupboards and drawers had been bare and there were no windows for her to try an escape. Not that she'd have gotten very far with her ankles bound and him waiting on the other side of the door with a gun.

Steeling herself for whatever lay ahead, knowing she had no other choice but to go along with this for now, Zoe had exited the bathroom and allowed him to cuff her hands again, this time in front of her. But he'd undone her feet, apparently impatient with her slow, shuffling steps. The dress would hamper her ability to get much leverage, but she'd kick him wherever she could if the opportunity presented itself.

Carlos's twenty-something accomplice, who was some kind of computer tech from India, had been asleep on the ratty living room couch of what she'd discovered was some sort of hunting cabin on a bayou somewhere. She had no idea whether they were still in Louisiana.

She'd expected Carlos to order her into the trunk but he'd surprised her by ordering her into the front passenger seat and tying her bound hands to the door handle.

You try anything stupid and I'll put a bullet in you.

The words had sent ice water sluicing through her veins. She couldn't see a gun but she knew he had one in here somewhere and didn't doubt the threat. She'd barely moved since leaving the cabin, instead staring out the window as her mind worked furiously to think two steps ahead. It was only a few minutes after four, so they had almost two hours until the meeting with Leticia.

He hadn't told her what he planned to do, of course, but so far he seemed to believe her that she was necessary for the meeting. She'd been trying to think of a way to warn Leticia and Xander if and when she saw them. Zoe didn't want Carlos to get either of them, but the thought of an innocent child being caught up in all this turned her stomach. She had to find a way to protect him.

Throughout the night she'd strained to hear whatever was being said on the police scanner Gill had on the kitchen table, but he'd had the volume down too low. Twice he'd woken Carlos, who hadn't slept more than a few hours, to report something. Zoe hadn't slept much either, wracking her brain for some kind of plan and thinking of Clay. His smile, the way his blue eyes warmed when he looked at her, the feel of his arms around her and the way he'd claimed her with his body.

He and Tuck would be searching for her right now. They'd be planning something for the meeting. She prayed it would all end quickly, without anyone getting shot.

Well, if Carlos happened to eat a bullet or two, she could live with that.

He was silent as he drove them along the

interconnecting waterways that made up the bayou, the tall cypress trees casting shaggy shadows with their fringes of Spanish moss hanging from the boughs. She'd lived practically her entire life in Louisiana and had only visited the bayous once in an airboat tour when she was eleven. It had an eerie beauty to it but she couldn't appreciate it now. Not when what might be the last two hours of her life were ticking away.

The radio was off, the only sound the hum of the engine and the bump of the tires over the rough, rutted gravel road. She could feel the frantic energy radiating from inside Carlos. Even though he'd barely slept he was wired, either from whatever he was taking to keep himself awake or because he was juiced at the thought of getting Leticia back. Maybe both. It made him that much more unpredictable, more unstable. Zoe had to be very careful with what she said and did from here on out. Her life depended on it.

He bypassed I-10 and took a series of back roads west toward Baton Rouge. They made it to the edge of town with about forty minutes to spare. He pulled over to the side of a deserted access road and turned off the car, plunging them into a taut silence broken only by the ping of the cooling engine. He tapped his thumb on the driver's window ledge in an anxious rhythm that grated on her nerves. All her muscles were tense, her stomach tightening by the minute as she counted down the time with the dashboard clock.

The ring of a phone broke the silence and he immediately pulled it from his pocket. He checked the call display and answered. "Yeah?"

Zoe watched him out of the corner of her eye, trying to hear what was being said on the other end but she only caught the occasional word. Whatever the person was saying to him, he was excited. His whole body went rigid, his gaze pinned straight ahead down the empty road.

"Are you sure?" he said, voice raspy. "What time was this?" He activated the accessory power and started the GPS. "What's the address?" He punched it in. "Shit, that's only ten minutes from here." He started the engine. "Thanks. I owe you." Ending the call, he shoved the phone back into his pocket and swung the vehicle around in a tight, fast circle, the tires spraying gravel.

Zoe didn't dare ask where he was going, but she already knew what would be at the other end. Leticia.

This time he took I-10 for a few miles before ducking off and taking a quieter route toward Baton Rouge. Brush and forest gave way to civilization, small communities of low income housing on the outskirts of town. A few minutes later they came to a small service station. Zoe shot him a sideways glance. The place was well-lit and the sun was coming up, and there was a car parked at the pump. There would be surveillance cameras. If he was risking all those things, Leticia must have been here.

He circled the station once, twice, his gaze pinging back and forth. In the pale early rays of sun now peeking through the trees across the road, she could see the sweat beading his forehead and upper lip, the droplets caught in the dark growth of stubble.

Zoe found herself searching too. If Leticia was here, then Carlos wouldn't need her anymore. Expendable meant she was dead. And from a few rantings she'd heard him make about Xander, Carlos saw the boy as a nuisance and a liability. She planned to do whatever she could to make Carlos let him go.

Think, Zoe, think! You have to come up with a way to make him keep you around if you can't get away. With him amped up on drugs and adrenaline, suffering from a combination of euphoria at the thought of finding Leticia and the mania of severe sleep deprivation, she would only risk attempting to run for it as a last resort.

Another partial circuit around the service station and Carlos cursed before yanking the car back onto the road. He stopped at the next intersection and seemed to be trying to decide which way to go, then suddenly turned right and headed down the road running parallel to the Interstate.

Up ahead in the distance, something appeared in the beams of the car's headlights. Someone walking. No, two people, their outlines illuminated by the headlights and the pale sunlight filtering through the screen of trees that lined the east side of the road.

"It's her." Carlos's voice shook with disbelief.

It was, Zoe realized with a start. Leticia *and* Xander.

Leticia stood frozen, looking back at the car, then took a step toward the trees as though she would run.

Carlos immediately stopped the vehicle. Leticia stopped too, still watching the car, wary as a doe scenting a hunter. A few moments later when Carlos stayed in place, she must have decided there was no threat to her or her son because she turned around and kept walking up the road at a brisk pace.

Zoe stared at the woman's back, wishing she could warn her somehow. *No! Get off the road, Leticia!*

"You're going to bring her to me," Carlos told her.

Zoe barely had time to process that before he cut the lights and jerked the car to the shoulder. With one quick movement he pulled a knife out from beneath his pant leg and reached over the console to grab her legs. Zoe stiffened and tried to tug her bound hands up to shield herself, but they were tied tight and all he did was shove her legs aside then lean down and slice through the carpet beneath her feet to retrieve a matte black pistol.

Sheathing the knife, he loaded a round into the

chamber as he spoke to her, never taking his eyes off Leticia up ahead, his excitement palpable. "I'm going to roll down the window and you're going to call her name to get her attention, then start talking to her, tell her you're here to help. Make sure she comes to you."

Zoe stared at him in disbelief.

"She trusts you," he said, beads of sweat visible on his forehead as he stared through the windshield. "She'll come to you. But if you warn her or try to run, I'll put a bullet in your spine and leave you on the side of the road to bleed out, and I'll still get her. Understand?"

So she had to lure them both into the trap, because Carlos knew Leticia would bolt the moment she saw him. He wanted Zoe to abuse the trust Leticia had in her, pretend everything was okay and lead them to a madman. Zoe swallowed, nodded, because she had no choice. Her heart pounded against her ribs, a cold sweat breaking out beneath her arms. Maybe once Carlos got out to go after them she could scream a warning. If she could get free and make a break for it, the forest might provide enough cover to shield her from a bullet—

"But first I'll kill the kid while you watch," he threatened.

She sucked in a breath, all her hope evaporating. Having to choose between the chance to gain her freedom and preventing an innocent child from dying was beyond cruel. Because there was no question which she'd choose. She wouldn't be able to live with herself if Xander died because of her. And Carlos knew it, the bastard.

Gathering her courage, she waited until he'd lowered her window and started easing the car forward. The dash lights were off, keeping Carlos hidden in shadow. At the sound of the tires on the gravel, Leticia paused once more and peered back at them over her shoulder.

Pulling in a shaky breath, Zoe fought for the courage to go through with this. With every second she prayed that someone would drive past them, give her the chance to warn Leticia and give them time to get into the woods before he caught them.

But the road remained deserted.

The morning air was cool and laden with mist. Inside she was freezing. Her jaw trembled, her thigh muscles rigid and wooden. Up ahead, Leticia stopped walking, her gaze pinned on the car.

Zoe wasn't sure if Leticia recognized the vehicle but she could feel Carlos's desperation, his anxiety. His hand flexed around the grip of the pistol. She took a deep breath. There was nothing else she could do. *Please help us,* she prayed. "Leticia!"

The other woman jerked, half-turned as she set Xander behind her in a protective gesture that broke Zoe's heart.

No choice. No choice now. "It's Zoe," she called out, her voice rough.

Leticia turned to face her fully now, stared for a second then started toward the car. Xander followed. *No, no,* Zoe silently begged her, not bothering to try and disguise the fear that had to be written all over her face. Hoping it would somehow warn her in time. *Stop. Don't come any closer. Please.*

"Keep talking," Carlos commanded, tension pouring off him in waves.

But Zoe couldn't force any more words out of her tight throat.

In the early light Leticia was a shadowy silhouette, occasionally lit by bars of gold that seeped between the trees. Then she stepped into a puddle of sunlight and when their eyes connected Zoe could see the smile of pure relief that spread across the other woman's face.

Her heart twisted. *Run, Leticia. Get out of here*

214

while you still can.

"Hey," she called out with a soft laugh, grabbing her son's hand and walking faster toward Zoe. "How did you find me? And who's that with you in the—" She trailed off, her expression freezing as she finally saw Carlos behind the wheel. She jerked to a halt, swung a wild glance at Zoe just as he hit the gas and sped toward them.

Leticia whirled and bolted for the trees. "Xander, run!" She shoved her son toward the forest and took off, even though it was already too late.

Carlos gunned the car up the road, the tires spraying gravel. With the window rolled down he'd heard every word and knew Zoe hadn't blown his cover, but Leticia wasn't getting away from him this time. His heart thundered in his ears as he drove to where she'd darted away from the road like a deer, his gaze pinned to that spot.

Mine. You're all mine.

He stomped on the brake, put the vehicle in park and leaped from it, leaving the door wide open in his haste to reach her. His boots thudded on the soft ground as he raced after her, reaching for the pistol in his waistband. He could see her up ahead, a flash of brown hair, her black flannel shirt making it hard to track her through the thick brush. Their sounds gave them away. They were crashing through the underbrush, giving him plenty of guidance to track them.

They hadn't gotten far, only a few dozen yards into the woods when he got a clear view of them up ahead and stopped, raising his weapon. He didn't care if anyone overheard him. He would make her come to him and get out of here within the next few minutes, way before the cops could respond if anyone called them.

"Leticia! Stop right there or I'll shoot him!"

His whole body was tight, amped up on adrenaline and the speedballs he'd taken earlier. He watched as she gave her son a desperate shove that sent him sprawling headlong into the brush and stopped, raising her hands.

The kid was the key to this first phase. Carlos had no use for him, a little bastard from another man. Every time he looked at the boy it reminded him that Leticia had willingly given her body and heart to another man. Carlos was sick of that and the way the kid monopolized so much of Leticia's time and focus. He wanted him gone. From his position he had a clear shot at both of them.

Keeping his weapon trained on Xander, he stalked toward Leticia. Fuck, his heart was hammering at the mere sight of her. He could see the tremors snaking through her, was glad she was afraid and was also looking forward to the chance to soothe her. His baby only ever had reason to fear him when she defied him, something she knew well. After her coming punishment, he'd give her the pleasure she'd always craved from him.

He was so hungry for that chance—for her—his hand shook slightly around the pistol grip. It would take a few days to iron everything out between them and start over, but they could do it. "Stay there," he warned. "I've got my weapon aimed at Xander's chest. Take one more step and I'll shoot him."

He angled slightly to the left and clearly saw the way she squeezed her eyes shut and bowed her head a little. He'd already won. Triumph surged through him. "Turn around and face me."

She hesitated for a second, then spoke to her son. "Xander, stay still. Don't move, okay? It's gonna be all right. Just stay where you are."

Always about her fucking son. Carlos couldn't wait

for him to be gone from their lives.

Finally she turned, slowly, and met his gaze.

The impact of those green eyes hit him in the chest like a sledgehammer, and for a moment he couldn't breathe. "Why'd you run?" He couldn't hold back the anger and pain in his voice.

Her jaw tightened, those gorgeous eyes bright with tears. From where he stood he could see the bruising along her cheekbone and the edge of her mouth, reminding him of the argument they'd had the day before she'd left. A pang of guilt and regret flashed through him. "You know why."

Fury and fear erupted inside him at the accusation in her eyes, a toxic mix that blended with his frantic need to touch her, hold her close. "You knew better than to run from me, but to go to a shelter?" He shook his head, feeling the rage bubble up once more, her betrayal a bitter taste in his mouth. "Come here." His weapon remained trained on the boy, huddled in the undergrowth, eyes just like his mother's, the only part of him that resembled her, gazing back at him with fear and loathing. He'd never shot a kid before. Would hate to have to start now, even if he didn't like the little bastard.

Leticia stared at him for several moments, her eyes hardening like green glass. "And if I don't, you'll shoot my son?" Her voice shook on the last word, the fear and pain there almost weakening his resolve.

"I wouldn't enjoy doing it, but I will. The choice is yours." She had to know he would do it, that it wasn't an empty threat, otherwise she would never leave the kid and come with him. But he also knew that if he did, she'd never forgive him. Leticia was a strong, spirited woman and that was a big part of the reason why he'd fallen so hard and fast for her. No other woman had even come close to her. He wanted them to have their own kids together, make a family. Xander didn't fit into that equation.

Carlos couldn't live without her. And he wouldn't let her live without him.

Her face fell and her shoulders sagged. She lowered her hands to her sides, looking back at her son. "I love you, baby. So much. No matter what happens, I need you to remember that."

Xander lurched up onto his knees, his face stricken, chin trembling. "Mom, no—"

"Be brave, Z. I'll be okay. Just stay there until…" She looked back at Carlos. "You want me to leave him here alone in the middle of the woods and just walk away?" Her voice broke and Carlos hardened his resolve, reminded himself that he had to stay the course he'd begun. It was way too late to go back now. Forward was the only option, for all of them.

"It's already daylight. He'll be fine and the interstate is only a few minutes' walk that way." He nodded to the east. "Now come on." He gestured with the pistol and she took a grudging step toward him. His free hand itched to touch her. That silken, golden skin, her shiny hair. He wanted her to look up at him with joy the way she used to, with trust and the knowledge that she was lucky to have him for her man. To have that chance, he'd have to let her kid go.

A sudden, terrifying thought hit him; that she'd never look at him like that again after this. No. He shoved it aside, using all his restraint to stay where he was and make her come to him. It was the only way. He'd start by using force, but to win her heart again he needed her to *want* to be with him.

As soon as she was within arm's reach he lowered the pistol and grabbed her, hauling her into his arms. She gasped and pressed her hands flat against his chest, her entire body stiff with rejection. Ignoring that for now and the pain it shot through him, Carlos groaned and buried his face in her hair, breathing in her scent. Sweet, clean. His baby. Christ, he was shaking at just the feel of having her in his arms again. So soft and warm.

When he eased back she swallowed and looked up at him, her eyes full of torment he longed to erase. "Y-you swear you won't h-hurt him."

Xander. Always goddam Xander getting in between them. Carlos had never imagined resenting a ten year old so much.

The kid was standing now, watching them uncertainly in the spot Leticia had left him. But he'd fulfilled his purpose now. Carlos had needed his life as leverage for the most difficult part, getting Leticia to come to him. He didn't need the boy anymore for the rest, he had Zoe, and letting him go now would go a long way with Leticia. Whipping his head to the side, Carlos scanned for the car. He couldn't see much through the screen of trees. She'd better still be sitting where he'd left her.

He looked back at the boy. "Go," he barked, and clamped a hand around Leticia's upper arm to drag her with him back to the car. She didn't dig her heels in, but it was clear she wasn't in any hurry to follow him. She kept glancing over her shoulder at her son, her distress clear. "He'll be fine," he said gruffly, moving faster now, annoyed and frustrated by her devotion to her son when he wanted it all for himself. "He can go to the service station. And we've gotta be gone before he gets there and calls the cops. So move it." It was implied that he could still make good on his earlier threat if that happened.

Leticia hitched in a breath and made a funny little sound in her throat. The grief in it sliced him. But it wasn't like the kid was going to die out here alone, this close to civilization. It was going to be hard for her to accept life without him though. Maybe after things settled down and she was bound to him again the way she had once been, she'd see this was for the best. Once they were out of the country things would improve. First he'd have to get rid of Zoe though. She wasn't going to stay quiet so there was only one way to silence her.

He planned to do that as soon as they got back to the hunting cabin. He'd kill her, dispose of her body, then take Leticia across the border while things cooled down. His Mexican friends were going to take them across the Gulf before first light tomorrow, and grant them entrance into cartel territory until things settled. Leticia would have plenty of time to adjust to her new reality then.

Moving quickly, he took Leticia to the edge of the trees and glanced toward the car. The front seat was empty and Zoe was nowhere to be seen. He swore, dragged Leticia parallel to the road so they were still hidden by the trees. How the hell had she gotten free?

There. Movement in the trees on the opposite side of the road. "Zoe!" he bellowed. "Get out here or I'll do what I said!"

No response. He stilled, listened. Could he have misjudged her? No. There was no fucking way she'd leave and put the kid's life at risk. Only birdsong and the sound of the leaves moving in the breeze surrounded him. Beside him Leticia was pale and stiff, darting her gaze around.

"You think I won't do it?" he yelled, starting to sweat again. They were too close to the service station. If Zoe got there she would absolutely call the cops and he had no doubt that she'd memorized the license plate. He didn't have time to find another ride and steal it. Not with an uncooperative hostage in tow.

Fuck. "Zoe!" He needed her for what came after this getaway. He'd planned on having her for a bargaining chip with Leticia, as a backup. From the rigid set of her features, he was going to need it.

A slight movement across the road caught his gaze. Zoe, trying to escape. "Freeze!"

She didn't. He raised his pistol, took aim and fired just ahead of her trajectory. The sound of the shot was loud in the quiet. Bark exploded from a tree trunk right in front of Zoe. Leticia cried out and cringed away from him. The movement stopped.

"Next one's going through you," he threatened, meaning every word.

A moment later Zoe materialized on the opposite side. Hands bound in front of her, eyes shooting poison arrows at him. A shitload of tension drained away inside him. Everything was going according to plan. This was still going to work.

Expelling a hard breath, he jerked his head toward the car. "Get in. *Now*." He kept his pistol trained on her, tracking her progress to the vehicle as he and Leticia rushed over. He put Leticia in the front seat and quickly bound her hands to the door handle so she couldn't try to escape or interfere.

Zoe edged closer, wary as a wild animal, features pinched. Rounding the back with his weapon aimed at her, Carlos seized her by her bound wrists, twisting them down and to the side at a sharp angle. Zoe yelped and rose on tiptoe to try and lessen the pressure, the binding making it impossible for her to get free. He tucked the pistol back into his waistband and secured her hands behind her this time, then opened the trunk and roughly shoved her into it. Slamming it shut, he hurried around to the driver's side, got in and fired up the engine.

He slung the car around and headed south down the deserted road. Once they crossed back over to the south side of I-10 it was an easy twenty minute drive back to the cabin. It was isolated enough that the cops would have trouble finding it. He'd take the women there, get rid of Zoe, and start wooing Leticia before it was time to leave and begin their new life together.

Chapter Seventeen

Tuck's voice came through his earpiece. "You guys got anything?"

"No," Clay answered from his position in the front seat of the SUV he and Schroder were sitting in. They'd parked it on the other side of the construction zone beside Nairn Park, next to the trailer that served as the contractor's office on site. His team's job was recon only, to assist the other agents on scene. He and the others had their fatigues on and their kit handy, their weapons stowed in the backs of the vehicles they occupied.

Going by the burning sensation in his gut that wouldn't ease up, he was going to have a fucking ulcer soon. Not knowing where Zoe was or what had happened to her was eating him alive from the inside out.

He lowered his binos to glance around. Schroder was watching the opposite side. It was quarter to six already. None of the agents posted in the surrounding area had reported any sign of Leticia yet, let alone Ruiz.

Pushing out a breath, Clay rubbed at his eyes. He hadn't slept much. He'd spent the late afternoon and evening getting the insurance thing rolling with Celida's help, then replaced Zoe's exterior and bedroom doors himself and put on sturdy new locks. The project had helped save him from losing his mind with worry, but only just barely.

He'd added something to secure the front gate as well, had intended to strip the bed and put on fresh sheets for her but he'd caught her scent on the pillowcase and decided to leave it. Throughout the night he'd kept checking in with Tuck and DeLuca, and each time they'd had no updates.

At first he'd sat out on the balcony, but that only reminded him of what they'd done on the daybed. When he'd finally turned in for the night at one in the morning and crawled into her bed, the faint scent of her perfume on the sheets, all he could think about was her and what might be happening to her. He'd dozed off and on, lying on her side of the bed with her pillow hugged to his chest, thinking he'd have given anything for it to be her in his arms instead.

Now they had a whole taskforce of agents and cops out looking for her and Ruiz, and so far had dick-all to show for their efforts. It was driving Clay fucking insane.

Settling back into the seat once more, he raised the binos and scanned his sector. The other agents were doing a pretty good job of staying hidden out of sight because he could only spot a few of them. One was doing stretches on a yoga mat spread onto the grass and another was doing laps around the field with a little dog. Celida was with her boss and a couple other Feds half a block away, and Tuck was with Evers, Vance and Blackwell about an eighth of a mile from them.

Schroder was silent as he kept watch. The minutes kept ticking past and the only new arrivals to the park were a couple of joggers and one person walking their dog.

Normally Clay could wait for hours in position without moving or getting antsy, even in extreme weather. This time it took all his discipline to sit still. At twenty-five minutes past six, he was all out of patience, frustration eating at him from the inside like acid. He tapped his earpiece. "What's the word," he asked Tuck.

"DeLuca said no one's reported any sightings yet."

His jaw tensed. Somebody should have at least spotted Leticia already. "They're not gonna show. Something's wrong." He just prayed it didn't mean Zoe was already dead. The thought alone made his stomach lurch.

"Stand by." Clay didn't know who Tuck had gone to talk to, but he'd bet it was either DeLuca or Celida. He came back on a few minutes later. "We'll withdraw and head back to the local field office."

Clay didn't want to leave in case someone did show up, but he also knew it was just wishful thinking. Either Leticia had gotten cold feet and bailed, or Zoe hadn't told Ruiz about the meeting. If the latter was true, it meant there was a good chance she was still alive. "Roger that."

Clay started the engine while Schroder slid from the back into the front passenger seat. Only part of Clay's attention was on the road as he drove, his mind filled with images of Zoe.

Please be okay, raven. We're doing everything we can to find you. I need you to hold on.

Fuck, his throat was starting to close up.

Swallowing, he gripped the wheel tighter and drew in a deep breath. It didn't help ease the pressure in his chest any.

"You need anything?" Schroder asked as Clay turned onto the highway. "Want me to grab some coffee, something to eat?"

He shook his head. "No thanks." He'd forced himself to eat a piece of toast before leaving Zoe's. It was currently sitting in his stomach like a piece of concrete. He didn't want to eat or sleep or do anything but find her. All they needed was one good piece of intel that gave them a decent lead. Just one fucking decent tip to point them in the right direction.

They were a mile away from the local field office when Tuck spoke again. "Get back to the RV point. Locals just got a tip. How far out are you?"

Schroder answered. "About seven minutes."

"Four," Blackwell answered from the other vehicle.

"Okay. I'll get more details and brief you all when you get here."

Clay shifted against the seat, his fingers tapping an anxious rhythm against the steering wheel. *Come on, come on*, he urged the driver in front of him silently as he sped along, weaving his way through the traffic on the highway. When they arrived at Tuck's location, he and their other teammates were standing with Celida and DeLuca. Clay and Schroder jumped out and hustled over.

"What've you got?" Clay demanded as he reached them.

"Local cops just picked up Leticia's son," Celida answered, the shadows beneath her eyes telling him that she hadn't slept for shit last night either. "He says he and his mother were walking down a road when Zoe called to them from a car."

Clay's heart kicked into overdrive at the mention of her name but before he could ask more questions Celida continued.

"It was a trap. Ruiz chased Leticia and the kid into the forest, held them at gunpoint and threatened to shoot the kid if she didn't go with him. She did, leaving her son there. The boy said he heard Ruiz shout Zoe's name and then a single gunshot before the car drove away."

For a moment Clay couldn't breathe. *Oh, shit. Shit, no, not Zoe.*

"Kid waited for a few minutes and went back to the road, then found his way to a service station. He didn't get a look at the plates but he gave a general description of the car. Four door sedan, older model, dark gray."

Clay shifted his stance, growing more agitated by the second. "Any word from the people on scene?" Authorities would be using various programs right now to search for the vehicle.

"Nothing yet. They've got a team out now to search the area and—" She stopped talking as her cell rang, stepped away to answer it. Clay didn't take his eyes off her.

His heart was fucking pounding as she talked to whoever had called, imagining Zoe either bleeding or dying in the woods from a gunshot wound, or wounded and dragged back into the car with Ruiz. His teammates stood silently while she finished the call and hurried back to them, her face tense.

"They found a bullet hole in a tree but no traces of blood anywhere, and they've got a set of prints leading back from that side of the road to where the tire tracks stop." She met Tuck's gaze, then Clay's. "Zoe was still alive when they drove off."

But that didn't mean she was still alive now.

Celida didn't have to say it, and Clay knew everyone here was aware that her chances of survival dwindled with every passing minute. If Ruiz had Leticia, he no longer needed Zoe, making her expendable.

He dragged a hand through his hair, turned away as he sucked in a deep, steadying breath. It didn't help. The fucker now had two hostages. Clay wanted to be the one to hunt him down.

"We're putting out a description of the vehicle now

and checking CCTV footage." Her phone dinged with an incoming message. She glanced at it, nodded. "They've got a couple frames with a car matching that description and have a partial plate to go on." She looked back up at them. "I'll keep Commander DeLuca updated with anything new, but I gotta get back into the office." She kissed Tuck before climbing into a waiting SUV.

As the vehicle drove off, Tuck looked around at his team. "I'm calling the sniper teams in to meet us. In the meantime let's get our gear together, do a weapons check and be ready to roll."

Yes.

Might not be the action Clay wanted, but if the call came and they were deployed, they'd be ready.

****

Zoe clamped her teeth together to keep her jaw from trembling as the back of the vehicle bumped over the ruts in the rough road. They'd left the relative smoothness of the highway long minutes ago and each bump sent her bouncing around the trunk. She'd already smashed her head against the top and sides twice, no matter how hard she braced her feet and bound hands on the interior. Her wrists were raw from when she'd wrestled the rope from the door handle.

The full-blown panic she'd experienced when that bullet had torn into a tree not five feet in front of her had now eased, but the fear was as strong as ever. She was expendable now. Logically she couldn't figure out why Ruiz hadn't killed her and left her body in the woods. Either he'd been in too much of a rush or hadn't wanted to leave more evidence at the scene, but she had no illusions that he would let her live long now.

The back tires thudded into a pothole, sending her into the roof of the trunk. She grunted, braced her forearms above her and lashed out at the right taillight with her heels.

She'd lost count of how many tries this made, hoping to dislodge it enough that someone might notice it, or maybe she could stick her fingers through it and signal for help. Her bound hands made it impossible to move her wrists and fingers enough to search for the trunk release that was supposed to be in here somewhere, let alone to find the wires and disable the brake lights.

Zoe kicked at the taillight again, ignoring the pain in her bare feet. It didn't budge.

Dammit! Scrambling around to get aligned properly, she kicked at the other one. Three times. Four.

Something cracked. A surge of hope filled her. She lashed out again, felt it give this time.

The car began to slow.

Zoe braced herself as Carlos took another turn, then another a few seconds later, and stopped. The engine shut off. Her heart thudded in her ears in the sudden silence.

A door opened and slammed shut. Footsteps approached the trunk.

She tensed, gathered her strength. Once that lid lifted, if he planned to shoot her she'd only have one chance to use the element of surprise and kick the gun out of his hands and try to escape. She drew her knees up, feet together, using her upper arms to brace her against the trunk.

The trunk popped open, revealing a strip of daylight, then the lid lifted.

With a snarl locked in her throat she kicked out at the hand reaching for her, landed a glancing blow. He cursed and reached in to grab her, tying something around her ankles as she fought and bucked. Cruel fingers bit deep into her upper arms as he flipped her onto her stomach and dragged her out backward.

Zoe threw her head back and tried to sink her teeth into his neck but he hit her across the face so hard it dazed her, and dumped her onto the ground with a bone-jarring thud. Wincing, she tried to roll over but he merely grabbed her by the hair and began dragging her toward the same cabin they'd been in last night. Her feet scrambled to keep up with him, the grip on her hair pulling strands out.

"Carlos, don't!" Leticia screamed from the car.

He shoved her through the door and into the hallway. He stilled, seemed to look around. "Gill?"

The computer tech guy that had been here when they'd left. He was obviously gone and Carlos wasn't happy about it. Swearing viciously, he all but threw her into a closet and slammed the door shut. The sound of a lock clicking into place came just as she got to her knees. Then his receding footsteps.

Heart pounding, she rammed her shoulder against the lock. Again. Again, until she was biting back cries of pain from the impact. The lock held fast. She lay on her back and tried kicking at it. Nothing.

The front door creaked open and she heard more footsteps coming down the short hallway. Carlos was talking to Leticia softly, his voice ten times as creepy because of the soothing tone he was using. Zoe scooted to her knees and bent until she could peer through the tiny opening in the lock.

Carlos had Leticia in the kitchen. All the blinds were drawn on the windows but he had turned the overhead light on. Her hands were bound behind her, her head bowed. Carlos cupped her face in his hands and tipped her head back, thumbs moving gently across her cheeks in a tender gesture that turned Zoe's stomach.

"It's okay now, baby, I've got you," he murmured. He bent his head and began trailing kisses over Leticia's bruised face, lingering on the marks he'd put on her. She remained rigid and unmoving, her eyes closed in dread. Zoe swallowed, wishing she could shoot the motherfucker in the back right now.

Carlos raised his head and smiled down at Leticia, stroked one hand over her hair. "I'm going to leave your hands tied while we talk. Do you need anything first? I'll feed you."

Leticia didn't answer.

He cupped her jaw. "Baby? You hungry? Thirsty?"

Her face crumpled and her shoulders shook with silent sobs.

"Hey. Hey, it's okay," Carlos told her, drawing her close and kissing the top of her head. "Come on, don't cry." He picked her up and carried her to an old armchair set in the corner of the room, sat with her in his lap and cradled her there while she cried. For her son, for her loss of freedom. And for what was coming.

Zoe's heart ached and her eyes stung. He was sick. So sick he couldn't—or wouldn't—accept that for Leticia it was *over*.

"Shh, baby." He stroked her shuddering back while she cried, murmuring things Zoe couldn't hear and didn't want to. Then, "We'll get through this. It'll be fine, you'll see. I've got it all worked out for us. By this time tomorrow we'll be in Mexico and we can start over there."

Zoe stopped breathing. *What*? He was seriously going to smuggle her out of the country against her will?

Leticia's head snapped up. "M-Mexico?" she asked in disbelief.

Carlos nodded. "Some of my friends are gonna set us up there. We'll have our own house and everything, right on the ocean. You'll love it."

Zoe watched as Leticia drew back, her spine stiffening with outrage. "I'm not leaving my *son*! I'm not going anywhere with you!"

Zoe flinched, expecting Carlos to explode at any moment. His face tensed but he managed to stay calm as he answered. "Yes, you are. Tonight."

At that, Leticia vaulted off his lap like she'd been hit with a cattle prod. She shook her head frantically, staring at him. "I won't do it. You can't make me."

Zoe instinctively drew back at the rage that suffused Carlos's face. "Can't I?"

Oh shit, oh shit... Zoe scrambled back as far as she could against the closet wall, not wanting to see what happened next. She closed her eyes, desperately tried to think of something that might get her out of here, but when the chair creaked and harsh footfalls sounded in the kitchen, coming toward her, her eyes sprang open.

Terror forked through her when he suddenly unlocked the door and wrenched it open. Before she could do more than cower he'd seized her by the hair again and dragged her out of the closet on her knees. She struggled against his grip but froze when she felt the cold bite of a gun muzzle against her temple.

Zoe's gaze flashed to Leticia. The woman stood unmoving, her tear-bright eyes wide and locked on Zoe in horror.

"Go into the bedroom," Carlos ordered her in a low voice that made the hair on Zoe's arms stand up.

Leticia focused on him, her throat moving as she swallowed. "Don't. Please don't hurt her. It was my decision to leave, not hers—"

"Don't fucking remind me of what she did and didn't do in this mess," he snapped.

She shook her head, her expression pleading. "If you kill her there's no going back. We'll never be able to get our lives back."

The pressure of the muzzle stayed firm against Zoe's temple. "We can in Mexico."

"*No*. Please, Carlos. For me. You're not a

232

murderer."

Zoe felt him go eerily still behind her. She held her breath. "You don't think I've killed before, baby?" he said in a silky voice.

The words hung in the air, the unspoken threat that he had no problem killing again all too clear. Zoe was too scared to move, afraid to breathe. He'd killed her neighbor yesterday. Shot him down in cold blood without any hesitation. There was no question he'd done it before and could do it again. She closed her eyes and prayed. *Please, God. Please, not like this.*

"Please don't." Leticia's voice cracked on the last word.

Her distress seemed to bother him. Carlos heaved a sigh. The pressure of the muzzle eased slightly, then vanished. Zoe sagged in relief, would have hit the floor if he hadn't been holding a fistful of her hair. "I'm not making any promises about her yet. Whether she lives or not depends on your behavior. Now go into the bedroom and wait for me so we can finish talking."

There was no mistaking what he meant by that, and it had very little to do with *talking*.

Oh god, she was going to throw up. Zoe shook hard, the bile rising in her throat. She couldn't imagine having to endure what Leticia was going to.

Casting her a long, resigned look full of acceptance and apology, Leticia turned and walked toward the bedroom.

Immediately Carlos wrenched on Zoe's hair, sending tears of pain to her eyes. He dragged her back to the closet. "Don't make any noise," he growled, shoving her inside and locking the door once again.

Huddled in a ball on the floor, Zoe thought of Clay to block what was happening to Leticia right now in the bedroom. Completely the opposite of the unforgettable experience she'd shared with Clay only yesterday. She'd give anything to see him again, feel his powerful arms around her so she'd know she was truly safe.

Shaking all over, chilled to the depths of her soul, Zoe wondered whether this nightmare would end with them being rescued, or Carlos putting a bullet in her head.

Chapter Eighteen

C lay set the rifle he'd been cleaning aside and jumped to his feet when Celida barged into the FBI field office room at just after five that afternoon. He'd already cleaned it and checked it before but he'd needed something to keep him busy and occupy his mind or he would go insane waiting for word on Zoe.

"Think we've got him," she said, her expression filled with excitement as she set a laptop down on a small table.

DeLuca and Agent Travers entered the room a moment later and everyone gathered around while Celida pulled up a GPS map and put it on the big screen on the wall.

"Got a few tips from some insiders, people Ruiz has used as contacts over the past few months. An anonymous tip said he was at this remote cabin last night and that he had Zoe there. Agents have already been dispatched to confirm whether Ruiz is there now, and of course they'll be covert. They understand how sensitive this matter is and that he can't know we're watching."

Clay leaned in closer to get a better look, heart thudding. *Zoe.* The cabin was in a remote area situated on a finger of land extending out into the bayou. Tall trees blocked a good view of the structure but there was enough detail in the image for him and the rest of the team to start coming up with a tactical plan in case they got the call.

Another agent poked his head into the room and looked at Travers and Celida. "Got something." Both agents stepped outside to hear what it was, and Clay got busy examining approach possibilities with the others, part of him desperately wanting to know what was being said out in the hall.

The door opened a minute later and DeLuca marched back in, his expression all business. "Listen up." They all straightened around the table, focusing on him. "Just received intel that some of the people Ruiz is cozy with down in Mexico are planning to run him and Leticia across the Gulf by boat at around oh-two-hundred tomorrow. This group's a real bunch of winners. A drug lord's soldiers are planning to ferry a few of their Islamic jihadist heroin suppliers to shore here. The guy found dead at the hotel the other day? Member of the same group. They're going to come ashore here when the others pick up Ruiz." He nodded at the big screen. "Right now that's our target location, and if we get confirmation that Ruiz is there, we'll be deployed to bring him in. So let's get at it. I'll call the sniper teams and brief them while you guys go over this."

Hell yes. A surge of adrenaline hit him. He couldn't verify whether Zoe was still alive or even at the cabin, but he could at least do this, plan for the moment when they'd go after Ruiz. And Christ knew, he needed something to focus him now and ease the horrible sense of helplessness he'd been battling for the past day. He refused to let himself think the worst, because even he, as mentally tough as he was, couldn't keep compartmentalizing this forever.

"There's a dock right here," Clay said, pointing on

screen for the others. There was something near the base of it on the edge of the bank. Looked to be covered by a tarp of some kind. A boat maybe? Another vehicle? "Think they'd pick him up there?" It was risky, coming to shore, but DeLuca had just mentioned they were planning to drop off some unwelcome passengers, so it wasn't that much of a stretch.

"Or he might be planning to leave by boat to meet up with them offshore," Tuck suggested. He ran a hand over his hair. "I don't see him traveling by car from this point. Not when he knows someone might have spotted it and not when he's got at least one hostage with him. He knows how we'll track him so he'll be avoiding any CCTVs he can."

Oh god, please let Zoe still be alive. He didn't think he could take it if he found out she was dead. The light she'd kindled within him would go out and what was left of his heart would shrivel up and die. If he could go back and do things differently, he'd have told her how he felt about her this morning.

Putting that out of his mind, Clay studied the image on screen. He agreed that Ruiz escaping by vehicle was unlikely at this point. They had to find a good entry point that would provide cover and allow for stealth.

There was only one road they could use to access the location. The surrounding area was heavily wooded with Cyprus groves and while the thick underbrush would provide good cover, it would also slow them down if they wanted to remain invisible or if they had to break cover and chase Ruiz down. And he would be watching all the land approaches.

"Gonna have to be the water," he said to the others. Ruiz would expect any water approach to be by boat. But he wouldn't expect what Clay had in mind.

The guys all looked at him. "Go on," Tuck said.

He pointed to the screen where a finger of land

jutted out into the bayou. "This is a good jumping off point. We can access it on foot from the road and still avoid detection. Looks like it's about..."

He calculated the distance to the shore where the cabin sat using the legend at the bottom of the screen. "An eighth of a mile or so from there to the target. The water's murky but we don't need to stay under for long and it's shallow there so we won't need tanks. He'll be listening for boats or helos and watching the road, not expecting us to come out of the water."

Evers and Vance nodded, staring at the screen. Blackwell glanced at him, his teeth flashing white against his dark skin as he smiled. "I like the way you think, frogman."

Clay turned his attention to Tuck, who was still looking at the image on screen, and waited for an answer. Finally his team leader nodded. "All right, agreed. But you'll take point."

No problem. "Absolutely." They were all trained to operate in the water, day or night, but as a former SEAL, nobody was better than him in the water and Tuck was humble enough to acknowledge it. Just one of the reasons why he was the best damn team leader they could have asked for. Though with all the years he'd spent in SF then Delta, he was probably the closest to Clay in skill and experience with working in the water.

For the next hour they hammered out the rest of the plan and all its contingencies before running the final version past DeLuca. The CO listened carefully, asked a few questions and offered a few suggestions. Ultimately the final say on how this went down was Tuck's call, and everyone in the room knew it. Clay would be point man, Tuck would follow him, then everyone else and this time Evers would bring up the rear.

They called in the DEA Fast Team members, who would be responsible for overwatch and be ready to intercept any suspicious vehicles or boats approaching the cabin. The Coast Guard was placed on alert and was moving two ships into the area offshore to provide additional security.

Finally, when they'd analyzed the entire op and plan to death and had nothing more to add, Tuck glanced up and looked around the table at everyone. "All right, so that's it. Any questions?"

Clay shook his head, impatient to get moving. No one else had anything further to add.

"Okay, I'll start taking care of the details and get the paperwork ready. The rest of you go get your gear together," Tuck told them. The DEA guys filed out to brief their own people.

Clay turned and exited the room, heading down the hall to grab more of their equipment where they'd stashed their gear in another office. Halfway there he saw Celida and Travers step into the hall from an office at the end. She looked up, saw him, and smiled in a feral way that made the hair on the back of Clay's neck stand up and his heart rate elevate. She had something.

"Go tell the guys and get ready," she said. "Ruiz is there."

Yes. He glanced at his watch, saw it was only a few minutes after eight. They had just under six hours before the supposed pick up, wherever that was supposed to happen. More than enough time for them to carry out the op before Ruiz ever got around to leaving.

He looked back up at Celida, the sudden leap of hope a painful pressure in his lungs. "What about Zoe?"

Her smile faded. "We don't know yet. Not about her or Leticia. But until I hear differently, I'm saying they're both alive and with him."

He held her gaze, every muscle in his body taut, ready for action. Craving the chance to get Zoe and take down Ruiz. Clay wanted that fucker to pay for what he'd done. "If she's there, we're bringing her out."

Celida nodded, her eyes filled with gratitude. "I know."

Without another word, Clay turned on his heel and rushed back to tell the others it was time to lock and load. He was bringing Zoe home today.

****

Zoe's eyes snapped open in the darkness when she heard Carlos's raised voice coming from the bedroom down the hall, where he'd disappeared with Leticia what seemed like hours ago.

The bedroom door flung open with a crash.

Zoe tensed and scrambled to a sitting position, her heart thundering in her ears. But he didn't come for her. She could hear him moving around the kitchen, muttering to himself as he paced on the linoleum floor. He was clearly agitated and frustrated. Things between him and Leticia must not be going well, although what had he expected?

He stalked out of the room and Zoe braced herself to sit there and listen to Leticia scream or cry. It was quiet for a few minutes, then Carlos's voice rose and Leticia's along with it. She flinched when Carlos's bellow of rage echoed down the hall. Something smashed against the bedroom wall, shattered.

Carlos yelled again, his voice becoming more distinct when he exited the room into the hallway. "You're going to fucking talk to me before we get on that boat!" he shouted. Leticia shot something back and Carlos lost it. "Yeah? Well, let's see if you don't change your mind after this," he threatened.

This time when his footsteps sounded on the linoleum, Zoe knew he was coming for her. There was nothing in the closet for her to defend herself with, she'd already checked long ago. She crouched there in the dark, weight settled on the balls of her feet, bound hands in front of her, fingers curved like claws. Ready to spring.

The lock turned.

He swung open the door, a huge shadow against the dim light, and Zoe attacked.

Launching up with every bit of strength in her shaky legs, she lunged and went for his eyes with her fingers. Carlos yelped in surprise and staggered back a step when she hit him full force with her body, one hand flashing up to grab her wrist. But she'd managed to get him in the eye with her fingers.

Snarling with rage, he threw her off him. Zoe hit the floor on her side, her ribs and elbow taking the brunt of the impact. She winced, forced herself to quickly get to her feet and darted for the front door, the only exit.

A hand reached out, caught the ends of her hair as she ran. His fingers slid through it, just missing her. Zoe focused on the door handle at the end of the hall, vaguely aware of Leticia behind them, screaming at Carlos to stop.

It was going to cost her precious seconds to get the door open but it was the only way out. She had to get out. Instinctively she knew if he caught her this time, she would die.

The blood roared in her ears with every step, hope and desperation flooding her. She threw out a hand, grasped the lock. Turned it. Gripped the doorknob. Turned, yanked.

It started to open. She caught a breath of briny air as it whooshed open, had taken a step outside when he caught her from behind in a flying tackle. They flew through the air over the short set of wooden steps and landed on the damp, muddy grass with a bone-jarring thud, his weight atop her knocking the air out of her lungs.

Unable to breathe, she flailed as he wrenched her to her feet with a cruel grip around her throat and whirled her to face him. Her hands locked around his wrist as he squeezed, doubling the choking sensation. In the dimness outside his eyes were black pits, burning with rage.

Leticia stumbled through the door, still screaming at him, but froze and went silent when he withdrew his pistol and put it to the center of Zoe's forehead. And God help her, for just a split second that shamed and shocked her, Zoe found herself wishing he'd just pull the fucking trigger and get it over with.

The mere thought snapped her back to reality. She was a fighter. She wasn't going to be a lamb to the slaughter.

"No!" Leticia cried, her voice shrill. Zoe could see both her hands and feet were bound. "You promised!"

"I told you whether she lives depended on your behavior, and I've fucking had enough of her. So you can stand there and watch her die the way enemies of my Mexican friends do, and know it's your fault."

Zoe's knees turned to jelly. She hung in his powerful grip and shuddered, closing her eyes so she wouldn't have to see him anymore. Instead she thought of Clay, of Tuck and Celida, her parents and how hard it would be for them when they found out what had happened to her.

Ignoring Leticia's pleas, Carlos muscled her around. Her eyes popped open when he grabbed something crinkly and she saw the edge of the olive drab tarp in his hand. He yanked it off, exposing the machinery beneath and it took a moment for her to realize what it was. When she did, her blood iced up.

A wood chipper.

He was going to shoot her and put her body through a fucking wood chipper.

Fuck that. She'd fucking shove him through it first.

"Gators will be out soon to clean up the mess you'll make, and they're hungriest at night," he taunted as he threw the tarp aside.

Something snapped inside her. A strange, high-pitched sound came from her throat.

She was raw instinct, more animal than human as she turned on him. Her teeth closed around a chunk of flesh on the side of his neck, her hands gripping his throat.

She bit down hard. Blood spurted into her mouth. His howl of pain shattered the night.

A fist caught her in the side of the face. The blow stunned her but she didn't let go, sinking her teeth deep until they met with a clack, her thumbs digging as hard as they could into his windpipe.

Another blow, this one to the side of her head, and strong enough to send her reeling. She hit the ground and spat out the piece of flesh she'd ripped from him, gagging on the iron taste of warm blood as she rolled to her hands and knees and lurched to her feet.

Run. Run!

Terror and the will to survive drove her onward on a wild dash for the trees. He was right behind her, bellowing his rage as he gave chase.

Can't stop. Won't stop.

The muscles in her thighs burned. She darted left, narrowly avoiding the arm he threw at her. Her bare feet slipped on the muddy ground. It cost her everything.

Carlos slammed into her, an arm locked around her throat, choking the life from her. She clawed at his arms, nails raking his skin.

No air.

Her lungs began to burn, her eyes bulging from the pressure.

"What the hell's going on over there?" a male voice

bellowed from somewhere off in the distance to the left. The faint beam of a flashlight flickered at them through the trees.

Carlos froze, the crook of his arm still around her throat but the lethal pressure had eased.

"Who's there?" the man called out, sounding all kinds of suspicious and pissed off.

"Fucking *hell*," Carlos muttered to himself. He seemed to hesitate for a second.

"Help! Help us!" Leticia screamed from the porch. "Call the cops, he's got me and another woman held prisoner—"

The rest of what she was going to say was cut off when Carlos raised his pistol and fired one shot in Leticia's direction. She yelped when the bullet slammed into the side of the cabin, feet from where she stood, then dove for cover behind a pile of wood.

That muscled arm fell away from Zoe's throat. She dropped to the grass, her starved lungs sucking in a breath of air. Before she even realized what was happening Carlos was dragging her back to the cabin. He threw her inside and went back to grab Leticia, hauling her up the steps by the hair. He was back before Zoe could stagger to her feet. This time he opened a trap door in the floor and stuffed both of them in what had to be a cellar.

There was just enough room for her to kneel. Zoe immediately got to her knees and banged on the trap door with her bound fists, the wooden rectangle outlined by a pale line of light from above. It was cold and damp down here, smelled of mildew and mold. The darkness surrounded her, disorienting in its completeness.

Leticia scrambled to her knees and shuffled over to her. "Oh my god, Zoe, are you all right?"

No, she wasn't all right. She was shaking all over, her stomach heaving. If that man hadn't called out and interrupted Carlos, she'd be dead right now. A shudder ripped through her. Leticia slipped her arms around her, awkward because of her bound hands. "H-have to g-get out," she rasped.

"I know," Leticia whispered. "I'm hoping that guy will call the cops."

Zoe prayed she was right. But maybe that Gill guy had turned on him and alerted authorities already. The FBI and cops would be out searching for them. "Wh-where's Carlos?"

"Don't know. I think he's gone to make sure the guy didn't get close enough to see anything."

"H-help me br-break the lock," she gritted out through chattering teeth. She wasn't sure what he'd barricaded it with, but they had to find a way to get out.

Leticia lifted her arms off her and turned around, a tight fit in the cramped space.

"Kick it," Zoe whispered. "*Now.*" Together they kicked the door, right at the edge that had closed last, where that line of light was. Pain shot through her heels, up her legs, but she ignored it. They had to escape. While Carlos was outside. There would be no second chance.

"Ag-gain," she commanded. Their next combined blow made the wood creak. It gave Zoe hope.

Another kick. *Bam.* The door thudded under the force, the wood cracking this time. Zoe bent her knees and drew her legs back again, ready to smash through the wood. Determined to. One more might do it.

Heavy treads on the outside steps reached them from above. They both stilled, listening in the pitch darkness. More movement.

Zoe's heart thudded against her ribs.

"Oh shit, it's him," Leticia whispered, her voice laced with terror. She trembled so hard Zoe could hear her muscles shuddering.

No. Zoe squeezed her eyes shut and fought back a scream of denial as the front door opened and closed. Ragged breathing sounded in the hallway, then ominous footsteps heading toward them.

Carlos had returned. And now there was no escape for either of them.

Chapter Nineteen

Carlos paused in the act of readying the aluminum fishing boat to swipe the back of his forearm across his sweaty forehead. The bite wound in the side of his neck stung like fucking hell and his shirt was stained with blood. More dripped down the side of his neck, trailing over his chest and shoulder. She'd gotten him good, the bitch.

He cast a glance back at the nearest tree line. The sun had gone down almost an hour ago so it was dark outside but with that nosy neighbor likely still sniffing around for the past fifteen minutes he couldn't afford to wait here any longer. He'd have to move him and Leticia to a different hiding spot to wait.

He was sure that old bastard next door had called the cops to check out the place, and he was probably prowling around with his shotgun right now. If he'd called, cops would arrive in as little as twenty minutes from now. Carlos had to be long gone by then and the boat was the safest way to move him and Leticia. The countermeasures he'd set up previously on the property would buy him some time, but it wouldn't hold them off for the three hours remaining until his friends were due to transport he and Leticia across the Gulf.

Carlos yanked the final knot on the rope tight, tying the boat to the dock. There was enough room in it for him, Leticia, some weapons and other supplies like water and food and medical stuff, just in case. But dammit, none of this was working out the way he thought it would.

Yes, he'd expected her to put up resistance at getting back together and he'd known she would pitch a fit about leaving her son behind. He kept fighting the irrational yet growing fear that he'd never reach her the way he once had. That the magic he'd found only with her was dead and would never be resurrected.

His hands shook as he threw a duffel full of supplies and weapons into the bottom of the boat. He'd intended to have more time with her to soothe her fears before they left but that wasn't an option anymore and he had no choice now but to leave.

Once he pulled Leticia out of the cellar and killed that interfering bitch Zoe, they'd be on their way and he wouldn't look back. He would have shot her already but he'd needed to stash both women where the neighbor and the cops couldn't see them, in case they surprised Carlos in the middle of his preparations.

The sounds of the swamp surrounded him as he grabbed the can of fuel he'd just filled the boat motor with and rushed back to the cabin—insects and nocturnal animals just beginning their nightly hunt. Shame they wouldn't have pieces of Zoe to snack on as he'd originally intended but he didn't have time to put her in the wood chipper anymore and the noise would only draw more unwanted attention and investigation.

The terror on her face when she'd realized what he intended had filled him with power. One that had quickly disappeared when she'd taken a chunk out of his hide.

He swore, batted away the insects swarming around

him, drawn to the fresh scent of blood. At the cabin he splashed the remaining gas on the porch and doorway, careful not to get any on him.

His breathing sounded over-pronounced to him as he pulled the front door open and paused inside the threshold to take stock. All was quiet, and dark except for the lamp he'd left on in the corner of the kitchen. His gaze shot to the rectangular shape of the trapdoor cut into the linoleum floor.

No noise from the cellar, but he knew they wouldn't have stayed locked in there quietly. Anxiety pulsed through him at the thought of what was coming. It was going to be near impossible to get Leticia to come with him willingly now. He'd have to drug her. That didn't bother him as much as the thought of her closing off from him forever.

Screw it. Nothing he could do about it at this point and he wasn't waiting around for the cops to show up, even if he was more than ready for a shootout to get Leticia away from here.

He yanked out the piece of wood he'd jammed into the handle to lock the women inside and tossed it aside with a clatter before jerking the door upward. Although he'd braced himself for the possibility of an attack, neither one tried it.

In the blackness below him he couldn't see either of them but he could hear their breathing, shallow and nervous. Both women had good reason to be scared, but Zoe especially. His jaw clenched. She was going to pay for what she'd done, both to his and Leticia's relationship, and for the chunk missing from the side of his neck. Plus she'd overheard his plans and had witnessed everything. She had to die.

Blood continued to trickle over his skin, hot and sticky, its smell nauseating in the muggy air. Crouching down next to the opening, he caught a glimpse of brown hair off in one corner. He reached in one hand and grabbed Leticia by the shoulder. "Come on. We've gotta go."

"Just leave me alone," she rasped out, trying without success to pull out of his grasp.

Ignoring her, he hauled her up and through the trap door, his muscles straining to lift her because she was a dead weight. Carlos set her on her feet, his heart constricting at the sight of the tear tracks on her face.

She didn't just look sad, she looked devastated. And the hatred he saw burning in her eyes was like a punch to the diaphragm, momentarily shoving the air from his lungs.

No. He would win her back, no matter what it took or how long. Once they reached Mexico she'd have no other option but to turn to him and he would use it to his advantage.

He wasn't letting her scream for help all the way to the new pickup location, however.

Impatient and out of time, Carlos pulled out the bandana he'd put in his back pocket and used it to gag her. He was just tying the ends behind her head when the device in his front pocket buzzed.

The alarm for the sensors he'd placed at the northern perimeter of the property.

He pulled it out and checked the readings. Someone had triggered the northwest one, planted into the ground at the base of a large tree. At that spot they had to be on foot, so it gave Carlos only a few minutes to get out onto the water. Maybe the neighbor, who'd obviously still been on his own property when he'd heard them fifteen minutes ago, otherwise he would have triggered the silent alarm then.

Or it could be the cops. Whoever it was, if they tried to infiltrate past the inner perimeter he'd set, he'd know soon enough.

He shoved the device back into his pocket and grabbed Leticia, putting her over his shoulder in a fireman's hold. She wriggled around and squawked but he held her in place easily enough.

Now to give Zoe what was coming to her.

Turning for the door, he pulled his weapon from the back of his waistband, aimed it into the cellar. When he caught a flash of movement below, he adjusted and fired twice, back-to-back. Leticia reared up against his back, her muffled scream battering his left ear as he rushed for the front door. He didn't stop to see if she was dead, because after what he was about to do next, she would be soon enough.

Adrenaline punched through him as he readied for the run for the boat, his body primed for action. His hand had just closed around the doorknob when a loud boom behind him at the inner perimeter shattered the night.

****

"Be advised, we just heard two gunshots from inside. Over."

Clay's heart nearly stopped at the announcement from one of the snipers through his waterproof earpiece. *Zoe.* He faltered beneath the water for an instant before forcing himself to move forward and refocus. It was dark and murky, making it difficult to see but his training kept him oriented and he'd navigated in far worse conditions than these.

He mentally pushed away any thought of Zoe and focused on the task at hand. He was leading this op. The most dangerous part was when they had to transition from water to land on the opposite bank, leaving them exposed, then move in on the cabin.

He consciously slowed his heart rate, reducing his body's demand for oxygen so he could hold his breath for longer. Something he'd learned and mastered during his long journey to making the Teams. The muddy floor of the bayou he was walking on began to slope upward as they approached the shore.

Soundlessly, with hardly a ripple, Clay's head breached the surface of the water. Keeping his mouth and nose above the surface and the scope on his rifle at eye level he crept through the shallows at the head of his team.

The cabin was less than fifty yards away at their eleven o'clock. A faint light glowed through one of the front windows. They couldn't see into the building because blinds covered every door and window. Their two sniper teams had also reported zero visibility from their positions in the woods prior to Clay and his assault team entering the water.

There was no movement. A small aluminum boat was waiting at the end of the dock.

You're not getting away that easily, motherfucker.

He zeroed back in on the cabin. The sniper teams had reported Ruiz running from the boat to the cabin when they'd first gotten into position. No mention of females or other hostages. Every intel report, including the informant who'd ratted out Ruiz, said Zoe and Leticia would be here.

Keeping to the deepest shadows lining the bank, Clay slid forward through the water. He was in his element now. This was his world and he was about to give Ruiz a violent introduction to what it felt like to be on the receiving end of an assault team made up of former tier-one operators.

The team moved as one unit, barely making a sound as they waded through the water. The steady hum of insects and croak of frogs surrounded them. A sudden explosion from somewhere behind the structure made him freeze in place. The faint flash had come from somewhere back in the trees. A second later one of their snipers came through his earpiece.

"Civilian just tripped some kind of booby-trap about thirty meters northwest of the target," the man murmured. "I'm calling for backup to intercept him."

They couldn't break radio silence without risk of giving away their position, and Clay wasn't surprised when Tuck didn't respond. In their various briefings they'd been told to expect booby-traps and for Ruiz to be heavily armed, likely wearing body armor. Still plenty of ways to bring him down, and that's what they were going to do. Their only concern was securing Ruiz and extracting his hostages.

With a hand signal Clay gave the order to advance and as one they moved forward once more, aiming for the edge of the bank ahead. He halted when the front door of the cabin suddenly burst open and Ruiz appeared carrying a woman over his shoulder.

She was limp, bound and gagged. Clay's heart stuttered but when Ruiz swung around to scan the area in front of him, the faint light from inside showed her hair was light brown, not black-and-purple.

No sign of Zoe. His gut sank. Had those two shots the sniper team reported been pumped into her?

A cold, deadly resolve filled him.

He was taking Ruiz down one way or another, whatever it took. He was getting Zoe out of there no matter what. Whether she was alive or dead he would carry her out himself, at least get to hold her close one last time.

No. Not happening. She isn't dead.

He slammed the possibility into a steel box in the back of his mind. Hidden by the shadows, he and the others stayed in place as Ruiz hurried down the steps. Once on the grass he paused only to pull something from his pocket and toss it toward the door.

Clay caught the flicker of a flame, realized it was a

lighter. He watched, helpless, as it hit the porch floor and ignited with a whoosh. A moment later the entire front entrance went up in flames as Ruiz turned and raced across the grass toward the dock.

****

Down in the darkness Zoe's heart was in her throat as Carlos's footsteps faded away overhead in the distance. She lay in the corner of the cellar where she'd been cowering, the warmth of her own blood trickling down her arm.

Those bullets had buried themselves into a wooden beam behind her, missing her by inches. Bits of wood had exploded, some of them piercing her skin. If she hadn't been moving when Carlos fired, she'd be dead or dying right now.

Her breathing was shallow and amplified by the sudden silence. She had no idea what that loud boom had been, but it couldn't be good. And she wasn't sticking around here for Carlos to come back and make sure he'd killed her.

The front door shut with a bang. She pushed up on wobbly legs and gripped the edge of the open trap door to boost herself through the hole, not an easy feat the way her muscles were shaking.

Her gaze immediately shot to the door. Carlos was outside, presumably running with Leticia toward the dock. Zoe was terrified for her, but she had no way to stop Carlos and the best way to help Leticia was to escape and inform the cops about everything.

I'm so outta here.

Shoving to her feet, she took off toward the door. He'd see her but she was counting on him being distracted with getting to the boat. She'd sprint out and veer around the corner before he could get a bead on her—

Something clunked on the front porch. She faltered, a bolt of terror spiking through her as she braced herself for the sight of him charging back inside. Then she heard a soft whump and caught a flash of light at the door, a wave of heat washing over her in the hallway. Followed by the distinctive, acrid smell of smoke.

Fire. He was torching the cabin with her in it.

Zoe whirled around and raced for the makeshift living room, the smoke following behind her like a lethal fog.

Chapter Twenty

S till in the water, Clay watched as Carlos raced across the grassy slope toward the dock, his body and Leticia's silhouetted against the orange and yellow flames engulfing the front of the cabin. As was the automatic rifle slung over his shoulder.

"Fire crews are en route," one of the spotters reported through his earpiece, "and another team is moving in to search for more hostages inside."

Shit, they'd never get here in time to save Zoe—if she was even in there.

Everything in him wanted to get in there and search for Zoe before the fire grew too large for them to enter, but he couldn't move from his position and race for the cabin without revealing him and the others, which would endanger everyone's lives. He had his teammates lives to protect. He couldn't break formation now, no matter who was inside the cabin. But goddammit, he'd never been this conflicted about an op before.

Behind him, Tuck reached out and tapped him firmly on the shoulder. Clay nodded and set his jaw, fighting like hell to stay in operational mode.

He was good at compartmentalizing, he'd been

trained by the best, but his brain kept focusing on Zoe. It took everything he had to lock that down, focus on what needed to be done. The quicker they took care of this, the faster he could search for Zoe.

Carlos was almost at the dock now. Just twenty yards away. He still hadn't seen them.

With another hand signal, Clay ordered them forward. Fuck, he wanted this over. They'd already gone over a contingency plan to cover the possibility of Carlos trying to escape during the assault. The plan called for them to split into two mini-platoons, Clay leading the group in the water and Tuck taking his group onto land.

Silently they split up and headed to their designated positions, cutting off both land and water escape routes. Clay dipped back beneath the surface, knew Schroder and Cruz were right behind him. Under the water the sounds from above were muted but he could see the eerie orange glow of the fire reflected against the top of the water and he clearly heard Ruiz's running footsteps as they thudded over the wooden dock ahead.

Close now. Just another few seconds and Tuck and the others should be in position...

He heard Tuck's warning shout to Ruiz. Instantly Clay shot to his feet, his upper body erupting out of the water like some lethal swamp creature, rifle aimed at Ruiz, the red laser dot resting in the middle of the bastard's chest. Cruz and Schroder popped up just behind him, flanking either side, their remaining teammates stacked in position between the cabin and the dock. Six more laser dots lit up Ruiz's chest.

"Put your hands up, now!" Tuck bellowed, taking a gliding step forward, weapon trained on Ruiz.

Ruiz had frozen in place, Leticia still draped across his shoulder. He whirled her around in front of him, using her for a shield, and raised his weapon at them with one arm.

Fuck.

"Freeze and get on the ground!" Tuck warned again, just as Ruiz wheeled toward Clay's position and pulled the trigger, unleashing a spray of bullets.

Clay ducked down, submerging, as rounds peppered the water to his right, missing him by only a few feet. *You stupid son of a bitch*, he thought, surging upward the moment the bullets stopped. He emerged from the water to see that Tuck had already taken a shot. Ruiz was on one knee, trying to gather Leticia back up in front of him.

Clay caught sight of the cabin in his peripheral vision. The entire front was on fire, and in a split second Ruiz would have his human shield back in place. *Fuck this.* He took aim at Ruiz's chest and fired. Simultaneous bursts of double shots rang out from both him and Tuck. Ruiz staggered back as the rounds hit him center mass, and fell to his knees on the dock. But he wasn't down.

Body armor.

Everything went into slow motion. Ruiz raised his weapon again, his face a mask of rage and panic, lit by the flickering fire up the slope. They couldn't take a head shot. The powers that be wanted this asshole brought in alive, so they could offer him fucking immunity if he agreed to testify on his drug cartel and jihadist buddies later on.

But there were always exceptions, and if it came down to taking Ruiz out to save his teammates, he'd do it in a heartbeat.

Clay aimed at Ruiz's right shoulder and squeezed the trigger.

****

Carlos screamed in agony as two bullets slammed into his right shoulder.

The force of it knocked him sideways, the pain making the world swim before his eyes. Leticia fell at his feet on the dock. But he didn't let go of his weapon.

He raised it with his left hand and squeezed the trigger, sending out a desperate spray of bullets, hoping to hit at least a few of the men shooting at him. He couldn't even fucking see the ones in the water.

All he needed was a minute. Just one goddamn minute to get him and Leticia into the boat and speed away from the dock. The aluminum wouldn't provide much protection but it was better than nothing and he doubted they'd keep firing at him without a clear visual for fear of hitting Leticia.

He spun around, ready to make a dive for the boat. Two more rounds hit his left shoulder, jerking him off his feet. He fell to his back, pain engulfing him. He couldn't move his ruined arms, couldn't get the muscles to cooperate when he tried to reach for his weapon once more.

The men were shouting at him to stay down, get on the ground. He knew they were here to take him alive, otherwise they'd have killed him the moment he raised his rifle at them.

He wouldn't allow it. Wouldn't let them take him in, offer him some deal to get him to testify against his friends. Then he'd wind up in fucking WITSEC and lose Leticia forever.

"On the ground, hands where I can see them!" a man shouted at him from the foot of the dock. There were four of them, Carlos saw now, backlit by the burning cabin.

He turned his head, his gaze swinging to Leticia. She was huddled on her belly on the dock, her eyes huge with fear as she stared back at him.

A pang of sorrow hit him in the heart. She was worried about him. She *did* still care.

But he wasn't going to let them take him.

Ignoring the shouts of the men closing in on him, knowing he had only seconds, he held her gaze for a heartbeat, grief filling his lungs like concrete. "I love you," he rasped out. "I'm sorry."

He looked down into the black water. Gathering the last of his waning courage, Carlos got to his knees and pitched forward.

"Stop!" the same man yelled from up the dock.

A bullet thudded into his thigh an instant before he hit the water. His mouth opened in a howl of pain. Water flooded in, foul and dirty. He choked on it, couldn't fight his body's reaction, making him thrash around in an attempt to surface, drag in air.

His ruined shoulders refused to move. The ballistic vest weighed him down. Pain engulfed him along with the panic. He started to sink, falling down, down.

Rough hands caught him. A hard arm clamped around his chest and suddenly he was rocketing upward. He broke the surface and let out a horrible gasp, struggled to get free but he was already too weak.

The man towing him reached the edge of the dock and shoved him upward. Someone else grabbed him, dragged him up and over the edge, ignoring his scream of pain. They secured his hands behind him and flipped him over onto his back.

Shaking, coughing, Carlos struggled to open his eyes. Someone was lifting Leticia into their arms. Seeing another man caring for her was ten times more painful than the bullet wounds slowly bleeding him dry. Other men were already racing up the dock, back toward the cabin.

Strong fingers grasped his chin and his head was jerked around. Carlos blinked, stared up into a pair of enraged blue eyes. The man was soaking wet, water dripping from his camouflage-painted face and dark uniform. It took him a moment to recognize him.

Zoe's lover.

Zoe's lover had pulled him from the water.

The man bared his teeth at him in a feral snarl. "Where's Zoe?"

You can't have her now. Carlos had lost his woman and now this man had too.

Zoe's lover leaned down until their noses almost touched, his expression deadly. "Where *is* she?" he bellowed, fingers tightening around Carlos's jaw with crushing force.

An ironic laugh bubbled up from inside him, but it came out a wheeze. "Gone," he muttered.

The man's eyebrows crashed together. "What?" But Carlos saw the naked fear his answer put in the man's eyes.

He turned his gaze to the cabin, now almost entirely engulfed in flame, and felt a surge of triumph. "She's burning."

The back of his skull thunked against the dock as the man shoved him and raced toward the cabin.

****

The smoke was so thick she was choking on it.

Zoe coughed and squinted through the thick, dark veil hugging the ceiling. She was crouched on the floor to take advantage of the clearer air down below but she knew she didn't have much time left. The fire was already in the kitchen and the smoke would kill her long before the flames reached her.

Crawling to the end table by an armchair she yanked the cord of the ceramic lamp out of the outlet and hurled it at the window. It shattered, raining bits of ceramic down on her, littering the floor. Another lamp, a paperweight and the TV were lying broken on the floor beneath the window.

She'd already thrown the smaller pieces of furniture she could lift and she was running out of ammo. The glass pane was broken but the frame was reinforced with bars on the outside and so far she hadn't been able to bust through it with anything.

Gunshots sounded from out front. Zoe's heart leaped. It was either the neighbor or the police. They'd get Carlos and help her. She didn't know how much longer she could withstand the smoke though.

Out of desperation she grabbed pieces of firewood and started throwing them at the window. They bounced off the metal bars without making so much as a dent. She ducked back down, coughing in ragged bursts as her lungs tried to clear themselves. Her eyes were streaming, the heat of the fire licking at her back. Crawling forward she grabbed a thick log and rose to her knees, reaching up to smash it repeatedly against the metal. The bars wouldn't give.

Zoe fought back sobs of fear. This was her only exit and she couldn't fucking use it.

More shots from outside.

A few minutes more. Someone would get to her. They had to.

She cast a frantic glance around the hellishly glowing room. She'd thrown everything possible at the window. There was nothing left to try and she couldn't stand up to yank on the bars without risking succumbing to smoke inhalation.

Zoe scrambled for the farthest corner of the room and laid flat on her stomach, yanking the front of her dress over her mouth and nose to act as a filter, feeble though it was. Her heart was lodged in her throat, every second a separate agony of suspense.

Then she heard it. Someone shouting her name.

She got to her knees and shuffled toward the window. Drew a smoke-filled breath and screamed as loud as she could. "I'm in here! Help me!" Smoke clogged her lungs. She doubled over, hacking and gasping, her eyes streaming.

"Zoe?"

"Here!" she shouted back, because that voice had been nearby. This was her only chance to get their attention. Dragging in a shallow breath, fighting not to cough, she held her breath and shot to her feet with a log in her hands, banging it as hard as she could against the metal bars.

Clang, clang, clang.

The sound echoed around the room, reverberating above the crackle of the flames, licking steadily nearer.

She smashed the wood against the bars again.

Clang, clang.

Her fatigued muscles gave out, her lungs screaming for oxygen. Out of air, she dropped the log and fell to her knees, dragging in a desperate breath. There was no clear air. She was choking now. Suffocating.

She cast a panicked glance up at the window.

"Zoe."

She couldn't answer. But through the smoke she saw hands grip the bars. They rattled the grate. "Help me get this off!" the man shouted to someone.

Another set of hands appeared. Together they yanked and yanked while Zoe locked her watering eyes on them and prayed with every heartbeat.

Then the metal creaked and gave way. The bars popped free and a man's head and shoulders emerged through the frame. The smoke thinned for an instant. A pair of hazel eyes zeroed in on her from a camouflaged face.

Zoe reached blindly for him. He shot his hands out, grasped hers and hauled her up with brute strength. The rough edge of the window ledge scraped against her belly, hipbones and thighs as he dragged her through it into the cool night air.

Zoe coughed and gagged for what seemed like minutes as he put her over his shoulder and ran away from the burning cabin, the other man right behind him. Her starved lungs sucked in breath after desperate breath of clean air, and soon she was able to breathe again.

The man ran toward the road where emergency vehicles crowded the turn to the property, their strobing lights lighting up the darkness.

"*Zoe!*"

She whipped her head up at the sound of Clay's voice behind her. Tried to answer but couldn't catch her breath.

"I've got her! This way!" the man carrying her yelled at him.

When they reached an ambulance the man eased her off his shoulder and set her onto the stretcher the paramedics had brought out. Zoe lay on her back and wiped her stinging eyes, still wracked by bouts of coughing, and blinked up at the stranger.

Before she could say anything the man behind him came up, and beneath all the camo paint she was startled to recognize Schroder.

"Hey," he said as he took up position next to her. He pulled off his gloves and put an oxygen mask over her nose and mouth, bending close. "Good to see you."

Zoe looked away from him, searching for Clay. He hadn't been far behind them. Where was he?

Pounding footsteps reached her, then Clay burst out of the darkness into the circle of light created by the emergency vehicles. "*Zoe.*" His painted face concealed his expression but she could see the anguish in his startlingly blue eyes as he drew near.

A funny sound, half-whimper, half-sob escaped from her throat. She sat up, reaching for him and a second later she was engulfed in his arms.

Zoe buried her face against his wet chest and squeezed her eyes shut, shaking all over. *Thank you, thank you.*

"God. *God*, Zoe," he whispered against her hair, his arms clamped around her like he was afraid someone would try to tear her away.

She nodded in agreement against his damp uniform, clutching at the front of it with desperate fingers. He pressed his face to her hair and held her, the way his arms trembled telling her just how scared he was that she'd died.

And just like that, everything faded away but him. Even through the faint smell of the swamp water and smoke on him she could smell the scent of his skin and it comforted her. Clay had her. She was safe.

A sob jerked her chest. Then another. And another.

"Ah, baby, I know," he murmured, cradling her closer.

Zoe couldn't stop it. She let the tears burst free, secure in the protective circle of his arms. She didn't know how long she cried but when the sobs eased at last, she barely had the strength to move.

"Bauer. Let me check her over."

Clay lifted his head at Schroder's voice, then gazed down into her face as he wiped the tears from her cheeks. "I'm not going anywhere, okay? He'll take good care of you, but I'm not going anywhere."

Zoe nodded, quivers still wracking her body, and lay back on the stretcher as Schroder moved in. Clay stood at her side, smoothing her hair back from her forehead. His touch helped center her.

"Let's start with getting these out of the way." With a pair of medical scissors Schroder cut the plastic cuffs from her wrists.

Immediately she reached up and locked her fingers around Clay's hand. He wrapped his hand around hers, squeezed tight and didn't let go. "Th-thank you," she said to Schroder. She'd hated having her hands bound, it made her feel helpless.

The corner of his eyes crinkled as he smiled. "Don't thank me, it was Cruz who pulled you out the window."

Zoe turned her attention to the other man, offered a teary smile. "Thanks."

"Don't mention it," he said with a shrug, and tucked a blanket over her.

"You hurting anywhere, Zo?" Clay asked, still stroking her hair with his free hand.

"Sh-shoulder." Her mind was filled with a thousand questions, but the shock was setting in. She was shaking all over, she realized. Rapid jerks of her muscles she had no control over.

Schroder set a hand on the side of her face. "Anywhere else?"

Zoe sighed. Just her lungs, the bits of wood in her shoulder and the scrapes she'd gotten. The few bruises Carlos had put on her face barely registered now. None of it life-threatening, unless she was way deeper in shock than she realized. She shook her head, the motion unsteady.

His eyes met hers. Calm. Sure. Zoe found her heart rate easing. "You've got lots of blood on your face," he said.

"Not m-mine," she managed, her jaw shaking along with the rest of her. "Bit him."

"Good for you. Bet he tasted like fucking hell, too," he said, rummaging through a kit he had with him.

"Y-yes." She couldn't wait to wash the taste of his blood out of her mouth.

Schroder pulled back the blanket and swept his hands over her, checking for more blood. "Your right shoulder?"

She nodded, grateful for the pressure of Clay's hand

around hers. Solid. Steady. Anchoring her.

"Just lie still for me, okay? I'm gonna clean you up a bit and see exactly what we're dealing with. The other paramedics are busy treating Ruiz at the moment, so you'll have to suffer making do with me."

Zoe half-chuckled at his teasing tone. "I'd rather it be y-you." She stayed still while he began cutting her dress off, only a little embarrassed at having him see her in her underwear. He was a highly trained medic and he was so unbelievably calm. She tilted her head back to look up at Clay. "Is Ruiz dead?" she finally asked.

"Unfortunately, no," he answered with a scowl as Schroder shifted her to get a better look at her shoulder. "He's in custody and bleeding from a few bullet holes though."

Good. She hoped he was fucking suffering.

"I'm gonna pull these splinters out. Hold on tight to Bauer's hand. I'll be as quick as I can."

She nodded, tightening her fingers. Pain she could handle, but she'd never felt this emotionally raw before. "W-what about Leticia?"

"She's fine. Paramedics are checking her out right now too," Clay said.

It really was over.

Relieved, Zoe closed her eyes and tried not to flinch as Schroder began pulling the splinters out of the back of her shoulder. The tiny wounds stung like hell when he cleaned them with something. She clutched the blanket to her chest and tried not to think at all, floating above the pain as occasional coughs wracked her.

"Don't think any of these need stitches," he said, "but you're not gonna want to move this arm very much for the next day or two."

"She won't need to, because I'll be with her," Clay said.

Zoe clung to his hand, grateful that he was going to

stay, but didn't open her eyes. A few minutes later Schroder put a bandage on her, wiped her face and gave her water to rinse her mouth with. "There," he said with a smile. "You look much better. Although that blood gave you a real creepy Goth look."

It surprised a laugh out of her. She coughed, jackknifed into a sitting position as it jolted through her. Clay grabbed her, bracing her against his body, his arms around her. Finally they subsided, leaving her sagging in his hold. God, she ached and throbbed all over. And she was suddenly exhausted.

"Zoe."

She opened her eyes at the sound of her cousin's voice. Clay eased back to give Tuck room and her cousin immediately engulfed her in a hug. She flinched as the wounds in her shoulder protested, but didn't say anything. It felt so good to have Tuck's arms around her.

Tuck pulled back and took her face in his hands, his eyes searching hers. "How are you?"

"Been better," she answered, a sudden lump in her throat, his familiar drawl washing over her.

"No doubt." He pushed out a long exhalation, shook his head, then turned his attention to Schroder. "So? How is she really?"

"Great. Little banged up and she'll have to go to the hospital for more smoke inhalation treatment, but I think that's it." His hazel eyes met hers. "She's lucky."

Zoe knew it. It was still so hard to take everything in that had happened. She didn't even know how to begin processing all of this. "Leticia's son, Xander," she said to Tuck. "We left him in the woods—"

"He's fine, darlin'. Cops picked him up and he'll be taken to the hospital to meet his mom. Happy endings all around."

The side of her mouth that wasn't cut pulled upward in a half-grin. "You know how much I love happy endings."

Tuck smiled. "Yeah, I do. I'll call Celida and your parents to update them."

Zoe nodded her thanks and sighed, letting her eyes close as a wave of exhaustion rolled over her. She was hanging on by a thread emotionally and it wouldn't take much for it to snap.

"I'm going with her to the hospital," Clay said, lying her back against the stretcher as the paramedics came to load her into the ambulance. No one argued and just before the doors shut he climbed inside, perched his big frame beside the stretcher and took her hand in his.

Chapter Twenty-One

M att DeLuca turned away from Celida and Agent Travers when his phone chimed with an incoming text. He didn't recognize the number but the message itself made everything go still inside him. It gave the name of a terrorist on the FBI's Most Wanted List and an address.

A terrorist rumored to be a higher up in the cell Ruiz had been waiting for tonight, the same cell the dead tango at the hotel had belonged to. Talk about high fucking value.

From one of the good guys, it read. No name, no clue as to who'd sent it. Hardly anyone had his private number, so someone sending him a message to this number meant something important.

He glanced over at the others. "Excuse me a minute." He walked a short distance away and called an analyst he'd worked with on previous cases. "Need you to trace this number and get me a visual of an address," he told her, and gave her the details. "Call me back when you've got something."

Putting the phone in his pocket, he turned back and surveyed the scene. Celida and Travers were speaking to three other agents. Bauer and Tuck had gone to the hospital with Zoe and Leticia. Schroder had snagged a ride there with a cop. Ruiz was on his way to the hospital as well, and as soon as he was treated he'd be transferred to a holding facility for questioning. Fire crews had put out the fire and forensics teams were on scene gathering evidence.

One double agent tango in custody, none of his guys were hurt, and they'd secured both female hostages. As far as ops went, the mission had been a total success. The scene was secure. Everything was locked down and taken care of, barring a shitload of paperwork and several debriefings. Given that Tuck and Clay were in the middle of taking care of Zoe, DeLuca had no problem letting the formalities of protocol slide until tomorrow.

Travers raised his eyebrows at him as Matt walked back toward them. "What've you got?"

"Maybe al-Tunisi." Rumored to be at the helm of all the sleeper cells in the area, and closely linked to the activity going on in Juarez, including the men who were supposed to link up with Ruiz tonight. Possibly manipulating all of it.

At that Celida stopped talking to the other agents and stared at him. "No freaking way." She frowned. "Who's it from?"

He shrugged, pulled out his phone and swiped in the code before handing it to her. "Dunno." One of the good guys, the message said. Rycroft maybe? Had to be someone with ties to the intelligence community.

"We've been hunting this bastard for almost a year now," Celida muttered, excitement in every line of her body as she re-read the message. She looked up at him. "You sure it's not a setup?"

"Checking that out now." al-Tunisi was a high value target. If he was there, they had to expect he'd be well armed with small arms and maybe explosives. Matt wasn't leaving anything to chance. "Can you get me a warrant?"

"Sure," Travers said, and got on his own phone.

A second later Matt's phone rang in Celida's hand. He grabbed it from her and answered. "Yeah."

"Number is from a burner phone," the analyst said without preamble. "The address is in a suburb of northern Baton Rouge, listed as owned by a company called Victory Enterprises. So far I can't find anything about it. No web presence, no tax information, like it doesn't exist, so it could be a front. Might be a shell company though, so I'll keep checking. I'm sending you the link to the satellite images I just pulled up."

"Thanks. Stand by, I might need something more."

"You got it."

"Well?" Celida was practically squirming with anticipation as he ended the call.

"Burner phone. Place is in the northern part of town, owned by some company there's no apparent trace of. An analyst is tracking it now. I'm pulling up recent satellite images she sent."

Once he had them on screen he angled it so the three of them could look together. The images showed a subdivision of townhomes in a suburban neighborhood, bordered by a thick greenbelt on two sides. Very private, appeared to be upscale.

But then, al-Tunisi was a chemical engineer by trade, and they made pretty good coin. Of course there was also the influx of money donated by admirers and supporters overseas. Matt wondered what they'd think of their donations being spent on such luxurious housing for one of the cell members.

While he waited for word on the warrant, Matt called Rycroft. The NSA agent answered on the second ring with a gruff hello.

"It's DeLuca. I got your message."

A slight pause. "What message?"

"About al-Tunisi."

"What about him?"

Cold settled in Matt's stomach at the confusion in Rycroft's voice. "I'm looking at a satellite feed of his townhouse in northern Baton Rouge. We're about to act on the tip you sent me."

"Interesting," Rycroft said. "But I didn't send you any message."

Matt frowned and ended the conversation. He glanced at Travers, who was still on his phone. A warning tingle started at the base of his neck. If Rycroft hadn't sent him the tip, who the hell had?

Travers lowered his phone and nodded at them. "Got the warrant." He sighed. "This feels too good to be true but just in case it isn't, I don't wanna waste time getting a team together and briefing them all from scratch. Can we use your guys to do the recon?"

"Yeah. Gimme a few minutes to alert them." He'd already been thinking the same thing, and his guys were the best, but without knowing who'd sent him that text, there was a very strong possibility it was a trap. His boys weren't going in until they were sure it wasn't.

Matt got back on his phone. In cases like this where a HVT was involved and the intel was perishable, he had the authority to move in fast. He'd leave Bauer and Tuck at the hospital and have one of the sniper teams cover for them.

He had everyone assembled and briefed within half an hour, and they split up into three vehicles.

Celida grinned as she headed for the one Matt was driving. "Shotgun," she said to him.

"I get shotgun," Travers argued, hurrying after her. "I'm your boss."

"Too late, already called it," she called over her

shoulder. She hopped in the front seat while Travers climbed in back and Matt settled behind the wheel.

He plugged the address into the vehicle's GPS system and led the way, driving the sixteen minutes to the north side of Baton Rouge. They turned down a quiet side street one block over and parked the vehicles where they'd be concealed by a screen of trees.

His boys filed out, organized themselves, then covertly infiltrated the area and got into position around the residence to do some up-close surveillance. Matt watched them via satellite link, each member's heat signature showing up bright green. They'd use camera wires to verify nothing was rigged and take a good look around inside before reporting back to him.

"If he's here I'll... Hell, I don't know what I'll do," Celida muttered from beside him in the passenger seat. "We've searched this area before, practically all of southern Louisiana, three months ago. Nothing turned up. And you mean to tell me he's been living right here?"

It seemed improbable, but stranger things had happened.

His cell buzzed with an incoming text. Bauer, reporting that Zoe was being released, Leticia had been reunited with her son, and Ruiz was in surgery.

Take a few days off and look after your girl, he texted back. *You've earned them.*

"Zoe's being released," he told Celida.

The other agent sighed in relief. "That's great news, thanks. Was that Bauer?"

"Yeah. He'll stay with her."

She shook her head, an ironic smile on her face. "Gotta say, I didn't see that one coming. Her and Bauer."

"Don't think any of us did." It did him good to know that the hard-assed Bauer had met his match in a woman strong enough to stand up to him, and beside him. Matt had been lucky to have a woman like that at his side for nearly nine years. If Bauer was smart, he'd recognize what he had and hold onto her.

He shifted his focus back to the screen showing the live feed. Twenty minutes later, Evers, who was acting as team leader for the op, spoke over the team radio link. "We got eyes inside. Looks clear, no trip wires. We good to go?"

"Green light," Matt told him. Heart rate picking up, he watched his guys ram the back door in to execute the search warrant. The moment they entered he lost sight of them on the satellite feed, but he could still hear them as the team swept the first floor.

"First floor clear," Vance announced in a whisper a minute later. "Moving up to the second."

"Copy that," Matt said and held up one finger to Celida and Travers to indicate the first floor was clear.

"Clear," Evers said soon after that. "Heading to third floor."

"Copy," Matt responded, holding up two fingers for the others.

Celida and Travers were silent, their gazes riveted to the screen of his phone as they awaited word about the third floor. Either al-Tunisi was hiding up there, or he'd somehow gotten wind of the warrant and slipped away before the team had arrived.

"Found him," Evers said two minutes later. "Third floor's secure."

"He alive?" Matt asked, already opening his door and hurrying to the townhouse.

"Nope."

He glanced at Celida and Travers, who were right behind him, and shook his head. Celida frowned and followed him to the back door in the cool night air. Travers was on his phone, calling the cops to provide a more secure perimeter. Neighbors were already starting to spill out onto the sidewalk in front, talking to the uniformed officer there.

Matt entered the back of the townhouse, stepping into the kitchen. All the lights were on. He could hear the TV going from the attached living room.

Something was cooking on the stove and a carton of orange juice was on the island in the kitchen. Everything suggested that al-Tunisi had just stepped out of the room for a moment.

Together with Celida and Travers, Matt started up the two flights of stairs to the third floor.

"In here."

At Cruz's voice from down the hall, Matt turned left and headed down a short hallway.

"He's in the master bathroom," Evers said from behind him.

Matt entered the bedroom and stepped up next to Cruz, who angled to the side and allowed him to see into the connecting bathroom. Al-Tunisi lay on the floor, two bullets in his chest and a hole in the center of his forehead, his pants down around his calves.

Assassinated while on the toilet. And from the way the blood hadn't yet congealed around him, not very long ago.

Letting out a low whistle, Matt eased to the side to let Celida and Travers see.

"Holy shit," Celida muttered. In the mirror she looked as surprised as Matt felt. "Who do you think did it?"

"No idea." But he'd love to find out. Right after he verified who'd sent him that text.

Travers got on his phone, had a short conversation and shook his head as the call ended. "Nobody reported gunshots to the cops. Neighbors must not have heard them."

"A suppressor," DeLuca guessed, both impressed and a little worried by this turn of events. He was glad al-Tunisi was dead, but who the hell had done the hit? Someone had got wind of it and tipped Matt off.

Confused, he went outside to look around, some sixth sense making the back of his neck tingle. Outside it was quiet, only the slight breeze in the trees disturbing the air. At the end of the walkway he stopped to scan the area. He didn't see anything suspicious, so he went back inside.

Two hours later when he was back at the field office with Celida and Travers, his analyst called with more intel. Matt put her on speaker.

"I searched through the satellite feed for the area and found something you need to see. Sending it to you now."

"All right." An image appeared on the big, wall-mounted screen at the far end of the room. All three of them stared at the picture, and the single heat signature approaching the rear of the townhouse.

"This was thirty minutes before your team's arrival," the analyst told them. "Watch what happens."

Matt stared in amazement as the figure climbed up the rear wall of the townhouse and entered the third floor window. A rifle was outlined against their shoulder.

"Who the hell is that?" Celida said.

"Can you get a shot of their face?" Matt asked the woman.

"Just a sec."

Another picture came on screen. From her end the analyst zoomed in multiple times and did more fancy tricks with the imaging program until a grainy image of the person's face became visible.

Shock reverberated through him as recognition dawned.

B.

Matt stared. She had on a skullcap and the image wasn't good enough quality for him to prove it was her, but he knew it was.

Holy shit. *She'd* done this? And contacted him because why? She'd somehow known he was with Celida and Travers, two of the top agents in the domestic terrorism division?

Matt didn't buy it. In his business, this kind of information was never free. She had to want something in return. A favor of some sort. What, he didn't know. And he wasn't even sure he wanted to know what kind of favor she'd have in mind for something like this.

"What, you know her?" Celida asked. Travers was staring at him too.

"Maybe."

"Who is she?"

He shook his head, his mouth twisting in a sardonic smile. "I could tell you, but then she'd have to kill you."

****

"You sure you wanna go back to your place? They're holding a hotel room for us," Clay said.

Still nestled in his lap in the back of the SUV Tuck was driving back to New Orleans, Zoe shook her head. "I'm sure." She wanted to go back to her place. The sooner she faced being there, where she was attacked, the better. "Gonna have to stay there alone when you leave anyhow."

Clay sighed and stroked a hand over her hair. "Okay."

No one spoke for the rest of the long drive and she was glad, able to drift in and out of sleep with Clay's arms around her. When they got into The Quarter Tuck parked at the curb beside her building. "I'll check in with you guys in the morning," he said to them. "Celida's gonna want to see you again, and your parents too."

They'd all come to the hospital to check on her. Her mother had been frantic but with Tuck, Clay and Celida there to run interference, Zoe had missed most of the emotional drama and had been able to soak up the hugs and fussing both her parents had given her instead. "Sounds good," she murmured and started to push up in Clay's lap.

He stayed her with a firm hand between her shoulder blades, pushing her back against his chest. Not having the energy to argue and loving the way he'd been taking care of her ever since he'd shown up at the ambulance, Zoe sighed and rested her head on his muscled shoulder. She was a strong, independent woman, but right now it felt good to be held.

Clay carefully lifted her out of the vehicle and carried her to her gate. It had a new lock on it, she noticed, stiffening as she braced herself for the sight of the blood on the old brick in the courtyard, where her poor elderly neighbor had been gunned down.

"It's all cleaned up," Clay told her, striding for the door. A new one. "I put a new door in but didn't paint it yet. I can do that tomorrow."

His thoughtfulness overwhelmed her. "Thank you."

"It's nothing."

Zoe twined her arms around his neck and kissed his jaw anyway, because it wasn't *nothing* to her. After everything she'd been through, it was amazing to come home to this.

He got the door unlocked and disarmed the security system before reaching back to lock it behind them. "What do you want right now?" he asked, striding for the stairs.

"Shower," she said. "And a toothbrush." Not necessarily in that order.

"Sure."

In the bathroom he set her on her feet and started up

the shower. Zoe waited until he stepped out to give her some privacy before using the toilet, then washed her face, brushed her teeth and swished mouthwash around to get rid of the lingering taste of Carlos's blood she swore was still in there. After rinsing the sink, she finally confronted her image in the mirror. She definitely looked like hell. Or at least like she'd been through hell.

But she was lucky to be alive.

Traces of black eye makeup were still smudged beneath her eyes, her face a little swollen and discolored where Carlos had hit her, her lower lip bruised and a tiny cut on it that stung every time she talked or touched her tongue to it.

Her wounded shoulder throbbed but Schroder had been right and they hadn't given her any stitches at the hospital. The burning in her throat and lungs would lessen in the next few days, they'd told her. Right now she wanted to get clean then curl up in Clay's arms and sleep for the next week straight.

Turning away from the sink, Zoe sighed as she stripped out of the XXL T-shirt and sweatpants one of the guys on Clay's team had loaned her at the hospital. In the shower she tipped her head back and groaned in mingled pleasure and relief at the feel of the hot water sluicing over her, and set about rubbing shampoo into her hair.

She looked over her shoulder as the shower curtain slid aside and Clay stepped into the tub, stark naked. Her heart gave a hard thump at the sight of all those powerful muscles bared to her gaze, but she was too damn sore and exhausted to enjoy him properly at the moment. Not to mention mentally drained.

Without a word he moved in behind her, the tub suddenly seeming tiny with him crowding the small space. He took her hands and pulled them down to her sides, his fingers wrapping around hers.

"Are you really okay?" he asked, staring into her eyes, his expression full of concern.

"Mostly," she admitted. It would take time to deal with everything, but she was strong and she had lots of support. Support she wasn't afraid to ask for when she needed it. Beginning with Clay. "I'm so glad you're here."

Clay pushed out a long exhalation. He gave a terse shake of his head, his eyes tormented. When he lifted a hand to brush a wet strand of hair back from her face, she was shocked to feel the tremor in it. "I thought I'd lost you." His voice was rough.

Zoe swallowed, blinked back tears. "I thought you had too." She'd never forget how close those bullets had come to hitting her, or how near those flames had been. That sick feeling of desperation and helplessness at not being able to escape.

He didn't look away, kept stroking the side of her face. "I wanted to run in there and find you. But I couldn't without exposing all of us on the team." He pulled in a deep breath, his anguish clear. "God, knowing you might be in there and not being able to help you was…"

Zoe set her hand against his and pressed her cheek against his palm, her heart twisting at the pain in his voice, on his face. "They got me out. And I understand why you couldn't leave. You had to get Carlos."

Clay closed his eyes as though he couldn't bear it. "Jesus, don't even say that fucker's name."

"Okay." She pressed a kiss to the inside of his wrist. "Just hold me."

His eyes opened. The hand cradling the side of her face tightened slightly, his expression fierce. "I've never felt like that before and I wouldn't want to again. Do you even realize what you mean to me?"

She smiled, totally undone at how emotionally

vulnerable he was allowing himself to be with her. "I think so."

He shook his head slowly, as if he didn't believe her. "I swore I'd never let another woman in again, but you... I couldn't keep you out even if I tried, and I don't want to."

Tears stung her eyes at the frank admission. "I'm glad you don't. And I've never let a man in this far before either. Ever. Only you." Not even her ex-husband. She realized that now. She'd loved and trusted him, but maybe she'd been subconsciously holding back because some part of her had known he wasn't completely trustworthy. After being officially involved with him for only a day, she'd let Clay in past every defense she had. He'd seen the proof of that in the bedroom.

Something ignited in his eyes at her admission. Pride. Triumph maybe. Whatever it was, it made his gaze more intense than she'd ever seen it. "I won't ever let you down again."

Oh, God, Clay... Zoe swallowed back tears. "I know you won't."

He nodded, gave her a little half-smile that turned her inside out before his face became serious again. "I'm not good at this, Zo. Saying how I feel. But I need you to know I'm trying. I'm sure I'll fuck up along the way so just...be patient with me, okay? You mean so much to me and it took almost losing you to make me confront that. I want this to work. I want to see where this goes and so I'm just gonna say it. I need you, all right? I fucking *need* you."

Zoe swallowed hard, his words touching her more deeply than any romantic gesture ever could have. She could see how hard he was trying to convey what he felt for her, could see his sincerity.

Gazing up into his earnest eyes, Zoe felt her heart

go into freefall.

I love you.

The words were there, crowding her mouth, but she didn't say it. Not yet, because it was too soon. He'd already come so far and after what had happened things were emotionally intense for both of them.

They'd also only been together for a ridiculously short amount of time, even though they'd been building toward it for months. She could wait a little longer to tell him, didn't want to spook or push him for more now. And she also felt he needed to be the one to say it first.

"I need you too," she said instead.

Clay groaned and cupped her face in both hands. His blue eyes searching hers, he kissed the tip of her nose, the corner of her mouth. The other corner. Her chin. Her cheeks. Every single spot that hurt or throbbed. As if he wanted to erase the marks. Soft, slow kisses. Sweet, tender kisses that melted her and turned her heart inside out.

When he finally settled his mouth over hers he did it gently, sealing their lips together before gliding his tongue across her lower lip. She opened for him, sought out his tongue with her own, a deep, searching kiss that made her tingle all over. But then he broke the kiss and lifted his head, his hands sliding across her jaw to the back of her neck and up to her head. "Let me take care of you."

She wasn't about to argue, and she could feel how badly he needed this, almost as though he needed to make up for having to leave her in the cabin, even though he'd had no choice and she didn't hold it against him.

Zoe bowed her head as he began rubbing the shampoo into her hair and scalp. She winced when he hit a tender spot from where Carlos had yanked on her hair. Clay immediately lightened the pressure of his massaging fingers, sending streamers of pleasure through her battered body. On a grateful groan she rested her head against his chest and closed her eyes, letting him take care of her.

Another lump formed in her throat at the feel of his big hands working in her hair, rinsing the shampoo out then gliding the bar of her favorite soap over her wet skin. Slick and warm, they ran gently over her body, avoiding her bruises and cuts from the wooden shrapnel and where the jagged edge of the windowsill had scraped her.

She drifted in a contented haze as the water pounded down on her back and his heat surrounded her. "This feels so good," she murmured, never wanting him to stop.

"Good." He slid his soapy hands down her back, over the curve of her hips to her rear. That she didn't even want to act on the tingles his touch created told her how beat up she was. "Sore?"

"Yeah. But just think of how realistic I can make my action and suspense scenes now that I've experienced all this firsthand."

His hands stilled on her rear and she looked up into his face. He was staring down at her with an almost comical expression of disbelief. "What? Too soon?" she asked.

He grunted in reply, drew her head back down to his chest and resumed washing her, his motions caressing. Drugging. Her eyelids grew heavy.

All too soon the water began to cool. Clay reached past her to shut it off, snagged a towel from the hook on the wall just outside the shower and wrapped her up in it. She opened her mouth to argue that she could take it from there but he shot her a look that told her not to bother so she stayed quiet while he toweled her off then lifted her in his arms and strode for her bedroom.

Once again, her body stiffened, preparing for the moment when she entered the room where Carlos had attacked her. Clay had replaced this door too, she noticed, filled with gratitude for having such a wonderful man who cared so much.

Clay stopped walking. "We can sleep in the guest room," he said quietly.

"No, I want to be in my own bed. With you." It was the only way to replace the bad memory with a good one, and she wanted to hold onto it for the coming nights when Clay wouldn't be here. That was coming far too soon for her liking as it was.

He pulled the covers back and set her on the bed. She settled onto her side and snuggled deeper under the covers, inhaling the scent of fresh sheets. "You changed the bed," she murmured, feeling like she might cry all over again.

"Yeah, after I stayed the night here," he said, as if it was no big deal. But it was. Those little things he'd done, his consideration of her feelings and comfort, meant the world to her. He slid in next to her and eased her into his arms. Zoe moved fully into his body and rested her head in the curve of his shoulder, breathing in his scent.

Clay kissed the top of her head, ran a hand over her damp hair. "Need anything else?"

"Just this," she mumbled, his heat seeping into her. "So tired."

"I know. Let yourself go."

"You'll stay here with me all night?"

He snorted and tightened his arms around her. "A direct order from the Director of the FBI himself couldn't make me leave this bed, raven."

Zoe smiled at that, closed her eyes and fell headlong into sleep, aware at the deepest level of consciousness that she was safe in his arms.

And, even if he hadn't said the words yet, loved.

****

Clay jerked awake in the darkness hours later when Zoe shifted against him. For the most part she'd slept soundly but over the last hour or so she'd been restless. Three times she'd woken, immediately looking for him and he'd pulled her close and soothed her back to sleep.

She lay curled up in his arms on her side, her head resting on his shoulder, one bare leg thrown over his. Clay rubbed a soothing hand up and down her spine, the other cupping the back of her head to hold her close. While she'd been sleeping he'd been running over everything in his mind.

Every time he thought of how close he'd come to losing her it shook him. He lived with that kind of violence on a constant basis, ever since he'd joined the Navy. But that was his world, not hers. He hated that it had touched her.

"You okay?" he murmured, still overwhelmed by the need to soothe, to comfort. She'd been through hell and he would do whatever it took to help her.

"Mmhmm." She rolled a bit so more of her weight rested on him. He'd already been half-hard from having her naked in his arms, and now his erection was swelling rapidly against her belly but he ignored it.

The urge to roll her onto her back and claim her with his body was so strong his muscles twitched. He wanted to push into her and watch her fly apart beneath him so badly but that wasn't what she needed right now. She needed to be held and he'd do it for as long as she needed him to.

Sighing, Zoe snuggled in closer, her fingertips drawing little patterns across his bare chest and shoulder. Tracing his tat. Bathing him in the warmth of her soft curves, her clean scent. "So I want to tell you something but I don't want to freak you out," she said quietly. "I was going to wait but I just can't anymore, and you know how I like to say what's on my mind."

Did he ever. And while anything that came with a warning like that wasn't something he wanted to hear right now, her thinking he might freak out was downright insulting. Especially considering what they'd been through the past few days, not to mention what he did for a living. "Okay."

Her fingers paused on his chest, her touch still sending tingles through him. She tipped her head back and looked into his eyes. "You sure?"

"Yeah." Whatever she wanted to say, he could handle it. Except if she didn't want him in her life. After the way he'd opened up to her earlier he wasn't sure if he could take that.

A mischievous little smile played around her mouth, making her eyes sparkle in the half-light. "We're falling in love with each other," she murmured. "I just thought you should know, in case you weren't aware."

It was so unexpected and lighthearted that he couldn't help but grin. "Yeah?" And he was extremely aware of the falling in love bit.

She nodded, seeming completely confident about her statement and not at all hurt or thrown off when he hadn't agreed. "I write about falling in love for a living, so in a way that makes me an expert on the subject. I recognize the signs when I see them. And it's happening to us right now."

He wasn't going to deny it, because it was true. He toyed with a lock of her hair, then stroked a fingertip down the length of her straight nose and nodded once. "Yeah, I think you're right." She sure as hell was. He'd never felt like this in his life. She made him feel alive in ways he hadn't in a long, long time.

Her smile widened, showing even, white teeth. "I

know I am."

He chuckled at her smugness. She looked up at him with such joy and pleasure, it twisted him up inside. And he was so grateful that she didn't seem to expect the actual words from him yet. He felt them, wanted to say them soon, but when he did say them he wanted it to be all on his own, without her feeling like she'd coaxed it out of him.

"We'll take the plunge together."

God, when she said things like that he just wanted to squeeze her tight and never let her go. *Already plunged, raven.*

It still startled him that he'd fallen for her after he'd sworn never to do it again, but then, Zoe was unlike any other woman on this earth. He was going to make damn sure he was worthy of her.

With a soft murmur of contentment Zoe leaned her head back to kiss his fingertip, then forward to press her lips to the center of his chest. She worked her way up his throat, over his chin to his mouth. "I like knowing we're in this together," she whispered against his lips. "Then it's not so scary."

"I'm not scared." Wait, was *she* scared? He looked down at her.

She pulled back a few inches to stare at him in the dimness. "You're not? Not even a little?"

He shook his head. "Nope." The only thing he was scared of was screwing this up and losing her somehow. And that was a major revelation in itself. "Are you?"

She bit her lower lip. "I was a little, until you said that." She blinked fast.

He grinned. "Didn't mean to make you cry. C'mere and let me kiss it better." He cupped the back of her head so he could kiss her properly. The way she opened for him, her tongue twining with his, made his aching cock swell even more.

No. Not yet. She needed something other than sex right now.

With his cock screaming obscenities at him Clay ignored it and cradled the side of her face with one hand. God, just looking at her made him ache. He was already dreading leaving her. "I can stay for a few more days, maybe until Wednesday. But when I go back to Virginia, I want you to come with me. To stay for a few weeks, or however long you want." He didn't want to pressure her into doing something she wasn't ready for, but he hoped she'd want to go.

She gave him a serene smile. "I'd like that."

Tension released from his shoulders. "You can stay at my place—well, Tuck's place, but he won't be there because he's at Celida's mostly. If you'd rather stay with them, though, I understand." Wasn't his first choice but having her in the same city was a good start, and a helluva lot better than her staying here in New Orleans.

Zoe reached up and put her hand against the back of his, holding his palm to her cheek as she searched his eyes. "I want to stay with *you*, Clay, not with my cousin or my bestie, even though I love them both to death."

His heart nearly imploded at the trust and yearning in her face. "Okay, good." Damn, he couldn't wait to have her with him, at his place. There when he came home from a long day of training or a work trip, her in his bed every night, her head on the pillow beside his when he woke up in the morning. It was way too soon to ask her to move in with him, but that's what he wanted eventually. And maybe, someday down the road when they were both ready, he'd ask her to marry him.

It would have to be a Gothic-style ring, he decided. Something with black and red or maybe blue or purple. Definitely not a diamond for Zoe, but he'd give her those too if she wanted them.

Zoe settled her head back on his shoulder with a

little sigh. He rubbed her back, savoring the softness of her skin. "Go back to sleep." She gave a sleepy murmur, let her body relax.

Clay held her as she drifted off. He still couldn't believe how optimistic she was about life and didn't know how she'd become such a die-hard romantic in the first place. But he was grateful for both of those things because she'd done the seemingly impossible and shown his jaded, cynical heart that there was still plenty of light and good in the world. There was nothing on earth he wouldn't give her if it was within his power. And while that realization still amazed him, he'd never felt more certain of anything than his feelings for her.

Zoe was his and he was hers. End of story.

Speaking of stories...

Clay kissed the top of her head and smiled to himself in the darkness. They were opposites in so many ways. She was a romance author who, despite the world being a fucked-up place full of imperfect people, somehow still believed in happily-ever-after.

Now, because of her, he believed in them too. And it was the most incredible feeling to realize he'd found someone who made it possible for him to have a happy ending of his own.

Epilogue

Six weeks later

Breathing a sigh of relief at getting in out of the cold wind and rain, Zoe stepped inside the front door of her new condo and locked it behind her. She hung up her coat on the hook and set her purse on the black, bat-shaped table she'd placed in the entryway.

"Clay?" she called out. His truck had been in its parking spot but he wasn't in the kitchen or living room.

He slept here more often than not, since he was helping Tuck with renos to get his place ready for when he and Celida moved in together in a couple months. Their wedding was scheduled for the beginning of April, depending on their shifting schedules. Zoe had just come from dress shopping with Celida. The moment her friend had put The Dress on, they'd both known it and Celida's eyes had gotten misty. Then of course Zoe's had too.

"Where are you?" she called.

"Back here," came the reply, sounding like it had come from the bedroom.

They'd tried the long distance thing for nearly a month before deciding it was sheer stupidity to stay apart, and once she'd made the mental plunge to move up here to be close to him she'd felt a calm she hadn't experienced in forever. Things were finally settling into place again, and not just for her.

Leticia had taken her son home to Tennessee. She'd kept in touch with Zoe since their horrific experience with Carlos and they talked on the phone once a week. She and Xander were both doing as well as could be expected given all they'd gone through, and moving forward with their lives.

As for Zoe, she belonged with Clay.

Being a writer, she could work from anywhere, and since Clay needed to be near Quantico, logic dictated she be the one to move. Plus, he'd asked her to, saying he wanted her to be closer so they could spend more time together. It was a huge step for him, and she'd recognized that. His request alone had made the decision easy.

He'd helped find her a place and he and some of his teammates had moved in all her furniture she'd had shipped from New Orleans. Halloween was only a few days away, her favorite holiday of the year, and he'd even given her a hand decking the place out with all her decorations. Bats, goblins, witches, pumpkins and spiders dotted the condo in splashes of black, purple, green, orange and yellow. When Tuck and Celida moved into his house in another two months or so, she was hoping Clay would move in here with her. She planned to ask him soon because she sensed he was ready to take the next step in their relationship.

The dark hardwood floor was cool against her bare feet as she made her way down the hall, past the guest bath and bedroom to the master suite. A hot bath with her apple cider bubble bath and her Witches' Brew scented candle burning on the bathroom windowsill seemed like the best idea she'd had in a while.

Especially if she could convince Clay to climb in with her, though she probably wouldn't have to try very hard. The man had very talented hands, and his demanding work schedule meant they hadn't seen much of each other for the past five days.

She tingled at the thought of his slick, soapy hands sliding over her wet skin, lingering on her most sensitive places and finally slipping between her thighs. *Mmmm*... "Are you having a nap?"

"No." He sounded alert enough.

She turned the door handle, pushed it open, and halted in her tracks.

Clay was on the massive four-poster bed she'd had shipped from New Orleans all right, but not because he was tired.

He sat perched on the foot of it, wearing a white button-down dress shirt and charcoal gray suit slacks. He had both forearms braced on his spread knees, the sleeves of the shirt rolled up partway, revealing several inches of roped muscles. His muscular thighs strained the material of his pants. The top two buttons of his shirt were undone, showing the upper delineation of his pecs and a tantalizing sprinkle of dark hair.

When she managed to stop gawking and look up at his face, her mouth went dry and a shock of heat burst inside her at the molten desire she read in his eyes.

"Did you have a meeting?" she croaked out. A miracle, considering how dry her mouth was and how hard her heart was pounding. That outfit made her want to undress him, torturously slowly, and lick him from head to toe.

He shook his head, a little smile playing around the edges of his mouth as though he could tell what she was thinking. Then he raised a hand and crooked a finger at her, never taking his eyes from hers. "Come here, raven."

A bolt of desire shot through her at the quiet command in his voice, which sounded an octave lower than normal. His voice did crazy things to her insides at the best of times, but when it got all deep and intimate like that, every cell in her body melted. Her breath caught as she realized what he was doing.

Suit porn, she thought dizzily.

The man had remembered what she'd said all this time and was giving her her suit porn fantasy. She put a hand on the edge of the doorframe to keep her knees from wobbling.

Already light-headed with anticipation, she sauntered toward him. The sensual glint in his eyes intensified as she neared, his appreciation of her body and her willingness clear. She stopped within arm's reach in front of him, watching his eyes, but he merely gazed up at her and waited.

She was a little breathless at the prospect of him bringing one of her favorite, hottest fantasies to life. But *day*-um, that calm, authoritative and knowing look he gave her made it feel like she was melting from the inside out.

"Take off your dress." Again, that quiet, commanding tone, the one that said he expected her to obey and knew she would. A light shiver rippled over her skin.

Yes, sir. She was only too happy to comply.

Slowly, drawing out the moment and making him ache for it as much as she did, she reached behind her to undo the zipper in the center of her black, Victorian-style lace dress. When it parted she eased the halves down her chest and arms, spellbound by the way his eyes raked over her body, pausing on the black lace bra. It was such a rush, seeing this man so hungry for her.

She slid the dress inch by inch over her hips, caught the way his eyes flared when she was left standing in nothing but her bra, panties and black high heels, the ones that had sexy straps around the ankles and a cute little bat ribbon at the top of each heel.

Clay held out a hand, palm up, the gesture controlled. Expectant.

She placed hers in it, her abdomen flipping when his long, strong fingers closed around hers in a firm but gentle grip. He had a way of touching her that always made her feel protected and cherished at the same time. A gentle tug downward and she followed the unspoken command, going to her knees between his splayed thighs, putting her at eye level with the bulging erection straining the front of his slacks.

On her knees, anticipating the moment when she'd get to pleasure him, she felt as powerful as a goddess. Strong, erotic, beautiful. He made her feel all those things with a single look, one simple touch.

It was no wonder why she'd gone and fallen head over heels for him.

Licking her lips, Zoe looked up into his face, her entire body humming.

"Undo my belt and hand it to me."

And then it hit her.

The scene she'd written a few days ago. He must have read it while she was working and hadn't noticed because she'd been so caught up with what was happening on her mind's screen. But knowing that Clay was about to do those deliciously erotic things to her?

Oh my god...

Her toes curled in her cute little bat heels, desire coursing through her like an electrical current. Her nipples went rock hard and her sex swelled.

Her hands were trembling, slightly clumsy with excitement as she did as he said, sliding the cool, slick leather out of the loops and placing it in his grasp.

There was no hesitation in her at all. She trusted him without reservation and knew he'd never use it to hurt or harm her.

Instead, he'd use it to restrain her and drive her out

of her mind by taking her to the edge of release again and again, only letting her come when she was writhing and begging and pleading. Or he might do the opposite and keep going, driving her from one orgasm to the next while ignoring her cries for him to stop until she was mindless from pleasure overload and too weak to move.

She couldn't wait to find out which it would be tonight.

The room held a hushed intimacy as they stared at each other, as if a spell had been woven. In the charged silence that followed Clay reached out with his other hand to touch her cheek, and for the first time she noticed the tie in it. Red silk, just like in the book.

Zoe sucked in a quiet breath, knowing that at some point that silk would become her blindfold. She adored his penchant for noticing details, and though she knew he had set this whole thing up for her, judging by the thick erection she couldn't wait to get to, he was enjoying this as much as she was.

Dying to see what he'd make her do next, Zoe raised her head and met his gaze. He was staring down at her with a mixture of desire, adoration and tenderness so powerful it stole her breath. He stroked the backs of his fingers down her cheek, the added caress of the silk tie sending shivers through her body.

Oh yeah, he'd planned this out carefully. Knowing him, probably the same way he would when planning an op. Detailed. Methodical.

One look in his eyes and she knew this was going to be a night she'd never forget. From experience she knew he'd take what she'd written in that scene and add in a few of his own surprises. She squirmed in anticipation, heart tripping when one side of his mouth quirked up in amusement at her obvious eagerness.

"Soon, baby girl," he promised, then leaned forward and took her face in his hands. She curled her fingers around his wrists, soaking in his heat and strength and vitality. "First I want to tell you something, but I don't want you to freak out," he said in a quiet voice.

A huge lump formed in her throat as his words registered, echoing what she'd said to him that night at her place in New Orleans. She tried to swallow around it, nodded.

He stared directly into her eyes, his gaze revealing everything he felt for her, nothing held back. "I love you, raven."

Even though she'd guessed it was coming, tears flooded her eyes and a sob caught in her chest. For this powerful, jaded man who'd been hurt so badly to trust her that much and be the first to say it, completely leveled her emotionally.

She'd been waiting to tell him she loved him, wanting to be patient and give him time to settle into their relationship, not wanting to push him. Now she wanted to say it back to him so badly but couldn't get a single word past the hot ball of emotion in her throat.

Thankfully he seemed to understand because he smiled and brushed her tears away before they could fall, never taking his hands away from her face. "You're not freaked out, right?"

She shook her head, trying to stop her tears.

He grinned. "Good." He bent to press a slow, lingering kiss to her lips. "Now be a good girl and unzip my pants before I bust a seam down there," he murmured against her mouth. "I've got a tie and a belt waiting here, and I'm not afraid to use 'em."

Zoe gave a watery laugh and tipped her face up to kiss him properly. Overflowing with love for this incredible, brave man, she opened herself to him completely and let the fantasy unfold.

—The End—

Complete Booklist

<u>**Romantic Suspense**</u>
Hostage Rescue Team Series
Marked
Targeted
Hunted

Titanium Security Series
Ignited
Singed
Burned
Extinguished
Rekindled

Bagram Special Ops Series
Deadly Descent
Tactical Strike
Lethal Pursuit
Danger Close

Suspense Series
Out of Her League
Cover of Darkness
No Turning Back
Relentless
Absolution

<u>**Paranormal Romance**</u>
Empowered Series
Darkest Caress

<u>**Historical Romance**</u>
The Vacant Chair

Erotic Romance (writing as *Callie Croix*)
Deacon's Touch
Dillon's Claim
No Holds Barred
Touch Me
Let Me In
Covert Seduction

Acknowledgements

I couldn't write books without a great team behind me to perform quality control.

Katie, my sister-from-another-mother, you know I love you!

To Kim and Kate, my fantastic beta readers, I greatly value your input.

My fantastic editor, Joan, who polishes the manuscript.

And my hubby, whose attention to detail is second-to-none. Thank you all!

About the Author

NY Times and USA Today Bestselling author Kaylea Cross writes edge-of-your-seat military romantic suspense. Her work has won many awards and has been nominated for both the Daphne du Maurier and the National Readers' Choice Awards. A Registered Massage Therapist by trade, Kaylea is also an avid gardener, artist, Civil War buff, Special Ops aficionado, belly dance enthusiast and former nationally-carded softball pitcher. She lives in Vancouver, BC with her husband and family.

You can visit Kaylea at www.kayleacross.com. If you would like to be notified of future releases, please join her newsletter.

Made in the USA
Lexington, KY
30 August 2015